eval IV

ves in South Wales with his wife and dog.

rating on historical fiction books, espe-
man and Medieval eras, he found signi-
th the India Summers Mysteries, a series
a librarian and her Special Forces partner,
into history to solve modern-day prob-

MEDIEVAL IV

Ring of Steel

K. M. ASHMAN

CANELO

First published in the United Kingdom in 2013 by K. M. Ashman

This edition published in the United Kingdom in 2022 by

Canelo
Unit 9, 5th Floor
Cargo Works, 1–2 Hatfields
London, SE1 9PG
United Kingdom

A CIP catalogue record for this book is available from the British Library.

Print ISBN 978 1 80032 449 7
Ebook ISBN 978 1 80032 448 0

Cover design by Black Sheep

Cover images © Shutterstock, Arcangel

Look for more great books at www.canelo.co

Printed and bound in Great Britain by Clays Ltd, Elcograf S.p.A.

1

MIX
Paper from
responsible sources
FSC® C018072

Prologue

Since Llewellyn's death in 1282, Edward the First of England, also known as Longshanks, spent a fortune in time and money subduing the Welsh nation. To do so, he awarded lands and titles across Wales to those nobles and warlords who swore fealty to the English crown.

To support the occupation he also embarked on an unprecedented building programme erecting huge castles across Wales, the like of which had never been seen before. Each was unassailable in its own right but together they formed his famed ring of steel, an impregnable chain of oppression from which his forces could maintain their tyrannical grip upon the troublesome country.

For ten years the castles and those loyal to the King held an entire nation beneath their heel and despite the occasional uprising from those frustrated by their masters' brutality, the rule of Longshanks was never seriously challenged. However, as the decade ended some of the more nationalistic Welsh lords started to talk once more of liberty and though such conversations had taken place many times before, this time there was a realism to the plans.

Edward dismissed the threat and concentrated on his forthcoming campaign to France but as the castles were stripped of cash and indeed manpower to fuel his campaign, the Welsh lords saw a window of opportunity. Resistance grew across the country and gradually an air of rebellion evolved into the beginnings of a full-scale uprising and Cynan ap Maredudd, a warlord from the hills of Mid Wales, gathered an army about him to prey on the supply lines of the castles throughout the country. Meanwhile in the north, a noble by the name of Madog ap Llewellyn claimed royal lineage from Llewellyn ap Iorwerth, or Llewellyn the Great, as he eventually became known and also set about raising a force with which he could resist the occupation.

The move took the English by surprise and within weeks, not only had Castell du Bere, one of Edward's favoured fortresses fallen to Cynan but also the unthinkable had happened when Caernarfon, one of the most impressive castles on the north coast, was besieged and captured by Madog.

The message soon got back to Longshanks and though it meant postponing his French campaign, he knew he had to wipe out the Welsh threat once and for all. As the winter of 1294 approached, the Welsh celebrated within the giant walls of Caernarfon and as there was no immediate reaction from the English crown, many thought Longshanks had no stomach for a fight.

So it came to be that while Madog and his men enjoyed their impressive victory, across the border, Edward Longshanks, King of England, slowly but surely, drew up his plans.

Chapter One

Brecon Castle – 1294

The screams of the dying man had long faded into silence and Garyn could only guess at the pain the poor victim had suffered before a merciful death had overwhelmed him, the unseen torturer's echoing laughter accompanying him on the journey to whatever afterlife he believed in.

The dark corridor set deep within the castle walls was lit only by small candles at either end and echoed with the sound of the jailer's footsteps as he patrolled back and fore, his face a picture of boredom as he waited for the change of guard that was long overdue.

Garyn lay curled on a rotting mat that stank of human waste, yet was still better than the coldness of the cell floor that seemed to reach deep into his very bones. A wooden bucket sat in the far corner, a rarely emptied receptacle for his toilet but since his incarceration three weeks earlier, he had been fed so infrequently, his body had little to pass.

His body was black and blue, for his jailers were generous with fist and boot and on several occasions, he thought he would be beaten to death but always they pulled up short, their ears ringing at the orders of the gaol commander.

'Enough, the Castellan wants this one alive.'

3

When finished they would usually throw a bucket of water over him and leave him to shiver in the pitch darkness as they walked away laughing, his plight already forgotten as they contemplated their next tankard of ale.

Garyn knew his situation was desperate for the continued beatings and lack of food meant he grew weaker by the day but though the pain was constant, the possibility that Gerald had been telling the truth and he did indeed have a son, kept him striving for life, hoping against hope that circumstances would allow him the grace to cast eyes upon the boy, even for the briefest of moments.

His mind went over and over the events of the last few weeks. His discovery of the famed Sword of Macsen, or the Liberty Sword as it had become known, should have proved a unifying moment where all Welshmen could unite under a common cause and drive Longshanks from their country, but fate had stepped up in the shape of Gerald of Essex and that opportunity had been lost forever. The sword now lay in the hands of the English, for even as Garyn and his comrade Derwyn were in sight of Caernarfon castle, Gerald had found him and informed him of the existence of his son now incarcerated within the walls of Brecon castle and unless Garyn handed over the sword and returned with him immediately, the boy would be put to death at the hands of the sick Abbot of Brycheniog, Father Williams.

At first Garyn hadn't believed the English knight but Gerald was convincing and Garyn realised that if there was even the slightest chance he was telling the truth, then he had no option, he had to return. Unwilling to have the death of his own son on his hands, Garyn handed over the sword before riding back to Brycheniog as Gerald's prisoner.

He lay in the darkness, desperate to catch whatever moments of sleep he could in the damp cell, no matter how fleeting. Sleep was the only escape from this continued hell but he knew as long as the abbot stayed alive, then his own life was safe, albeit miserable. The only reason he hadn't already been handed over to the torturers was because Father Williams had left express instructions that he was to die by his hands only, a double-edged sword with only one outcome.

The sound of hobnailed boots echoed down the corridor and Garyn sat up as he heard a key rattle in his cell door. A soldier entered holding a burning candle and placed it on a shelf before forcing Garyn back against the far wall with the point of his blade.

'Stay back, Welshman,' he said, 'and don't try any of your trickery.'

Behind the guard another man entered the cell and looked around in disgust.

'It stinks in here,' said Gerald before turning to the guard. 'Get out and lock the door behind you, I will call when I am done.' The guard left the room and when the door was locked, Gerald wandered around the cell before picking up the bucket and emptying the contents onto the floor, turning it over to use as a seat.

'So,' he said eventually, turning his attention to the sorry figure of Garyn, 'here we are again, Welshman, how have you found our hospitality?'

'Your thugs are well trained, Essex, I'll give you that,' he answered.

'Yes,' said Gerald, staring at Garyn's face, 'I see they have been giving you some attention.'

'Why don't you just kill me and get it over with?'

'You know why, blacksmith,' said Gerald. 'Our mutual friend has ensured your life is his to take. If I had my way, your innards would have been strewn along the castle walls long before now, juicy morsels for the ravens. Still, there's plenty of time for that.'

'What do you want, Essex?' asked Garyn. 'Spit it out or leave me to my misery. The air was decidedly cleaner before you came in with your treacherous stench.'

'Hmm, it seems you still have spirit,' said Gerald, 'perhaps we should increase the frequencies of your beatings.'

'Do what you will, Englishman, I will not beg for mercy.'

'No, I don't think you would,' said Gerald. 'A pity really, that would have been quite amusing.'

'So what do you want?'

'I want you to tell me more about this,' said Gerald producing a package wrapped in coarse sack cloth.

Garyn recognised the item, it was the Sword of Macsen, still wrapped in its original protective wrapping.

'The Liberty Sword,' he said eventually. 'What about it?'

'I want to know all about it, the significance, where you found it, where it came from,' he paused and looked across at Garyn before adding, 'and how much the Welsh would be willing to pay for its return.'

'Is that all that matters to you, Essex?' asked Garyn. 'The weight of everything in silver pennies.'

'I admit I have a healthy respect for money,' said Gerald, 'and am not averse to selling the occasional holy artefact but this is different, it is little more than rust and splinters. Why was it of so much importance?'

'You wouldn't understand,' said Garyn.

'Try me,' said Gerald.

Garyn turned back to face the knight.

'Why should I aid you, Englishman? You are the opposite of everything my people believe in and the fact you see no significance in a thousand-year-old sword speaks volumes that no monk could hope to ever scribe.'

'Perhaps so,' said Gerald, 'but my interest is roused and I would know its story.'

'Then ask one of the traitorous Welshmen under your command. Many know the tale; you will hear it not from me.'

'You are correct and some have already shared their understanding but each has a different version. However, they all share one similarity and that is that each claim the grave would contain the treasures of an emperor. You found that tomb, Garyn, and I would know where it lays. Tell me the tale from your own lips and in return, I will ensure your conditions improve.'

'In what way?' asked Garyn, sensing an opportunity.

'A dry cell, perhaps with a window, a hot meal each day and a set of clean clothes.'

'Can you guarantee my safety?'

'Alas that is beyond me for the abbot is a powerful man, but at least however many days you have left can be lived

7

in relative comfort. In addition, I will call off my men. No more beatings, Garyn, how does that sound?'

'It sounds like one more of your empty promises,' said Garyn, 'yet another lie to obtain what it is you desire.'

'Lies?' said Gerald. 'When have I lied to you?'

'You told me I had a son,' said Garyn, 'an untruth spun like a web to get me back here. Well congratulations, knight, I fell for your lies once but never again.'

Gerald laughed in the darkness.

'Garyn ap Thomas,' he said eventually, 'I have indeed lied during my life, usually as a means to bed some other man's wife, but I can assure you, in this case I told the truth. Your son sleeps within this very tower and it must be said, he gives me far less trouble than his father.'

'I don't believe you,' said Garyn.

'Believe what you will, my words are true.'

'Prove it,' said Garyn thinking furiously.

'And why do I need to prove anything to you?'

'Let me see him,' said Garyn. 'Allow me ten minutes to speak with him and if I find he is indeed who you say, then I will tell you everything you wish to know.'

Gerald sat back and stared in amusement.

'Your words are indeed a cunning weapon, Garyn, for I came armed with a bargain only to find myself upon the receiving end. A clever trait in any man.'

'Well?' said Garyn. 'What do you have to lose? Whatever happens, it would seem I am to die in the near future anyway so surely it is a small price to pay.'

'You would exchange ten minutes with a person you have never met instead of the comforts I just offered you?'

'No, I want them both. The better conditions and time with the one you claim is my son.'

8

'You push your luck, Welshman,' said Gerald. 'I may just withdraw my offer and get back to my mistress.' He stood up to leave.

Garyn also stood up and they faced each other across the cell.

'You were right, Gerald,' said Garyn loudly as the knight banged on the door, 'I did find the tomb of Macsen complete with his body.'

'And did you see any treasures?' asked Gerald turning around.

'I did not for anything of value had been taken by those before us but I will say this. The body was still wrapped in his shroud and I have heard tell that emperors were buried complete with their finery. He lies there still and as far as I know, he may yet be adorned with jewels befitting an emperor of his status.'

Gerald approached Garyn and stood directly in front of him, staring deeply into his eyes. For several seconds nobody spoke but finally Gerald broke the silence.

'If I find out you have lied to me Welshman, I will make you watch your son die the most painful death my torturers can envisage and trust me, they are very inventive.'

'It is not a lie,' said Garyn. 'The body of Macsen is intact within his coffin and the shroud lies unopened.'

'So be it,' said Gerald, 'you will have your way. I will have you moved and, on the morrow, you will meet your spawn.' He turned to the waiting guard. 'Get me out of here,' he said, 'this place disgusts me.'

Chapter Two

Caernarfon Castle

Madog and Meirion walked into the hall and looked around. Before them sat over a hundred men at arms, lords and lesser nobles from all across Wales. Some had been involved alongside his own men in the assault on Caernarfon, while some faces were new to him, and had journeyed many days to heed the Prince's call.

Messengers had been sent far and wide, extolling Madog's astonishing capture of Edward's most prestigious castle and inviting men to join the Prince in his struggle against the English.

Over the past week the victors had been busy burying the dead and repairing what defences they could in case of any counterattack by the English but no such retaliation had come and gradually the tension had eased as the implications of the victory sunk in.

As he stared around the room, one man got to his feet and looked toward the Prince. His full beard was grey and his hair was tied back from his face. His long moustache dripped with ale and his enormous hands made the tankard look small in their grip. His leather chest plate was dirty and bloodstained and Madog guessed correctly he was one of the minor warlords from Mid Wales, more used to fighting than banqueting. For a moment both men stared at each other in silence but just as Madog was about to speak, the grey-haired warrior slammed his fist onto the wooden table, making everyone jump in surprise.

For a second there was silence and the man repeated the action, following it swiftly with more strikes, making the table shudder with each impact. Over and over again he smashed his fist on the table and within seconds, all the men in the hall were banging their fists and tankards on the tables, displaying their admiration for the young prince's unlikely achievement. Soon voices joined the banging and men cheered loudly, deafening all present with their support as Madog looked around in astonishment. These men were the backbone of the resistance across Wales and here they all were, together in his presence paying homage to him, Madog, Prince of Wales.

Madog put up his hands for silence but the rapport between the men went on for several minutes more before gradually dying away. As it did, the original man climbed up onto the table and called for silence. The hall fell quiet as the men returned to their seats and as the noise abated, the warrior turned to face Madog.

'My lord,' he announced, 'my name is Martyn of Flint and I have ridden from the army of Cynan to share in this celebration of your victory on his behalf. For more years than we care to remember, most men here have risked their lives leaning against the yolk of the English. Individually we risked death from the King's men yet still we soured his path. Some preyed upon their supply lines whilst others ensured his forces were kept busy chasing shadows amongst the hills of our fathers.

'All this time we resisted alone, a broken force without a common banner between us. Though we did what we could, we knew it was a mere scratch on the armour of Longshanks and more was needed if we were to provide a true resistance. Many were the nights when men sat around the fires, praying for the time we would be united in one cause. For an age it seemed we wasted our time, yet what you have done in the last month is to mould us into a formidable army as surely as a sword smith moulds a blade. My lord, I raise my tankard to few men but here in front of these fellow warriors, I lift it now in honour of you and what you have done. Praise be to Lord Madog of Ynys Mon, warrior, leader of men, and Castellan of Caernarfon Castle.'

As he lifted his tankard to drain the contents the men erupted into cheers once more as Madog's comrade leaned across to speak into his ear.

'My lord, I note he did not voice acknowledgement of your title. Do you want me to address this oversight?'

'It was no oversight, Meirion,' said Madog, 'for he is Cynan's man and as yet undeclared. Cynan may have pledged not to fight against me but will wait to see what transpires over the next few months before declaring allegiance. Besides, that Martyn no doubt has many comrades within this hall, we would not want to set Welshman against Welshman so soon after unifying so many.'

'Understood,' said Meirion and sat back as Madog got to his feet.

'Men of Wales,' he called, 'Martyn of Flint. You have my gratitude for attending this day. We have indeed inflicted a dent upon the honour of Longshanks but make no mistake, in the greater scheme of things it is no more than a flesh wound. At this very moment he will be smarting from the humiliation of losing such a great fortress but do not sit upon your laurels for I can assure you that as surely as winter follows autumn, he will be gathering his strength to win back this great prize.'

'Never,' called out some of the men, 'the castle is ours.'

'It is,' agreed Madog, 'and I have no intention of delivering it into his hands just yet but that is the point of this assembly. You men before me are the real leaders of the people, the warriors they call on when they are dispossessed or treated unfairly. It is you who they turn to, not a prince or a crown, but the warlords they grew up admiring. All we have done here is take the fortress by surprise, aided by circumstance.'

'And the blood of brave men,' shouted a voice.

'Aye,' said Madog, 'and that is the greatest price of all but see it not as the final outcome of this struggle, for their sacrifice is but the first step and that is why we have gathered here this day. Between us we can raise perhaps ten thousand men at arms willing to fight against Longshanks. They are to be feted and thanked for their support but make no mistake, for everyone who carries arms on our behalf there are ten more who have not committed. Some of those may harbour allegiance to Longshanks and we will never gain their support but there are many who still labour under the yolk and need help to break the bonds. These should be our next targets, not in the next few months but in the next few days. The hill before us is steep and we need every sword arm we can get to continue the struggle so I say this: despatch what men you can to act as recruiters in my name. Tell them to report to a designated place of your choosing and for every man taking up the

13

call, I ask that he is paid the sum of a silver penny for food and drink.'

'Since when do we buy allegiance?' asked Martyn.

'It is not for allegiance,' said Madog, 'but if we are asking men to leave their ploughs, they will need to be able to feed their kin. It may not last long but the other families will need to help those who have sent their sons to the cause.'

'Assuming that many heed the call,' said Martyn, 'we cannot maintain such a force for long. These men will need to be fed and watered.'

'We will issue decrees to the villagers asking for support,' said Madog. 'I know they already struggle but at least this time it will be with a common goal in sight, the end of Edward's rule.'

'And what will be the targets of such an army?'

'I have here some documents drawn up by my scribes,' said Madog. 'Each identifies a strategic target for our forces in the north and stretches as far down as Dolwyddelan. Cynan has a similar list identifying targets in the centre of the country down as far as Builth. Ten days from now, both armies will descend on these positions with everything at our disposal.'

'My lord,' said a voice, 'the winter is almost upon us. Surely we should wait until the spring?'

'We will not wait,' said Madog, 'for Longshanks will not wait. Already he has sent his own messages across England seeking recruits to his army. Luckily half his soldiers are already in France, but he seeks to gather enough strength to send a force into Wales to reclaim what was his and to crush our resistance.'

'It is a great ask to defeat the army of a king,' said a voice.

'It is, but the size of his army is also its weakness. To maintain and supply such a force, he will need the safety of his castles. Many are alongside the coast and can be supplied from the sea so what we need to do is make them inaccessible to Edward. If his soldiers are isolated from the safety of the ring of steel then we can pick them off as the wolf takes a sheep. We grew up amongst the hills of this country and know them well. With careful planning we can terrorise his columns and disappear before they have a chance to reorganise. Over time, they will grow tired of fighting the mist and retire to the safety of their castles on the English side of the dyke.'

'And how do you intend we deny him his castles in Wales?' asked a voice.

'By taking them into our possession,' said Madog. 'The taking of Castell du Bere as well as this one at Caernarfon, the greatest of them all, proves it can be done. Yes, we had good fortune on our side but now we are stronger and more organised, I see no reason why we cannot wrest the fortresses from his control. Many are understrength as the garrisons have been withdrawn to fight in France so pitched battles will be unlikely, however the walls are mighty and will need to be breached.'

'A mighty task in itself,' said a voice.

'But not impossible,' said Madog. 'Already we have identified engineers across the country and as we speak, they are assembling the trebuchets we will need for the assaults.'

The room broke into conversation and Madog allowed them the time to discuss the details, knowing the whole thrust of his plan needed the support of the men in front of him. Finally one man stood and waited for the noise to die down. Madog looked over and recognised Dafydd Merchant, a noble from the west coast of the country.

Madog held up his hand and eventually the last of the noise died away.

'Lord Merchant,' said Madog, 'welcome to my hall. You have the floor.'

'Lord Madog,' said Dafydd, 'what you have achieved in the taking of this castle is indeed impressive and was thought impossible by many men. However it has to be said that now the English are aware of your prowess, they will surely double their defences. To ask us to throw ourselves against their walls is to ask many to die not knowing if their deaths will be enough to stop the main army.' He paused. 'That being said, I have never felt such an upsurge in fervour against the King. Just to be amongst such men in this hall is to bring the blood to a boil and set a man charging against a castle wall. For many long years we have knelt before the fist of Edward, always talking about the day when we will once more stand proud. Well I believe that day has arrived for there will be no greater chance than this.' He paused and looked around the room before returning his gaze to Madog. 'I pledge allegiance to your cause, my lord, and will raise an army of a thousand men before this month is out. In addition I will arm them and furnish whatever food is needed from my own cantrefs. This is my pledge.'

To a great roar the man sat down and Madog looked around the room. His eyes fell upon Morgan Talbot, a warlord from Mid Wales. Morgan was a renowned fighter and his allegiance would go a long way to capturing the support of the rest.

'Morgan Talbot,' said Madog, 'do you have something to say?'

'Aye, I do,' said Morgan, 'I have kept my counsel and watched from afar, for many have chanced their arm against the English before but all have failed. It would be better if you and Cynan stood shoulder to shoulder in this matter for united we are stronger. However, I understand his reluctance and know he will be like a deerhound on the flanks of the English, so I say this. We can wait forever more for circumstance to be in our favour yet no one can foresee the future. Look around you, men of Wales. Within these four walls sits every man of note from here to Builth and even though some have their doubts, the fact that you have come here demonstrates a longing to resolve our fate. Yes there are more questions than answers, but I say this is our only chance. So, Madog, Lord of Ynys Mon, I too will pledge my men and my resources to the fight and encourage everyone present to do the same. Act now, men of Wales, or keep your bleating for the safety of your own hearths.'

He sat down, again to a mighty roar. Another stood up from the crowd and as the noise abated, he made his decision.

'My lord, I am as one with Morgan Talbot. My men are your men.'

One by one all the most powerful warlords in the room stood to pledge allegiance until finally there were no more left. Madog got to his feet.

'Countrymen,' he said. 'My heart is gladdened at your resolve. But this is not about me or you, it is about our children and their children. Let the commitment in this room be the bedrock upon which freedom is built. Let free Welshmen generations from now look back on this day and tell stories about the night when a gallant few pledged to wrest their country from the grip of a tyrant. This day will be your legacy, this day and the freedom of Wales.'

For the last time the room erupted in cheers and this time did not abate. At a signal from Meirion, the doors swung open and lines of serving wenches walked in carrying trays of tankards.

Madog sat back alongside Meirion as the celebrations began.

'Well,' said Meirion, 'that went as well as you could have hoped.'

'It did,' said Madog, 'and for the first time since we took the castle, I once again enjoy confidence in our cause.'

Meirion looked around the room.

'It looks like this could get a bit messy,' he said.

'Let them celebrate, Meirion,' said Madog, 'for by the time this is over, I wonder how many of us will remain to see such times.'

Chapter Three

Brycheniog

Fletcher sat in the chair next to the hearth, warming his weary bones against the chill of the evening air. His wife sat in the corner, sewing patches onto worn clothing by the light of a single candle. On the flames of the fire, a diced hare complete with bones lay simmering in a pot along with onions and turnips, a meal meant to last them for at least three days. Half a loaf of bread lay to one side and the man leaned forward to pick off the stale edge before throwing it into the pot. Nothing was wasted in these hard times.

'I'll see if I can find some late roots tomorrow,' said his wife, Marian, 'with the dried apples from the dry store we can probably make it last a few extra days.'

'I need to collect some wood for the fire,' answered Fletcher, 'and reset the snares, you never know, we may get lucky.'

Marian got up and walked over to put her arms around the shoulders of her husband.

'Don't worry, Fletcher,' she said, 'another two days and I'll have the next basket from the manor. Perhaps I can persuade the cook to let us have some stew bones, there's always some meat left on them and the marrow is good for your blood.'

'It's just as well you are in gainful work,' said Fletcher, 'it has been a poor harvest and the store has too many empty barrels. Even though your payment is meagre, I foresee it will be your work in the manor's kitchens that will see us through this winter.'

'God will provide,' she said, hugging him tighter as she stared into the flames. For a few moments they stayed that way until the moment was interrupted by a loud knock on the door.

'Oh,' said Marian standing up, 'who can that be for it is already dark?'

'I will see,' said Fletcher and groaned as he got up from the solid wooden chair.

'Be careful,' said his wife, 'it could be anyone.'

'You fret too much woman,' said Fletcher, 'brigands don't knock doors they crush heads on lonely paths.'

'Still,' she said, 'it is always good to be wary.'

'Who calls at this hour?' asked Fletcher through the door.

'Sir, it is a family friend from your past, seeking shelter from the rain and perchance a crust from your plate.'

'Name yourself, traveller,' said Fletcher, 'for times are tough and hospitality is hard to give.'

'My name is Geraint,' said the voice, 'and I grew up alongside your daughter.'

Fletcher's brow furrowed as he strained to recall the name but Marian stepped forward and laid her hand on her husband's shoulder.

'Fletcher, if he speaks true then I know who he is.'

'I don't remember anyone called Geraint,' said Fletcher.

'You should,' said Marian, 'it is the brother of Garyn ap Thomas.'

Fletcher stared into his wife's eyes for a moment.

'Turn him away,' said Marian, 'we want nothing to do with that family.'

'Marian, since when do we turn away those who we know?'

'Since his brother deserted our daughter,' snapped Marian, 'why should we now give his family succour?'

'Because he may be able to help Elspeth.'

'What could he possibly do? Unless he is now a noble who can defend our daughter before the court of the people then I don't see how he can help.'

'I don't agree,' said Fletcher, 'and I will explore every opportunity to find a way out of our plight.'

'Don't open that door, Fletcher,' said his wife, 'it may not even be him; it could be a trick.'

Fletcher turned back to the door.

'If it is truly you, Geraint,' he said, 'what did your brother leave for my daughter when he went to the Holy Land?'

For a moment there was silence as the person thought about the answer but finally the reply came.

'A poem,' said the voice, 'declaring his love for Elspeth.'

Fletcher looked at Marian.

'Well?' he asked.

'Anyone could know that,' she said, 'send him away to return when it is light. At least his visit will be witnessed.'

Her husband paused but finally turned to lift the locking bar on the door.

'Fletcher!' warned the woman.

'Be quiet, wife,' said Fletcher, 'this is man's business.' He opened the door and looked into the hooded face of a figure blowing into his hands against the cold night air. Behind him stood another figure similarly clothed.

'Geraint,' asked Fletcher, 'is it truly you?'

The man pulled down the hood as Marian lifted a candle to see over her husband's shoulder.

'Well, young man,' said Fletcher eventually, 'you have certainly aged but those features are unmistakable; you are the image of your father. Come into the warm.' He stood to one side as the men entered and stamped the early snow from their boots. 'Marian, get some blankets, Geraint, remove your cloaks and get close to the fire, you look half frozen.'

'We were caught in the rainstorm earlier,' said Geraint, his voice shaking from the cold, 'and as soon as the sun went down the winter winds fell upon us like a hammer does an anvil. I did not intend to put you out but feared we may not last the night.'

'What about the tavern?' said Marian coldly, walking back into the room, 'there are lodgings to be had there and they are better placed to offer food.'

'Marian, that is enough,' snapped Fletcher, 'these men are now our guests and will not be made to feel beholden.'

'We cannot risk the tavern,' explained Geraint. 'Our purpose here must remain hidden from as many as possible lest we are imprisoned.'

'So are you outlawed as is your brother?' asked Marian.

'My lady, we are not but we are about business that would see us enchained by the English and perchance, lose our heads into the bargain.'

'And what business is so perilous?'

Geraint glanced at his comrade before turning back to face the couple.

'Ordinarily we would protect you from this knowledge,' said Geraint, 'but as it involves your family, you have a right to know. Allow us to thaw our bones and I will lay the story before you. Is that acceptable?'

'Of course,' said Fletcher, 'and your timing is opportune for there is a cawl upon the fire. Warm yourselves first and then we will take care of your insides. When the chills have been banished, you can share your tale.'

The two men set about removing their sodden clothes and wrapped the sheepskin blankets about them. Marian scooped out some of the hot broth from the bowl into tankards and they sipped it gratefully until the warmth returned to their extremities. When they had warmed up enough to relax, Marian fished chunks of turnip and meat from the cawl pot to fill two wooden bowls. She handed them over before adding the last of the bread.

Silently the men ate until finally they sat back and looked at their hosts with gratitude.

'It is a truly devilish night out there,' said Fletcher.

'It is that,' said Geraint, 'and I don't think it is far from the truth to say we may owe you our lives.'

'That may be a bit of an exaggeration,' said Fletcher, 'but it has to be said, you were in a sorry state.'

'Agreed,' said Geraint and turned to face his comrade.

'This is my good friend. He is known as Tarian and is the better man of us both. I trust him with my life.'

'Tarian, you are welcome,' said Fletcher. 'What town do you call home?'

'A place in the north,' said Tarian, 'a town called Dolwyddelan.'

'So what business brings you to Brycheniog?'

'It is a long story,' said Tarian, 'and the telling will be better from the mouth of Geraint.'

Fletcher turned to face Geraint and all waited for him to start.

'Well,' said Geraint, 'the first part of my story you know well, but I will start from the beginning so we are all made aware of the circumstance that led us to this day.

'I joined the army of King Henry when I was a young man but ended up in a dungeon in Acre through no fault of my own. Garyn, my brother, came to my aid and brought me home but not before making an enemy of a corrupt abbot, the same man who hides behind the cloth of the lord in this very town. When we returned, a Muslim girl came with me and though we could not be wed in the eyes of the church, we grew fond of each other and planned a life together. We did no one any harm and for a while we were accepted into the village. Alas when my health returned, I found my mind burned for the brotherhood that service brings and my heart was desperate for the freedom of campaign. I knew that if I was to settle down, then first I had to exorcise the spirits within me that demanded this freedom. I left upon a quest led by Tarian and together we found a land across the seas seen by no other living man.

'We courted both hunger and death but when we eventually returned, I was ready to pick up the threads of my past life. Alas it was not to be for I found Misha had been hung as a murderer and my brother Garyn had been outlawed as a brigand. I had nothing left so set myself to defending a young man whose destiny would be to unite Wales against the English crown. For more than ten years I carried out this task until at last he picked up the mantle and it is not ten days since I fought alongside him as he took Edward's castle at Caernarfon.'

'You were there?' asked Fletcher.

'I was,' said Geraint, 'as was Tarian. It was indeed a glorious victory but the celebrations were cut short when I found out my brother was still alive and had been taken prisoner by an English lord and cast into a dungeon deep.

'For all these years I had thought him dead but now, just when it seemed that my path was clear, this news cast clouds before my eyes and I knew that though he may be a brigand, I could not abandon him to rot as he did not abandon me.'

'So where is he now?' asked Fletcher.

'He lies a few leagues from here in the depths of Brecon Castle,' said Geraint, 'and I have made it my sworn duty to release him from the hell he must surely suffer.'

'If he is still alive,' said Tarian.

'Granted,' said Geraint, 'for he is not only in the hands of Gerald of Essex, but I hear the abbot also dwells within those walls. I will find out if Garyn is there and if he lives, then I swear by all that is holy, I will set him free or die in the trying.'

'You cannot,' said Marian.

All three men turned to stare at the woman.

'Marian,' said Fletcher, 'now is not the time.'

'Yes, it is,' snapped Marian, 'and I will have my say.' She turned to Geraint. 'You cannot free your brother, Geraint ap Thomas, for if you do it could be the death of our daughter and her son. She has been incarcerated within those walls on the false charge of treason against the king and awaits trial but if you assault those walls with your armies, the prisoners will be the first to die.

'I had no idea that your brother was also imprisoned there,' she continued, 'and indeed I thought him long dead, but even if I knew the truth of the matter then I would have given him no second thought. Such treatment is suitable for villains and brigands and he is surely such a man. It is an unfortunate coincidence that they share a jailer but if you pursue this course of action then I will not hesitate to seek an audience with Gerald himself and expose your fruitless quest.'

'Marian,' said Fletcher again, 'you will do no such thing.'

'Yes I will,' shouted the woman. 'This man's brother ran out on our daughter to save his own skin and never set foot within the village from that day to this. He broke her heart, Fletcher, as well you know. Why should we allow these men to try and save a vagabond at the potential cost of our daughter's life?'

'Because he is no coward,' said Fletcher quietly.

'What did you say?' asked Marian.

'I said he is no coward and did not flee to save his own skin.'

'Of course he did,' said Marian, 'he escaped the stocks and fled into the night aided by men of a similar ilk.'

'He did not,' shouted Fletcher, getting to his feet, 'for it was I who released him from his bonds that night. Myself and one other, the young man from the manor who travelled back from the Holy Land alongside him.'

'You speak of Dafydd?' asked Geraint.

'Aye, that was his name and I would not have shared it with you if he was not already dead, killed by an assassin in the pay of the abbot.'

'But I don't understand,' said Marian, 'you told me he ran like a coward, in fact you were his biggest denouncer and painted him a villain of the worst kind.'

'I had to,' said Fletcher. 'I am not proud of what I did but it was for the sake of our daughter. I cut him loose for he was going to be killed by Gerald's men, slaughtered while he was still in the stocks and unable to defend himself. I could not let that happen so I set him free but by giving him his life I took away his right to freedom for he had escaped the punishment set upon him by the manor. Whether it was just or not, he broke the law.'

'But why did you denounce him?' asked Geraint.

'So there was clear water between him and my daughter,' said Fletcher. 'The abbot knew she loved him and if he had thought for a heartbeat that she still had feelings for him or worse still, knew where he was, then she would have been labelled as an accomplice and faced the gallows. I could not let that happen and knew she had to set upon a new life without him. The only way to do that was to sour him in her eyes but I will say this. What I did, I did with the full knowledge of Garyn. He knew the price to be paid and though his heart was heavy he did what he had to do, live the life of a brigand so Elspeth could live the life of a free woman.'

Marion stared at her husband with a mixture of hurt and misunderstanding.

'All these years,' she said, 'I have thought him a knave and yet you knew differently. Why did you let me continue in my ignorance?'

'Because it was important Elspeth displayed a natural contempt if questioned,' said Fletcher. 'Garyn promised he would never return and after a few years, I also thought him dead. I saw no reason to stir it all again.'

Marian shook her head in disbelief.

'This is too much to take in,' she said. 'How will Elspeth react when she finds out that Garyn is not only a good man but is still alive?'

'It may not come to that, Marian,' said her husband. 'Let's just see what these men propose and take it one step at a time.'

Fletcher looked at Geraint who was also staring at him with a look of disbelief.

'Well,' said Fletcher, 'do you also hate me for my life of untruths?'

'I do not hate you, Fletcher,' said Geraint, 'though it is sad that a good man was separated from his home for all these years for the sake of a lie. For that, I blame Gerald of Essex, not you.'

'Then I am relieved,' said Fletcher. 'So, now I have opened my heart, perhaps you can finish your tale and explain what it is we can do to help?'

'Well,' said Geraint, 'the thing is we already knew of your daughter's incarceration. A messenger conveyed the tale to Caernarfon and we heard it first-hand. It would seem that the abbot claims Garyn is the father of Elspeth's child and he used the information to get my brother to return.'

'What do you mean?' asked Fletcher. 'Our daughter was imprisoned on a disputed charge of treason. We have not heard the evidence yet but our petitions are met with silence.'

'I fear the charges are nought but lies to imprison her and her son,' said Geraint. 'We were told that the abbot sent a messenger to Garyn and told him about the boy. He also said that if Garyn did not return to his justice immediately then both woman and child would be hung forthwith.'

Maria's hand flew to her mouth.

'And he returned?' asked Fletcher.

'He did, several weeks since,' said Geraint. 'However it seems the abbot is ill and has not had a chance to mete out his punishment.'

'And if he dies?'

'Then so does Garyn and your family. That is why we are here; we have to get them both out of there before he either recovers or dies from his illness.'

'How long have we got?'

'I know not, it could be weeks or it could be hours.'

'So what do you intend to do?'

'I have some thoughts,' said Geraint, 'but though I grew up in this area I have been away a long time and will need help from someone who knows the ways of the village, who can be trusted and who gives their allegiance to Edward.'

'Then I am your man, Geraint,' said Fletcher. 'I know everyone of note and belong to a group who leans against the control of Longshanks.'

'In what way?' asked Tarian.

'In whatever way we can,' said Fletcher. 'We short measure their purchases in the market, supply the dampest of the hay from the farms, and water the ale, that sort of thing. It is not much but we are all family men and can't risk discovery.'

'The smallest of raindrops lead to the greatest of floods, Fletcher,' said Tarian. 'Without people like you they would take even more of our lands from beneath our feet but fear not, the time for retribution is upon us. As we speak, the Lords of Wales gather their armies about them and Englishmen tremble behind their walls at the thought of the coming struggle. Caernarfon and Castell du Bere were but the first of many to fall and when Edward's soldiers are denied the false safety of their castle walls then they are but mortal men. Men that will fall before Welsh forged steel.'

'I thought as much,' said Fletcher, 'for though Gerald of Essex keeps a tight grip upon our lives, we still hear the tales of traders and troubadours as they travel through the village and our hearts lighten at the news. Despite the threat of retribution from the castle, even here the air is full of rebellion and we knew it was only a matter of time before the people turn against their brutal masters.'

'Well that time is upon us, Fletcher,' replied Tarian, 'and though we must hasten to join our comrades in the north, our quest to free Garyn and your daughter is no less important.'

'Then lay out your requirements, gentlemen, for though my sword arm tires through age, my heart is as strong as it ever was.'

Chapter Four

The Road from Bristol to Worcester

Edward was seated at a table situated under a temporary shelter set amongst trees at the side of the road. Around him, his personal guard took advantage of the break as did the rest of the column; over two hundred horsemen along with five hundred infantry and a hundred crossbow men, all taken from the invasion army assembled in Bristol waiting to sail to Gascony. They had been on the road only two days and had left Bristol castle to ride northward, gathering whatever men at arms they could from loyal landowners along the way.

For the past hour, Edward had been reading despatches brought to him from his lords in the south and west of Wales. His face appeared concerned at the news and he consulted regularly with his closest advisors. Finally he stood up and gave instructions to continue the march but as he did, two men rode into the makeshift camp and spoke to one of the guards.

A knight approached the King.

'What is your report, Henry Lauderville?' asked Long-shanks.

'My lord, two of the forward scouts have returned and reported a problem. Though the road is clear for ten leagues hence, there is a bridge down across a swollen river. They have engaged carpenters from the local villages to attend the problem as soon as possible but alas there is nothing we can do until the waters are lower. It could be many days before it is passable.'

'Is there another route?'

'Twenty leagues east, there lies another bridge, my lord, and we are told it remains intact.'

'This day is beset with problems,' said the King, 'but they will not weaken our resolve.'

'What is your command, my lord,' said the knight, 'shall we wait and hope the waters lower or take the longer route?'

'Whichever way we go, our journey is now longer,' said Edward, 'and we will not reach shelter before night-fall.' He turned toward the scout. 'Head upon the eastern road for another five leagues,' he said, 'and there set up my campaign tent for the night. Make sure there is water nearby for the horses and adequate forest to deflect the worst of the rain. The men have tents but I sense a storm coming our way.'

'My lord, we will find a farm and eject whatever family lives within. You and your court will sleep in a warm bed tonight.'

'No,' said Edward, 'I will stay amongst my men. Do as I command.'

'As you wish,' said the scout and turned his horse to ride away.

'Henry,' continued Longshanks, 'summon Fermbaud to attend me.' Moments later, Nicholas Fermbaud, Castellan of Bristol Castle arrived at the King's side.

'My lord, I was summoned?'

'Yes,' said Longshanks, 'take ten men as a guard and ride to Worcester in my name. Tell them to prepare for our arrival two days hence. I expect lodgings for my court and shelter for the men.'

'Are we not riding into Wales, my lord?'

'Not yet. I have today received disturbing news about the strength of the revolt and would take stock of the situation. It would be foolhardy to ride headlong into a hotbed of nationalism while their star is on the rise. We will let them enjoy the moment but, in the meantime, I will revisit the strength of the forces at my disposal. As soon as you arrive in Worcester, send word to the Earl of Warwick and the Earl of Gloucester. Tell them to attend me in haste.'

'As you wish, my lord,' said Fermbaud and turned to select his men. As he rode away, Henry Lauderville turned to address the King.

'My lord, if I may be so bold. Would it not be better to strike while the Welsh are distracted through ale and celebration?'

'Ordinarily I would agree,' said Longshanks, 'but the messages put before me this day tell of an uprising that stretches from the north to the southern coast and across the whole width of the country. A single column cannot put down such a widespread revolt so we will need a force of many fronts. The Earls of Gloucester and Warwick already have men to hand and I will seek their aid in this matter. First, we will muster at Worcester and take counsel. Once done, we will then decide the best way to extinguish this spark before it becomes a flame.'

Near the north coast of Wales, Reginald De-Grey, second Baron of Ruthin, sat in the hall of Ruthin castle within the cantref of Dyffryn Clwyd. His officers shared the same table and together they discussed the latest developments with the Welsh uprising in the north.

'So what news?' asked Reginald.

'Madog has laid waste to Ynys Mon,' said Gisbourn, one of his knights. 'He has burned Caernarfon town to the ground and taken possession of the castle. He has left a strong force within its walls and rebuilt the palisade but the main strength of his army has ridden out.'

'Do we know where?'

'We have not had a chance to secure any spies, such is the speed that he has manoeuvred, but it seems there was a meeting between Madog and the warlords of Wales a few days ago. There are rumours that each has a role on which they will focus. We do know there is a large force of men heading west and another coming this way.'

'To Flint?'

'We are not sure yet. The last we heard was they were certainly riding the eastern road but they could turn north at a moment's notice. If Rhuddlan is their target they could be here within days.'

'What is their strength?'

'Again, it is hard to tell as there are many different columns spread out through the country but I would say those coming this way are at least three thousand strong.'

'Three thousand?' gasped Reginald. 'Where would he raise such an army?'

'The Welsh are flocking to his banner. It would seem this time they have a determination about them as well as organisation.'

'Still,' said Reginald, 'his army is made up of farmers and peasants. The taking of Caernarfon is indeed a setback but the whole thing was fortuitous beyond compare. The Castellan of Caernarfon was in Portsmouth tasked with sailing to Gascony with the King as were more than half of his force. I also hear Madog used the cover of the monthly fayre to approach the town and took them unawares. That along with the unfinished walls of the castle all contributed to a set of circumstances that fell favourably at his feet.'

'Yet they still defeated the defending force and took the castle walls, my lord, and any man capable of doing such a thing should not be underestimated.'

'I accept the point, Gisbourn,' said Reginald. 'Good fortune may be his bedfellow at the moment but they will not find us unprepared. Send messengers to all the English landowners within the cantref and tell them if they value their lives, they will leave their manors immediately to join us here in Rhuddlan. They are to bring anything that may help should we suffer a siege, then food, water, weapons, indeed anything they have that can be carried quickly. I want them and their men within the town walls before the sun sets on the morrow. In addition, send word to Flint castle. Tell the constable there that we do not have the forces to defend Flint as well as we can Rhuddlan. Our town walls give us extra strength but Flint is open to attack. With immediate effect he is to gather what supplies he can unto the castle and lock it down for siege. In addition he is to burn the town to the ground to deny any attackers shelter or materials for siege engines.'

'What about the tenants?'

'Any of English birth are to be given shelter within the castle walls but be they Welsh born, turn them away unto the forests.' He turned to a second knight. 'John of Bath, you will take a well-armed patrol and see if you can buy us some time by holding up the advance of the rebels. We need three days and if you can secure us that, I feel we can muster a force capable of defending the cantref.'

'My lord,' said John, 'if opportunity arises, do you want me to engage the rebels?'

'No,' said Reginald, 'you will have the chance to face them in open battle soon enough but now is not the time. I know Edward gathers his armies as we speak and he will need a safe passage into Wales. He intends to muster in Chester and ride here via Wrexham. We are best placed to provide a safe route and I will not be distracted from that goal.'

'Aye, my lord,' said John, 'are we done?'

'We are. Gather your men and ride out immediately. Remember, harassment and delay only, we don't want them marching upon us until we are ready.'

The two knights left the room, leaving Reginald poring over his charts with his advisors.

'Well, gentlemen,' he said, 'I have long said these people will one day rise up against us. That's the problem with the Welsh, they don't know when they are defeated.'

—

The following two days were busy within the walled town of Rhuddlan. Constant caravans of English nobles came from within the cantref seeking the safety of the castle, bringing with them their families, supplies and of course, the much-needed fighting men. Mounted patrols were sent out by Reginald to check no enemy approached, and hundreds of archers were immediately deployed along the castellated town walls. Squires and pages were put to work supplying the defenders with the necessary tools needed to thwart any attack including poles to push away siege ladders, heavy rocks to hurl down at the enemy and, of course, thousands of arrows for the archers.

The population of the town were tasked with gathering what food they could from the many farms and villages in the area and within two days, Rhuddlan castle was stocked the best it could be considering the short period of warning.

–

Two days later, Reginald walked the town walls for the second time, checking on the preparations with his own eyes.

'You there,' he said to the sergeant in charge of the archers, 'place distance markers before the walls and get your bowmen to practise from dawn to dusk. The squires will retrieve the arrows after each man has shot a hundred shafts.'

'Aye my lord,' said the sergeant and set about his task. As he went, Gisbourn climbed the steps and joined the Baron.

'Gisbourn,' said Reginald, 'I heard you had returned. Did you relay my instructions to Flint castle?'

'I did, my lord, and at first the constable was loathe to carry out such a dire instruction but I explained the purpose behind your thinking and eventually he saw the sense in this matter.'

'And?'

'As we rode here this evening, the smoke from the burning houses of Flint darken the sky.'

'It is a harsh decision,' said Reginald, 'but the castle is strong enough and Edward De Laye should be able to last until Longshanks gets here.'

'The defences look ready,' said Gisbourn, looking around the walls.

'As ready as we can be,' said Reginald, 'but I know they will only delay any serious assault. Our main strengths are our numbers and the walls of the castle itself. Should we be defeated on any field of battle then we will reorganise within the castle until Longshanks arrives. I have had the north entrance secured with extra props and the bridge dismantled. I am happy to defend the southern gate but will deny them the luxury of options.'

He looked out at the road and saw a column of horses riding toward them. He recognised the banner and knew it was the diversionary force he had sent out a few days earlier.

'Open the gates,' shouted Gisbourn, 'it's John of Bath.' They both watched as the hundred lancers galloped between the gate towers and headed toward the castle. The lead knight turned his horse and dismounted before climbing up the stone steps to join the two men.

'Well, John,' said Reginald, 'how went the day?'

'My lord,' came the reply, 'there was indeed a force upon the eastern road and though their numbers were large, we managed to place doubt in their minds.'

'In what way?'

'When they went to ground to see out the night, we probed their perimeters with flaming arrows from a safe distance. Though we inflicted little in the way of casualties, the confusion amongst the burning tents was enough to make them lay up another half a day as they sent out patrols to check the road was clear. We did similar on the second night and in this way slowed their progress.'

'A task well done,' said Reginald, 'for it has given us time to prepare well. Ride on to the castle and seek rest and sustenance for your men. Once my inspection has been completed, we will meet in the great hall and you can brief me in detail.'

'Aye my lord,' said John and descended the steps before leading his horse up to the castle.

'Well, Gisbourn,' said Reginald turning to his comrade. 'We have almost five thousand men at arms under our command, a well-stocked stronghold and a fortified town perimeter. We've done all that we can so if Madog thinks he can take Rhuddlan, then let him come.'

—

Less than ten leagues away, Cynan ap Maredudd rode at the head of a column, keen to reach his destination before darkness fell. Martyn rode alongside him as they reached the crossroads, now defended by a hundred of his own advance party. They reined in their horses and looked down both paths, one heading north and one heading south east.

'North is the way of Rhuddlan,' said Martyn, 'people in the last village said that the Castellan has prepared well and has gathered a formidable army.'

'Rhuddlan is a target for Madog,' said Cynan. 'Let him worry about the strengths of the castle, our path leads southward.'

'To Denbigh?'

'Aye, to Denbigh. The town is well placed and if we can take the castle then any English patrols will be denied the chance of succour for many leagues and their resources will be stretched to the full. Pass the word to the men, Martyn, tomorrow we march upon Denbigh castle.'

Without another word, he turned his horse to the right and followed the path southeast.

In the heart of Snowdonia, the men guarding the northern approach to the hidden wooded valley looked up at the column cresting the far hill line.

'Riders,' said the first, standing up straight and loosening the clasp around the hilt of his sword.

'Stand down,' said the second guard, 'I recognise the banner of Maelgwyn. The column has returned from Caernarfon.'

'So it is,' said the first guard, 'but ride back to the camp anyway. Tell them to prepare for the arrival of our lord. The weather has been harsh and they will welcome hot mead and cawl.'

'Agreed,' said the guard and walked over to the horses tied to a nearby tree.

Ten minutes later, the column galloped past the remaining guard, most ignoring his salute. Their chainmail shirts and heavy tabards were covered with sheepskin jerkins and most wore heavy cloaks of oiled leather as protection from the rain. Those lucky enough to have furred collars had them tied tightly around their necks, and the guard could see they had ridden hard through the high passes of the mountains.

Maelgwyn ap Rhys ruled the western cantrefs from as far north as the high mountains down as far as Pembroke but though he was recognised as the local lord by the people of west Wales, his lands officially belonged to the crown, having been confiscated twelve years earlier after the death of Llewellyn. Despite this, he lived unchallenged in a manor amongst the hills and maintained a force of a hundred men at arms and twelve Welsh knights. Since Madog's success at Caernarfon, his numbers had swelled tenfold and a force of over a thousand men now secreted themselves amongst the deep valleys on the southern edge of the Snowdonia Mountains, being trained by Maelgwyn's regular soldiers.

He rode between the many makeshift tents and lodges that had been his men's home for the past thirty days and rode up to the conical tent that formed his headquarters in the field. He dismounted and handed the reins of his horse to a waiting servant before ducking through the entrance and into the heat of the interior, warmed by a log fire situated in the centre. A man waited for him and stood as Maelgwyn entered.

'My lord,' said the knight, 'welcome back. I trust the ride was not too arduous?'

'It was difficult, Gwylim,' said Maelgwyn, throwing his cloak toward a nearby chair. 'We rode via the northern bluff and suffered a storm along the way. The men are exhausted.'

'A strange choice of route at this time of year,' said Gwylim. 'The river pass is far more sheltered albeit a longer path.'

'It was a considered decision,' said Maelgwyn, discarding his sodden jerkin and extending his arms over the fire. 'It saved us a day and a night and we need all the time we can get.'

'I take it the meeting with Madog went well?'

'It did,' said Maelgwyn, 'and at last it seems that all men of influence are agreed with a common purpose. As we speak, any force of note throughout the country is about to unleash their strength upon any English position within the boundaries of their cantrefs. Before this week is out, Edward's positions will be under attack from every quarter. That is why we took the quicker route; it is imperative we move as quickly as possible so the attacks are coordinated. That way, each of Edward's castles will not have the chance to draw on the strength of another.'

'So is that the plan, to isolate and attack the castles?'

'Those and the manors,' said Maelgwyn reaching for a tankard of warmed mead. 'We will sweep southward and attack Cardigan castle with all haste. Should we succeed, our task is to then raid any English interests as far as Carmarthen, but I get ahead of myself. Summon the marshals and senior sergeants, I will give a full briefing within the hour.'

—

Deep in the rolling valleys of Mid Wales a smaller column of armed men rode hard southward led by Morgan ap Maredudd, a warlord from south Wales. For the past few years he had paid homage to Longshanks but having always been treated badly when compared with the English barons in the same area, grew more and more frustrated at the unfairness.

Madog's uprising in the north had raised his interest and though at first he had been sceptical, the fervour experienced in Caernarfon and the discovery that not one but two of Edward's favoured castles had fallen excited him enough to realise this was a genuine opportunity. Not just to seize back some of his stolen lands but to unify similar Welshmen in the same position and perhaps re-develop a position of strength and rule for his own family.

Though his garrison was relatively small back in Caerleon, he enjoyed good relations with his neighbours and knew the time was ripe for coordinated resistance. Many had been the night when they met in secret, bemoaning the brutality of Edward's rule and oft the talk had been of rebellion but never was the time right. Now however, it seemed the whole of Wales was waking from their slumber and standing up against the English. All he had to do was convince as many as he could to join him and then strike against the minimal English fortifications as hard as they could with the speed of a flying arrow.

He dug his heels harder into the flanks of his horse, desperate to reach the south as soon as possible. These were momentous days and he was keen to make history.

While the other rebel leaders were returning to their own cantrefs to take the fight to the English, Madog finalised his plans for the struggle in the north. He and Meirion sat in a room of Caernarfon castle, a jug of wine to hand on a nearby table and a fire roaring in the huge stone fireplace. Upon the table were charts of north Wales all the way down to Builth. Upon the maps, every castle had been marked and several circled with ink as targets for the

Welsh. The prince had been staring at the charts for over half an hour until finally he straightened up and called to his aide.

'Meirion, attend me, I would hear your thoughts.'

The man came over and looked down upon the charts.

'I have thought long this last week,' said Madog, 'especially about our position here in the castle.' He tapped the head of an arrow on the image representing Caernarfon castle.

'And your thoughts are?'

'I think our position is untenable,' said Madog. 'As you are aware, we are protected on the north approach by the Straits and by the river to the east. However, though that is a good thing for those familiar with the defence of castles, it is a burden for those unused to such situations, people like us.'

'In what way?'

'Should an attack come from Edward or any of his liegemen then they will have to come from the south or east but that is also the only way out. With a strong enough force, Edward can easily trap us here with no hope of escape. We are not an army of garrisons and fortifications, Meirion but of freedom and flexibility. We should not be barricaded in like a flock of frightened sheep but roam the hills like a pack of hungry wolves, modelling ourselves on the tactics of Llewellyn Mawr.'

'But surely if we are to pursue the claim of rightful self-government then as all such bodies, we will need a place from which we can proclaim our legitimacy.'

'You are right,' said Madog, 'but we are far from that time and there is much to do. However, in the meantime

I suggest Caernarfon has served its purpose and we move on to greater things.'

'My lord,' said Meirion, 'if we give up Caernarfon now then surely all those men who fell in the assault will have died in vain.'

'No,' said Madog, 'they haven't. The uprising is not about stone and mortar and never was. The assault of the castle was about more than that, it was about showing the people of Wales that the English have nowhere to hide, not even behind the walls of their so-called ring of steel. Yes, there have been many sacrifices, but for every man that fell in our cause another hundred rode to our banner. As we speak, the warlords across Wales are raising armies against Edward's rule and if this is the legacy of our fallen then a great legacy it is.'

'So what do you intend to do?'

'I think we should move our men out. The blow has been dealt and the message sent to Longshanks yet while we linger here, there are villages not even an hour's ride hence that still suffer under English rule. Our army grows every day, but if we leave it standing idle then it will surely dissolve as quickly as it appeared.' He pointed at a castle further south along the coast. 'I have received word that Dolwyddelan castle has no garrison to speak of and holds little interest for Edward. This is fortunate for not only is it central to our ambition but it is also the home of my ancestors. I suggest we relocate there to organise the uprising whilst using it as a hub from which we can operate. In the event of an assault, it will be easy to disappear into the hills before an arrow is fired.'

'I can see the strategic benefits,' said Meirion, 'but once there, what will be our goals?'

'I intend to split the army in three. The first half under the command of Alun Godwin will ride south-west and lay siege to Criccieth and Harlech castles. You, Meirion, will head for Dolwyddelan and set up an administrative centre. I will send a column of five hundred with you but expect no real resistance.'

'And the third column?' asked Meirion.

'I will lead it eastward,' said Madog, 'and assault Howarden castle.'

'Howarden castle? Isn't that dangerously close to Rhuddlan and the English border?'

'Perhaps so but that is why they will least expect it. My spies say it is lightly defended and while Reginald De-Grey expends precious resources fortifying Rhuddlan castle, it is surely at the expense of other fortifications. Howarden is an easy target yet will send more shivers through the bones of Edward himself and if we succeed, it reduces the number of places his patrols can seek succour.'

'An audacious plan,' said Meirion.

'It is, but that is why it has every chance of succeeding.'

'When do you intend to ride out?'

'It will take a day or so to arrange the supplies. I suggest the day after tomorrow at dawn's first light. Tomorrow night, the men are to burn what they can in the castle. Every coin that Edward has to spend rebuilding this place is a coin not spent on paying his soldiers to kill Welshmen. When we go, we are to leave this place barren of anything useful to the English.'

'So be it,' said Meirion, and drained his tankard of mead.

Chapter Five

Brycheniog

Garyn sat against the wall of the dungeon. A bucket of water and a bowl of potash soap had been provided as well as some decent hot food and a jug of watered wine. Combined with a change of clothes it meant that by the time the jailer returned to collect him, he at least looked a lot better. Finally the familiar rattle of keys echoed outside the cell and the door slammed back against the wall.

'Out,' came the order, 'your presence is required.'

Garyn got to his feet and walked slowly out of the cell. The jailer led the way up the winding stairs of the tower and through a narrow corridor built within the castle's walls, before taking him into a side room.

'Wait in here,' said the jailer.

Inside the room the conditions were far more comfortable. Tapestries hung on the wall and there was even glass within a window overlooking the castle courtyard. A jug of wine sat in the centre of a table along with four wooden tankards. A modest fire burned in the hearth.

Garyn walked over to the fire, taking the opportunity to warm his body for the first time in weeks. Finally the keys sounded again and he spun around to see a priest enter the room closely followed by a woman. Behind them came Gerald of Essex.

For a few seconds they all stared at each other before Gerald broke the silence.

'Sit,' he said and the priest sat alongside the knight on one side of the table. For a moment, both Garyn and Elspeth remained on their feet staring at each other.

'I said sit,' said Gerald impatiently and waited as Elspeth and Garyn took a seat opposite each other.

'So,' said Gerald eventually. 'Here we are. You see Garyn, I am indeed a man of my word and can make wondrous things happen.'

Silence fell again as Garyn stared at Elspeth, his mind racing as he recalled the brief time they had spent together all those years ago. Elspeth looked back, her gaze unwavering and Garyn detected a hint of resentment in her manner.

'Elspeth,' he said eventually, 'the years have been kind to you.'

'Have they Garyn?' answered Elspeth coldly, 'or is it that you see only my countenance for should you peer deeper within, you will see my heart is as aged as a crone. What brings you back here, Garyn, after all these years? Why have you returned after what you did to me?'

Garyn glanced at Gerald realising the knight hadn't explained the reason to Elspeth.

'Elspeth,' said Garyn, turning back to the woman, 'first of all I must say I am not here of my own free will but was coerced by others to return here on pain of death for...' He paused, realising that she may not know her life was in danger and he didn't want to add to her worry, '...on pain of death,' he said eventually and left it at that.

'Such is the life of a brigand, Garyn, and you should not complain, for after all this time your deeds have finally caught up with you.'

'It is not as simple as that,' said Garyn quietly.

'So where have you been all these years?' she asked. 'Or am I right in guessing you ran free with other outlaws, inflicting misery on the innocent while the rest of us worked hard to earn a crust of bread?'

'It wasn't like that, Elspeth,' he replied. 'Yes my path fell in with those outside of the law but it was the law of Longshanks, not the Welsh people. On not one occasion did I raise a fist against any I called countrymen.'

'You may not have,' said Elspeth, 'but those you left behind still paid the price of your actions and those of your fellows on a daily basis. Across the country, penalties are levied against the innocent whenever a loss is incurred by those loyal to the English. Don't you see? For every blow dealt by people of your ilk, twice the pain is suffered by someone who bears no guilt. Such is the way it is and such is the way it has always been.'

'Elspeth,' said Garyn, 'the situation was complicated. I had no other option but to leave.'

'You had every option,' snapped Elspeth. 'All you had to do was take the punishment issued to you by our laws and then come back to us. Instead, you chose to run like a thief in the night.'

'Elspeth,' replied Garyn, 'there are things which you know nothing about. All those years ago I planned a life with the woman I loved. Together we planned a future of honest work and family values. Our bond was tight and I thought no man could tear us apart but events overtook me and though my love burned no less brightly, I had to leave that night in the interests of everyone.'

'You mean your own interests,' said Elspeth. 'You ran from the stocks for humiliation bore greater importance than the love of the family around you.'

'That's not true,' said Garyn, 'there were other reasons why I ran.'

'Then share them, Garyn,' said Elspeth leaning forward. 'Cast light into the shadows of my mind for all I see is darkness and bitterness. Tell me why you ran without as much as a word of explanation and not one message since.'

Garyn glanced at the English knight but Gerald shook his head behind Elspeth's back.

'I can't, Elspeth,' said Garyn, 'it is not in anyone's interests to now dig up the past.' He reached out across the table and placed his hands upon hers but flinched as she snatched her own hands away.

'If this is so,' she said, 'then why have you come here, Garyn? What reason can you possibly have except to tear apart the fabric-thin happiness that we enjoy?'

Garyn sat back and realised he was fighting a losing battle. The woman he once loved was bitterly hurt and resented his very presence.

'Elspeth,' he said eventually, 'your pain is evident and I am not in a position to explain the circumstances but at least know this. I swear on the graves of my family that I never intended to hurt you and things came to pass that meant I had to leave. I know that is not enough but it is all I can offer.'

Elspeth stared at the man who she had loved with all her heart. For a second, her attitude softened as she remembered the good times.

'I don't know, Garyn,' she said quietly. 'Too much water has flowed under the bridge for me to be healed with soothing words. Without explanation then there can be no reconciliation.'

'I understand,' said Garyn, 'and I blame you not. All fault in this matter lies on my shoulders and I am not worthy of your forgiveness but as wretched as I am, I have a boon to ask.'

Elspeth shook her head in amazement.

'After all you have done, you come begging favours. What is it, Garyn? What could I possibly have that will ease your conscience?'

Garyn leaned forward and staring into her eyes, spoke softly.

'Elspeth,' he said, 'I would hear about Thomas.'

'My son?' gasped Elspeth. 'What about him for he is no business of yours?'

Garyn glanced across at Gerald.

'I have heard a rumour that I may be his true father.'

For a few seconds Elspeth stared at him, the anger growing behind her eyes.

'Whatever it is you thought, Garyn,' she hissed eventually, 'then you thought wrong. The father of Thomas is a barrel maker and though he has his faults, a better father no child could wish for.'

'I understand you married again,' said Garyn, 'and I doubt not the virtues of your husband but I must know for the sake of my sanity. Were you already with child on the night I left?'

Elspeth paused for a few more moments before giving her carefully considered answer.

'What if I was, Garyn? What if I was indeed carrying your child on that night? How does it affect our situation now for even if he was your son, do you really think I would let you set eyes upon him? The boy has a good life and once we get out of here, as we will, then he will return to the trade of my father, an honest fletcher. Whether I was carrying him on the night you ran is no business of yours.'

'But surely,' answered Garyn, 'if he is mine, don't you think he has the right to know who his real father is?'

'A lustful bed does not a father make, Garyn,' shouted Elspeth, losing her composure. 'Even if he had been created by your seed, there is a good man out there who fed him and played alongside him even as you preyed on the plight of innocents. Someone who was there when he was ill and worked in all weathers to bring back food to put upon his platter while you were probably frequenting the taverns of knaves and whoring amongst the women of the back lanes. You have no right to come in here and talk to me as if he has anything to do with you.' She stood up and turned to the priest. 'Take me from here,' she said, 'I am done.'

'Wait,' said Garyn as everyone else in the room got to their feet. 'Just one more question. If ever you held any feelings for me at all, I beseech thee to release me from my torment and clear my mind. All I ask is this one thing and I will turn away never to poison your sight again. Is he my son, yes or no?'

Elspeth stared at Garyn for the last time before taking a deep breath and giving him his answer.

'No, Garyn,' she said, 'he is not. Your source was mistaken. Now, if you don't mind, I have to leave.' She stood up and walked to the door. 'Take me back,' she said to the guard, 'this audience is over.'

'Elspeth!' called Garyn but the door slammed behind her. For a few moments there was silence until Gerald also stood to leave.

'Well,' he said, 'it seems I was mistaken.'

'Or lied,' said Garyn.

'Whatever you wish to believe,' sighed Gerald. 'Oh, I forgot to say, I have been informed that Father Williams has regained consciousness and is improving by the hour. It would seem the business between him and you will soon be concluded.'

'And what about our business?' asked Garyn. 'You said if I was to return you would set the woman free as well as her son.'

'Why do you care?' asked Gerald. 'She has made it clear she no longer has feelings for you and the boy is not yours.'

'It matters not,' said Garyn, 'her imprisonment was a lure to bring me back and now I am here and the abbot is recovering, there is no need to extend their captivity. You say you are a man of your word, Gerald, so let them go.'

Gerald considered for a moment before answering.

'Granted,' he said. 'I will have the charges dropped and they will be released immediately but don't forget your part of the bargain. You are to explain exactly where the tomb of Macsen is and be warned, if your information is proved false then they can be brought back within hours and next time I will not be so generous. I will leave you now for I have business to attend to, but will return with a scribe before nightfall. Make sure your memory is clear,

Garyn, or you will be returned to the cell whence you came with all speed. Come, priest, let's get out of here.'

Both men walked to the door but just before it closed behind them, Garyn saw the priest's hand reach back in the room and drop a piece of parchment on the floor. The door slammed shut and Garyn heard the key turning in the lock. He walked over quickly and picked up the parchment reading the simple words with fresh hope in his breast.

'Garyn, be upon your guard for at the twelfth
bell, friends will aim to set you free.'

He read the words twice before throwing the parchment into the fire, his heart racing.

—

An hour later, a man walked through the village of Brycheniog toward the house of the fletcher. After checking he wasn't being followed, he climbed over the fence holding in the family chickens and knocked upon the shutter in the rear wall. Inside the room, Marian jumped in alarm and Geraint looked nervously at Tarian.

'That must be him,' said Fletcher walking over to the shutter and undoing the clasp. He pushed it open a few inches.

'Who's there?' he asked.

'A friend,' came the reply.

'What can I do for you friend?'

'I am here to tell you the message has been delivered safely and the other arrangements have been made.'

'Is there anything else?'

'That is it. Good luck.'

'Thank you, friend,' said Fletcher and closed the shutters.

'Who was it?' asked Geraint.

'I don't know and don't want to know,' said Fletcher. 'There are many such people who lean against the rule of the English but each only knows one or two others. That way, if one is discovered then only a few are at risk and it minimises the amount of family men who have to run. It has been so for many years.'

'So has it all been arranged?'

'It has,' said Fletcher, 'an hour before midnight we will be met inside the castle by someone who can help us further.'

'And how do we get inside?'

'Leave that to me.'

–

Father Williams sat up in his bed for the first time in weeks. One of the serving girls fed him a weak broth from a wooden bowl and he sipped sparingly, gasping for breath between each mouthful.

'Father Williams,' said Gerald as he walked into the room, 'you are on the road to recovery, I hear. You must have incriminating knowledge on the devil himself for I have not seen a man come back from so near to death.'

'Gerald,' said the abbot weakly, 'you are back. Were you successful in your quest?'

'I was indeed,' said Gerald, 'and our quarry is incarcerated not a hundred paces from your sick bed as we speak.'

Father Williams managed a weak smile and pushed away the offered spoon from his mouth.

'Leave us,' he said and the serving girl scurried quickly from the room.

'Is it true?' asked Father Williams when they were alone. 'Is Garyn ap Thomas at last within my reach?'

'Oh, it's true,' said Gerald, 'do you want him brought to you?'

Father Williams thought for a while before shaking his head.

'No,' he said, 'not yet. I am still as weak as a babe and would not be able to wield a blade. Keep him safe for a few days, until I am strong enough to relish my victory.'

'So be it,' said Gerald, 'but I believe there is a small matter yet to be resolved between us.'

'You talk of my fortune?' asked the abbot.

'I do,' said Gerald, 'and would seek settlement before the devil finally takes you into his fiery embrace.'

'Fear not, Gerald,' said the abbot, 'I will honour my pledge and as soon as the blacksmith draws his last breath, I will reveal the resting place of the caskets.'

'Then let it be soon, holy man,' said Gerald, 'for I grow impatient.'

Chapter Six

North Wales

Madog crawled through the undergrowth and stared toward Howarden castle. Beside him was Emrys ap Martin, commander of his infantry. The first thing to capture their attention was the magnificent round keep soaring skyward from the mound at the centre of the fortress. Beneath it he could see the smoke rising from the hidden rooftops of the buildings situated within the castle grounds, usually used as barracks for any garrison stationed within the perimeter but Madog knew no such force currently occupied them and they were used by peasants and farmers seeking shelter from the winter's oncoming chills.

The gates in the outer wall were open and guarded by one man only, an old soldier bearing a spear. People came and went as they pleased and a constant line of locals passed between the castle and the village a hundred yards away.

'Do you see any sign of a garrison?' asked Emrys.

'I don't,' said Madog, 'only a few guards upon the walls. I think the reports of our spies are indeed true and, in his arrogance, Longshanks stripped most of his garrisons to fight alongside him in Gascony. In doing so he not only took a chance but treated us with contempt. Obviously, he thought this area needed little in the way of defence and left a skeleton force to keep his castles dry for when he returned.'

'I thought Howarden was of great importance to him,' said Emrys.

'It once was,' said Madog, 'when Dafydd ap Gruffydd took this castle in Llewellyn's campaign against the English twelve years ago, Longshanks was so angered that when the uprising finally failed, he had Dafydd hung, drawn and quartered with his remains displayed across the four corners of the realm.'

'No man deserves such a death,' said Emrys.

'Agreed,' said Madog, 'but since then it has become a favourite method of Longshanks when dealing with his enemies. It sends a shiver of fear amongst any who chance their arm against him.'

Both men fell silent as they stared across at the castle. Finally Madog spoke again.

'Are you clear about what has to be done?' he asked.

'I am,' said Emrys, 'and the men await your orders.'

'Good,' said Madog. 'We will wait until darkness and then unleash our wrath upon them. With fortune on our side, they will be so distracted, they won't see the true nature of our intentions.'

An hour later Madog sat in his saddle. Behind him, a further hundred cavalry waited for the signal along with a hundred archers and five hundred men at arms. Though it was an impressive force, another thousand had slipped quietly from the dense forest, keeping to the deep riverbank as they circled around the back of the castle.

'Sire the gates are closed,' said a voice.

'Good,' said Madog. 'Let them settle into their false security. When we assault, I want there to be maximum confusion.' He waited for another hour before giving the signal for his force to spread out along the treeline facing the castle.

'Don't forget,' he said to those in earshot, 'I want as much noise and disruption as possible but don't risk any of the men unduly. This is for appearance only; the real damage will be done by others.' He drew his sword and held it up.

'Men of Wales,' he roared through the darkness, 'attack.'

Within seconds hundreds of screaming men ran across the open fields toward the castle, each shouting as loudly as they could for maximum effect. The guards in the gatehouse towers immediately manned their positions and though it was dark, could see hundreds of lights advancing toward them, the result of the fire pots carried by the archers.

'Alarm,' shouted one of the guards, 'we are under attack.'

The message was repeated throughout the gate towers and within minutes a dozen men ran up to the battlements to take their place along the walls. Though they were few in number, they knew they were relatively safe for the walls were formidable and it would take the attention of many siege engines to breach them.

'Lewis London,' shouted the senior sergeant in charge of the defences, an older man by the name of Watkins, 'get a message to the keep. Tell them we are under attack.

Man the doors in case we are breached, but wait as long as possible so we can seek the safety within.'

'Aye sir,' shouted the man and ran off into the darkness.

'Bowmen,' shouted Watkins, 'load the crossbows but hold your fire. I know not their strategy for a night assault is unheard of. Someone waken the servants and have them bring supplies from the armoury immediately. We may be few, but by God we will give these barbarians a good account of ourselves.'

As he finished, the first of the Welsh attackers came in range and the sound of arrows flying over their heads made the defenders duck behind the castellations.

'You two,' shouted Watkins toward two of the younger men, 'check the bars on the gates. Ensure the upper and lower bars are also engaged, if they should try ramming them it will take nothing short of a mangonel to secure a breach.'

'Aye sir,' came the reply and they ran down to carry out their orders.

All around him, Madog saw his men running toward the walls with the siege ladders. Their cries echoed across the fields and the darkness was lit by hundreds of flaming arrows splitting the night sky. Behind him a cart brought up a small mangonel and lost no time in launching its stone missiles and fire pots over the walls of the castle. It was a noisy and impressive sight but any man with battle experience knew it was a futile attempt for without trebuchets or siege engines to master the walls, the attackers had little chance of success. Even the ram now hammering against the giant gates was but an attempt to gain the defenders' attention. He watched as the few siege ladders they placed against the walls were easily pushed away from the walls by the defenders, casting the men upon them to the floor. Despite this, some of his men were killed by the crossbows from above and he knew he couldn't keep up the pretence for long.

'Bowmen,' he called, 'keep their heads down. Another few minutes and our job will be done.'

Up above, Watkins peered between the castellations, trying to work out the enemy's tactics.

'It makes no sense,' he said, 'we can hold them back for weeks if this is the extent of their strategy.' A man came running out of the darkness and crouched down beside him.

'My lord,' he gasped, 'I came as soon as I could. The reserve are deployed on our flanks but there seems to be no activity there. The enemy are focusing their attack on the front walls.'

'A futile approach,' said Watkins, 'they throw themselves at the wall as if knowing they have no chance of success.'

'A feint perhaps,' said the soldier.

Watkins' eyes widened at the realisation.

'Of course,' he said, 'it has to be a bluff. What force do we have on the rear walls?'

'Nought but a sentry, my lord, they all came running when the alarm was sounded.'

Watkins stood and stared at the far wall to the south of the keep but the night was dark and he could see nothing, not the body of the southern sentry with an arrow through his face, not the siege ladders leaning against the outside of the far wall and certainly not the hundreds of men running through the inner ward, their faces blackened with soot as they raced toward the keep.

'Something's wrong,' he said slowly, but as he drew breath to shout the alarm across to the guard on the keep doors, an arrow smashed through the back of his head, sending his body crashing to the floor.

His comrade shouted in fear but as he turned to face the way of Madog's diversion, a flaming arrow pierced his chest and he too fell screaming into the inner ward.

At the keep the guard took a step forward to get a better view but as he stared, he was seized from behind and a knife opened his throat.

'Inside,' roared Emrys and stood aside as hundreds of men stormed into the keep, killing anyone in their path irrespective of age or gender.

'You men,' shouted Emrys, 'follow me.' He ran down the mound away from the keep and headed toward the gates of the outer walls. Too late the defenders heard them coming and though they turned to confront them, they were hopelessly outnumbered.

'Open the gates,' shouted Emrys as the last of the defenders fell and as the huge wooden barriers swung slowly inward, he stepped through to greet Madog, waiting upon his charger.

'My lord,' said Emrys with a grin, 'your castle awaits.'

He stood aside as Madog galloped his horse between the gate towers and up the hill toward the keep. Already the tell-tale signs of smoke bellowed from the upper windows and he knew the day was already won. Howarden had fallen, the castle was his.

Throughout the night, Madog's men ran riot throughout the castle. Any enemy survivors were put to the sword or thrown from the top of the keep. Stores were plundered and by dawn the entire fortress had been ransacked. Madog had managed a few hours' sleep during the carnage but now he was on his horse and ready to be gone. The rest of the column was already formed up outside the castle walls, leaving Madog inside with a dozen men.

'My lord, we should leave,' said Emrys. 'Word would have reached Rhuddlan by now and unless you want a pitched battle with Reginald De-Grey's army, I suggest we are long gone before he gets here.'

'Agreed,' said Madog. 'Get these men to fire the castle. Leave nothing unburned or undamaged. I want nothing left for the English to use, not as much as a tankard, do I make myself clear?'

'Aye, my lord, you do. Leave it to me.'

'Good,' said Madog. 'Once it is done, join us on the road to Dolwyddelan but make haste, fortune has been with us so far but it is only a matter of time before we meet an enemy worth fighting. Without another word he turned his horse and galloped through the gate towers to join his column.

'Move them out, Marshal,' shouted Madog, as he emerged, 'take us to Dolwyddelan.'

Chapter Seven

Denbigh Castle

Cynan crested the hill and peered down at the scene below. The slope fell away to a fertile rolling plain, bisected by the main route from north to south Wales. Alongside the road lay a wide river, the source of all the drinking water for the substantial town that had been established in this important location. Cynan knew the town was mainly inhabited by English traders and there would be rich pickings for his men should they attack but at the moment his mind was focused on something greater, the huge circular castle sitting on the hill high above the town.

'Robert Byrd,' he said, summoning his second in command, 'before us lays the prize. What say you to our chances of seizing this bauble from the crown of Long-shanks?'

Robert adjusted himself in the saddle and stared for an age before responding.

'Well, my lord,' he said, 'I will reserve judgement until our scouts have returned with news of any outlying forces but based on the castle layout alone, I feel we have a heavy task upon us. The approach is uphill and though that matters not in the final assault, it means we are disad-vantaged when it comes to siege engines. Wheeled rams are out of the question as are siege towers. The only things that leaves us with are the catapults but the slopes stop us from getting close enough for maximum effect.'

'And the town itself?'

'I see no problem with the town walls for they are incomplete and short enough for siege ladders. If we hit them with maximum force, we can have our men over before the enemy have the chance to string their bows. No, the town walls are of little consequence but the castle is a different matter altogether.'

'Thank you, Robert,' said Cynan. 'Sound counsel as usual and not far from my own thoughts. However, despite the obvious risks, this fortress is important to me and I would have it in my possession as soon as possible. I will ride back to the army and have them rested. You will organise your scouts to get as close as they can without being seen. Report to me as soon as you can and in any event, no later than nightfall two days from now. I want to know the garrison strength. What are the weaknesses? Who is in command and what is his experience? Anything we can find out will help us in our aim.'

'It is a formidable fortress,' said Robert staring at huge castle.

'Castell du Bere was formidable,' said Cynan, 'but it fell to our fist. This is no different, it is just a bit bigger. I will have this castle, Robert, even if it takes a year or more. Do what I bid and report to my tent two days hence.'

'Aye, my lord,' said Robert and watched Cynan ride back down the rear slopes of the hill to return to the dense forests hiding his army five leagues away.

Cynan was in his campaign tent with his master of trebuchets when Robert Byrd reported back two days later.
He returned the salute of the two guards and ducked
under the sodden flap of canvas, glad to get shelter from
the constant rain, yet excited by the news he bore.

'Robert, you have returned at an opportune moment,'
said Cynan as his comrade entered, 'come into the warm
and dry yourself. It has been a wet few days.'

'That it has,' said Robert catching the linen cloth
thrown toward him.

'Our magister here,' continued Cynan, 'tells me he
can have trebuchets built capable of reaching the castle
walls from the flanks of the river. Isn't that correct Master
Reynolds?'

'Aye, it is,' said the man, 'but it will take a few weeks.
The few we already have can be altered but in itself that
will take several days and the strain will probably push
them beyond their limits. It is far better to start anew and
I can have my carpenters set about the task first thing on
the morrow.'

'As usual your commitment and knowledge are admir-
able, Magister,' said Robert, 'but your particular skills
may not be needed in this instance.' He turned to Cynan
and took the offered goblet of warm wine. 'My lord,' he
continued, 'I come bearing great news but spiced with
danger. Our spies have excelled themselves and found the
people of Denbigh loose with their tongues when plied
with ale.'

'And what have they found out?'

'One of my men befriended a mason from Conwy
within one of the taverns. As the ale flowed the mason
regaled our man with stories of his importance and how

he had been requested personally by the Castellan of Denbigh, a man called Henry de-Lacey, the third Earl of Lincoln, to join a work gang of similarly skilled people to build an extra tower outside his castle walls. Not only this, but the mason and his comrades were then to extend the existing walls to embrace the new tower.'

'A strange request,' said Cynan. 'It seems that the existing wall is of adequate strength and the whole structure would see little benefit from an extra tower.'

'I agree,' said Robert, 'as did our man. Subsequently he asked about the importance of the new tower and after many a coin passed the serving girl's way in return for full tankards, the mason revealed the importance.'

'Which is?'

'My lord, if the walls of the castle are adequate, why build an extra tower unless it was to protect something of great value?'

'But surely,' replied Cynan, 'any building that is to protect the Castellan's treasures would be better built within the walls?'

'They would,' said Robert, 'but though this treasure be greater than all the gold in the world, alas it cannot be moved.'

'You play games with my mind, Robert,' answered Cynan, 'spit out what it is you know. What treasure could possibly be greater than the value of all the gold known to man?'

'Water, my lord,' said Robert, 'the tower is to cover a well.'

For a few moments Cynan stared at Robert as the implications sunk in.

'Their water supply lies outside the castle walls?' he gasped in astonishment.

'Apparently so,' said Robert. 'It would seem there was a smaller well inside the inner ward which has long since dried up and though there is plenty of water in a much larger well nearby, it lays an arrowshot away from the outer walls. Thus the need for masons to encompass it within the castle.'

Cynan stood and paced around the tent, his mind racing.

'If this is true,' he said, 'we surely have an opportunity undreamed of. All we have to do is secure the well and hold out until they come forth or surrender.'

'We could poison it,' said Robert. 'A few rotting cattle carcasses will render it undrinkable on pain of disease.'

'No,' said Cynan, 'I intend to use the fortress as a rendezvous for our forces in the area and though there is water aplenty in the river, a local source is essential in case of a siege, as the third Lord of Lincoln is about to find out to his cost.'

'My lord, the news gets better,' said Robert. 'Just this morning we saw a fully armed column of almost a thousand men muster within the town. They were soon joined by the Castellan and his entourage and rode out under full colours. It seems they have set out upon a mission and judging by the number of supply wagons, will be away for many days.'

'Do we know where they go?'

'No, my lord, but my spies follow at a safe distance. Once they set upon the return journey, a messenger will ride back at full gallop and give ample warning.'

'Then our path is clear,' said Cynan, 'we will attack at first light with full strength. Send word around the camp, tell the men to take whetstones to their blades for by tomorrow night, they will be dulled by enemy flesh.'

Word spread fast around the forest as messengers went from tent to tent. Excitement grew amongst the soldiers as once more they felt their blood stirred to battle. Outside one such tent, four men sat around their fire as the message came. Immediately one of them, a man called Griff, reached for his ration pouch and drew out any remaining strips of dried beef and the flask of best wine he had ransacked from Castell du Bere but had been keeping for a special occasion.

'What are you doing?' asked Alun, a newcomer to Cynan's ranks.

'If we are to fight tomorrow, boy,' said Griff, 'I am not going to risk dying hungry. I'm going to finish all this off tonight and you would do well to do the same. To die is bad enough but to do so whilst in possession of unused wine is surely a crime before God.'

The other two men laughed and reached for their own packs.

'What ails you friend?' asked Griff. 'Your face is as white as the snow upon the trees.'

'I haven't fought before,' said Alun, 'and my stomach turns circles in apprehension.'

'Fret not, Alun,' said Griff. 'You are young and strong. Keep your wits about you and don't think twice about your strike. If you hesitate, then you are a dead man.'

'Of course,' said one of the other men, 'as an untrained man, you will probably be in the van of the attack. Cynan will keep his best men for the second wave.'

'But that makes no sense,' said Alun, 'surely the best men should go in first?'

'Absolutely not,' said Griff, 'for the first wave always suffers the worst casualties. At that time the defending bowmen are at their calmest and their aim is true but by the time they have killed the first ranks they are more flustered and the aim becomes poorer. That's where the likes of us come into our own,' he indicated his other two comrades, 'we can seek cover behind the bodies of you youngsters and take advantage of the confusion. Makes sense really, don't you agree?'

Alun stood up and walked away from the fire.

'I think I'm going to be sick,' he said and as he walked into the trees, the three men at the fire burst into laughter.

After a few minutes Griff stood up.

'Where are you going?' asked his comrade.

'I'm going to find the youngster,' he said, 'perhaps we were too hard on him.' He followed in the boy's footsteps until he reached the area where many of the lancers' horses were tied. For a few moments he looked around until he saw the boy putting a saddle on a horse.

'Hold on there, boy,' said Griff walking over to him, 'don't you be doing anything rash now, desertion is punishable by hanging amongst this lot.'

Alun turned and walked toward Griff.

'I'm not deserting, Griff,' he said, 'in fact, I'm doing quite the opposite, I'm being true to my birth.'

'What do you mean?' asked Griff but before he could question further, he gasped in pain as the boy's knife thrust upward, plunging the razor-sharp blade up through the older man's innards and into his heart. Alun's left arm pulled his victim's head against his own chest to stifle the cries of pain.

'What I mean old man,' snarled Alun quietly, as he twisted the knife, 'is my true allegiance lies with Long-shanks and I have put up with the company of traitors for too long. My job here is done and before this day is out, my countrymen will be aware of Cynan's designs on Denbigh.'

Slowly Griff's struggles eased and Alun lowered the body to the ground before mounting the horse. Within moments the spy was galloping away from the forest to seek the nearest English outpost.

The following evening saw Cynan and Robert Byrd once more upon the ridgeline above Denbigh. The army was deployed amongst the dead ground away from any alert sentries and most took the opportunity to close their eyes as they waited for night to fall.

'The men are ready, my lord,' said Robert, 'and are as close as we dare approach lest we are discovered.'

'It is enough,' said Cynan. 'Once we have secured the outer wall, your focus is to be the well only. Ignore any other distraction and head directly for our target. Once there, go firm within a perimeter defence. Under no circumstance are you to withdraw even unto death, is that understood?'

'Aye, my lord,' said Robert, 'leave it to me.'

'Good,' said Cynan, 'then I see no point in wasting any more time. As soon as it is dark, I will lead the infantry into assault positions. At a given signal we will assault the walls and if successful, take control of the gates. As soon as they are open you are to lead your command through the town and up to the well at full gallop. Pause for no man for the well must be your sole focus. We will follow as soon as possible.'

'Consider it done,' came the reply.

'Let fortune be your comrade, Robert,' added Madog, 'and soon we will celebrate our victory with the best wine from the castle's cellars.'

'So be it,' said Robert and returned to his men.

Twenty leagues away, Madog led his column through north Wales toward Dolwyddelan. He had received reports from Meirion that the castle was in his control and had been taken without bloodshed. His army had pulled back amongst the trees to rest and though they were almost five thousand strong, the bulk of the men were out of sight amongst the undergrowth.

Madog sat against the trunk of a large tree and leaned his head back, glad of the break. His page came over and undid a leather wrap containing cold but soft strips of pork. Madog looked at the boy and smiled.

'Peter,' he said, 'are these for me?'

'Yes, my lord,' said the boy. 'I was given them by one of the soldiers at Howarden before we left. He stole them from the castle's kitchens but I have eaten enough and would share them with you.'

'That's very kind of you, Peter,' said Madog, 'but I will not eat the meat of comfort when my men eat meat of campaign. Together we will share some salted mutton and you can tell me of your grandfather. I hear he was a respected knight?'

'He was, my lord, but fell at Acre.'

'A sad tale,' said Madog, 'but all knights would rather die on campaign than rot at a fireside as their bodies grow old. Go, share the meat with your comrades, your selflessness has been noted.'

'My lord,' came a shout and Madog leapt to his feet as three horses galloped up the forest path. The first rider he recognised but the other two were unknown to him.

He grabbed the reins of the first horse as Emrys reined him in.

'My lord,' he said. 'I bear grave news; these two men are scouts of Cynan and followed an English column north. The column is led by the Castellan of Denbigh Castle and his absence left the fortress ripe for an assault from Cynan's army.'

'A fortuitous situation,' replied Madog. 'What causes you so much angst?'

'My lord,' said one of the men, 'this very morn we saw a horseman ride to join de-Lacey's column. We believe he was an informer for within the hour, the column turned and is riding back to Denbigh as we speak. We ride to warn him but they are not far behind and we fear our comrades will be unprepared. They could be slaughtered.'

'How far behind you are they?' asked Madog.

'About an hour,' said the rider. 'They follow the river path in the next valley. At the pace they ride they will be back in Denbigh by dawn.'

'Tell me,' he said, 'you know these lands, is there a place where we could engage them?'

The two men looked at each other before the first turned back to face Madog.

'I suppose you could use the farm of Tristan,' he said. 'It is an open plain flanked by wooded hills but it is narrow at one end and would be difficult to retreat from should the need arise.'

'That sounds perfect,' said Madog, 'I have no intention of retreating. Emrys, call the men to arms and follow these two to the place they described. Set our archers amongst the treeline and block off the narrow end of the valley like a stopper in a flask of wine. I will stay here with the horses and attack them from the rear.'

'Aye, my lord,' replied Emrys and wheeled his horse around.

'To arms,' he called as he galloped down the path, 'every man on his feet and prepare to march. Pass the word, leave all your possessions here, just carry your weapons and water. Quick about it, for there are Welshmen about to be slaughtered and we will not let that happen.'

Henry de-Lacey rode at the head of his column. Though the pace was slow, they were going as fast as they could without leaving the infantry far behind. Despite his frustration, he would need every man he could muster if he was to deny the rebels the castle but as the night approached, he knew they would soon have to make camp.

'Captain,' he called, 'continue the march beyond that far hill and then go firm. Tell the men to be on their guard for these hills are riddled with Welshmen.'

'Aye, my lord,' said the officer and rode back to relay the message to his sergeants. De-Lacey lifted his flask and drank deep of the watered wine but was only half done when he slowly lowered it to stare at the sight unfolding before him.

At the end of the valley, a column of foot soldiers trotted across the narrow strip of land between two hills and formed up line-abreast, barring any further advance. To either side, heavily wooded slopes meant any route out of the valley would be difficult. De-Lacey looked around in concern for it was clear the ground had been carefully selected for that very reason. For several moments he just stared at the enemy forming up before him but his officers were more experienced and immediately started organising the men.

'Drop your packs,' shouted one of the officers, 'and prepare weapons. Pike bearers to the fore, archers to the flanks.'

Another officer rode up and reined in his horse alongside de-Lacey.

'My lord,' he said, 'what are your orders?'

De-Lacey looked around him slowly, his mind cold and calculating yet angry that he had been so foolish.

'My orders are simple,' he said eventually. 'These are my lands and have been for ten years. I am not about to step aside and let this rabble walk all over them as they please. Bring all the foot soldiers to the fore, Fenwick. Assemble them line-abreast and have them ready to advance, I will give the enemy one chance to concede the road but be prepared for the worst.'

'Aye, my lord,' said the officer and watched as de-Lacey walked his horse forward to parley with the Welsh.

—

On the opposite end of the field, Emrys mounted his own horse and rode out to meet the oncoming lord. Within moments they were less than ten paces apart and both men stared as they weighed up their opponent. De-Lacey wore sheet metal armour with a brightly decorated tabard over the top. His arms and legs were protected by the brightest of chainmail and a red cloak fluttered in the wind behind him. The visor of his helm was open and, in his hand, he held a long lance, reaching upward toward the sky. His horse was draped in a heavy barding depicting the colours of his family crest.

Emrys looked him up and down before glancing down at his own attire of a chainmail shirt, leather leggings and dirty woollen cloak.

'Excuse me, sir knight,' said Emrys, 'if I had known this was to be a formal affair, then perhaps I would have dressed accordingly.'

De-Lacey ignored the jibe and looked over Emrys' shoulder toward the Welsh lines.

'Where is your master?' he demanded. 'I would talk with someone of similar standing.'

'Ah, that's a problem,' said Emrys, 'for my master is otherwise engaged so I will have to do.'

De-Lacey turned his attention to the poorly dressed man before him.

'You?' he sneered. 'Surely you are no more than a serf?'

'As are all of my comrades,' said Emrys, 'and though they be poorly dressed, I can assure you they wear the armour of free men.'

'Free men they may be,' said de-Lacey, 'yet all men are governed by the dictates of those they call master. Even I answer to the King so what makes you think you are any different?'

'We are happy to answer to our betters,' said Emrys, 'as long as they be Welsh. Now, enough idle chatter and say what it is you have to say, sir knight, so we can all be back about our business.'

'You know what I want, knave, you trespass upon my lands and block the road south. I have urgent business to attend and demand you clear the path.'

'I cannot do that, sir knight, for though these lands may belong to the crown, we differ about whose head that crown should sit upon. I am no traveller, my lord, but would wager Lincoln is a fair distance from here. Why don't you go home to your ancestral lands and leave us to ours?'

'These are not your lands,' growled de-Lacey, 'they belong to me, granted by the hand of Longshanks himself.'

'Longshanks gifted that which he did not own after he killed Llewellyn,' said Emrys, 'and we do not recognise the legitimacy of your claim.'

'I warn you for the last time, Welshman,' said de-Lacey, 'clear the path or suffer the consequences.'

'The path is ours, my lord, and we will remain upon it.'

'So be it, peasant,' said de-Lacey. 'Warn your army of farmers that English steel will soon be amongst them.'

'We look forward to it,' said Emrys and both men turned to return to their respective lines.

—

'How says their commander?' asked Fenwick upon de-Lacey's return.

'The man was nought but a peasant,' said de-Lacey, 'and my air was poisoned with his presence. Prepare the men for battle, Fenwick, and on my command, we will move forward to engage these upstarts. Let them see they are nothing but a fly to be swatted aside.'

'My lord, you do know the ground is not favourable?'

'The ground is irrelevant,' said de-Lacey. 'We outnumber them two to one and though they hold the territorial advantage, if we can engage them at close quarters there can be only one outcome.'

'If you say so, my lord.'

'I do, Fenwick, give the command. Line abreast, advance to engage.'

—

The Welsh lines watched the oncoming English, each man growing nervous as they realised they were vastly outnumbered. Slowly the gap between them closed until the enemy were no more than fifty paces distant. Suddenly the advancing lines stopped and de-Lacey stepped forward.

'One last chance, Welshmen,' he shouted. 'Yield the road or death will be the order of the day.'

'Go to hell, Englishmen,' answered Emrys and turned his head so his own lines could hear him better. 'Men of Wales,' he roared, 'present pikes.'

The front rank dug the hafts of their weapons into the ground and leaned them forward, a solid defence against any horse charge. The next rank placed their weapons over the shoulders of those before them, the whole thing presenting a wall of Welsh steel.

'Spearmen prepare,' roared Emrys and the rear ranks hefted their spears ready to throw. Each man had another three laying on the floor at his side.

Across the open ground, de-Lacey was also shouting at his men.

'Archers,' he roared, 'target the centre, release!'

Hundreds of arrows filled the air but Emrys had expected the tactic and within seconds had called out the counter command.

'Enemy arrows, present shields.'

Every man in the Welsh lines crouched low and lifted their shields against the hail of incoming death. Arrow points thudded into the laminated wooden boards and though some found their targets, most stuck in the shields with no more than an arrowhead protruding on the inside.

Over and over again the air filled with arrows and slowly the Welsh lines collapsed in a heap, their shield walls bristling with the shafts of thousands of arrows.

De-Lacey held up his hand and the arrow storm died away. For several moments there was silence as he stared at the decimated lines of the enemy strewn upon the field.

'Their bravado has been silenced by English steel,' he shouted, 'though beware the ones who feign death. Upon my command, advance to contact and should any regain their feet, plough straight through them for they are nought but peasants with ideas above their station. Ready. Advaaance.'

'Wait,' warned Emrys from beneath his shield, 'wait... ready... now!'

As one the Welsh army rose from the floor and regained the defensive positions they had held moments before. Emrys looked around, grateful to see that the number of casualties incurred was mercifully low.

'My lord, we should hold back the men,' shouted Fenwick in the English ranks, 'and use the bow men until the enemy numbers are weakened further.'

'No,' shouted de-Lacey, 'we waste too much time, our men will take advantage while there is confusion amongst their ranks.' He drew his sword and held it high. 'Onward men,' he roared, 'cut them down as the filth they really are,' and slowly the lines of infantry started the advance.

'Spears,' roared Emrys from the defending lines and instantly the air was full as the missiles flew to land amongst the attackers. Many were deflected by shields and though some men fell, the impetus of the attack was not affected. The English army started to run, keeping close together for maximum effect. By the time the two sides met moments later they were running at full pelt, each screaming their own battle cries as they smashed against the Welsh lines.

Though the attackers tried desperately to avoid the wall of metal spear points, many were impaled as the two armies met in a crash of metal, blood and screams of agony. The impact of the numerically superior English meant the Welsh lines were forced back several paces before they managed to regain a foot hold.

'Hold the line,' roared Emrys, knowing full well that a broken line meant almost certain defeat. He added his weight to the back of the defenders, pushing forward as hard as he could. In the front ranks, men were crushed without any possibility of wielding their weapons but those behind swung over their comrades' heads to strike at any enemy within reach. Blood and bone flew every-where as skulls were dealt crushing blows and wherever an opportunity presented itself, blades were thrust through gaps to find flesh on the opposite side.

The sounds of battle echoed around the field as men fought desperately, their battle cries only bested by the screams of the freshly wounded. Some men already dead stayed upright in the crush, the pressure unrelenting as both forces pushed forward and those in the first few ranks were soaked in the blood of friend and foe alike.

'Hold the line,' screamed Emrys again as his ranks took another few steps back, 'trumpeter, give the signal.'

The sound of a horn rang through the air and the pressure eased momentarily as the English looked around them in confusion. For a few seconds there was nothing to see but the sound of rushing air made Fenwick look up to see the sky darkened by more arrows, though this time of Welsh origin.

'Enemy archers,' he cried, 'present shields,' but it was too late, the volleys of steel-tipped ash thudded into the backs of the English before they had time to disengage and hundreds of men fell within minutes.

'Disengage,' roared Fenwick, 'retreat to the slopes.'

'Cancel that command,' roared de-Lacey, 'press on with the assault.'

'My lord,' shouted Fenwick, 'the men are being slaughtered. They will all be dead unless we do something immediately.'

De-Lacey hesitated and looked around but before he could answer another shout came from one of his men.

'Riders to the north, we are surrounded.'

He looked back up the valley and sure enough, dozens of cavalry were cresting the ridge, closing off their one avenue of escape.

'My lord, we need to do something,' shouted Fenwick.

De-Lacey snapped out of his stupor and made a decision.

'Fenwick, engage the archers on the left flank only. Return their attack with willow of our own.'

'My lord, they are hidden amongst the trees, the volleys will be in vain.'

'I will lead a charge through their lines,' said de-Lacey, 'and secure a route out of here for our men. All I need you to do is distract them for a few moments to aid our passage. As soon as we reach the treeline, withdraw the infantry but change the aim of our own archers onto the Welsh to prevent pursuit. We have moments only, Fenwick, so make it happen. Once we are amongst the trees, we can take on the archers hand to hand and lose ourselves amongst the forest.'

'Aye my lord,' shouted Fenwick and turned his horse.

In the distance he could see the Welsh horsemen had formed up into a straight line and begun their advance down the valley.

'Archers,' he called, 'new target, left flank. Volley fire at the front edge of the forest, loose arrows.'

The English archers changed the point of aim and sent volley after volley into the trees. Underneath the cover of flying willow, de-Lacey led his cavalry charging toward the enemy's hidden position, losing only a few riders on the way. As soon as they entered the wood, Fenwick organised the retreat and within minutes his infantry were racing toward the safety of the dense forest.

—

'They are escaping,' roared Madog from the centre of the Welsh cavalry line, 'increase the pace, advance.'

The horsemen urged their mounts into a gallop and the line broke up as each sought their own route over the rough ground. Soon the valley was covered with charging cavalry and though most of the enemy reached the treeline, the Welsh horsemen set about the slow and the wounded, cutting them down without mercy.

Madog rode to meet Emrys who was organising aid for his wounded amongst the Welsh infantry lines.

'How goes it, Emrys?' he asked.

'A few dozen killed, my lord, and twice that wounded. Your arrival came none too soon.'

'The marshes at the top of the valley hindered our progress,' said Madog, 'and I am pained to see so many of our men hurt.'

'It matters not, my lord, the aim was to prevent Lincoln's column from falling on the rear of Cynan's army unawares and despite our losses, I think we have succeeded.'

'Indeed we have,' said Madog, 'though I don't think de-Lacey's army are entirely routed. No doubt he will reform and make another attempt.'

'Are you going to pursue him through the woods?'

'No, it invites ambush upon our men. Let him go, at least we have bought some time. I will take the cavalry to Denbigh with all haste and warn Cynan of the risk.'

'What about us, my lord?'

'Bury our dead and patch up the wounded. There is a village an hour's march from here. Go firm there and await my return. Unless our strength is needed in the assault, we will be back by sundown tomorrow.'

'So be it,' said Emrys and returned to bandaging the arm of a wounded pike man.

—

Several hours later, dozens of men crept along the river outside the town of Denbigh, keeping their heads lower than the bank. Each pair carried one end of a siege ladder and they moved slowly so as not to alert any nearby dogs. Soon they were as close to the town as they were able to get and within the hour, almost fifty ladders were ready to be carried to the perimeter walls. Behind the ladder bearers came a thousand lightly armed soldiers, all dressed and equipped to move fast. Heavy battle wasn't anticipated and it was essential to inflict as great a surprise as possible upon the town folk if the assault was to be successful.

Hidden amongst the trees of a copse on the slope of a nearby hill was Robert Byrd along with another fifty horsemen. These however were heavily armed for theirs was a task that would face the most danger. The taking and defence of the castle's well.

Cynan crouched low behind the riverbank alongside his men. Though they were getting impatient, the warlord waited, looking to the cloudy skies as he was hoping for the conditions that would aid the assault. Finally the skies darkened and Cynan felt the first drop of rain land on his upturned face.

'Pass the word,' he whispered to the man at his side, 'get ready, we go within minutes.'

The message was passed down the riverbank and the nervous army said their final prayers in case they were about to meet their maker.

Within minutes the heavens opened and rain poured down upon the town of Denbigh. Cynan hesitated a few moments more, knowing that even the keenest of sentries would probably seek out a drier position upon the walls or even leave to find a cloak. Whatever the thinking, he knew this was the time to make any move.

He tapped the man's shoulder in front of him.

'This is it, soldier,' he said, 'lead us in.'

The two ladder bearers climbed up over the bank, and crouching low, ran as fast as they could toward the looming wall. As soon as they moved, the next two knew the signal had been given and followed their comrades out of the river channel. Within seconds, over a hundred ladders were being carried silently through the storm, closely followed by a thousand Welsh men at arms.

Cynan was amongst them and as he reached the wall, he looked around, pleased to see there were already hundreds of men scaling the ladders as far as the darkness would allow him to see.

'Let me through,' whispered Cynan and quickly climbed the ladder before him, reaching the battlements without incident.

As he landed on the walkway behind the wall, he crouched low to avoid making a profile, happy to see that all the other men already inside had adopted the same tactic. They had been trained well. Cynan could hardly believe his luck that they had got this far without being noticed but he knew the bigger test was to come.

'Over here,' hissed a voice and Cynan joined his men as they ran to a nearby tower in the defensive wall. As they ducked inside, he passed the body of a sentry with his throat freshly opened. Cynan glanced at the man responsible.

'Sleeping on duty,' whispered the soldier, 'his mistake, our gain.'

Cynan slapped the man gently on the back as a sign of his appreciation before descending the stairs and emerging onto the town road below. Several men knelt in a circle facing outward, each wielding a sword or an axe.

Cynan crouched to get his bearings.

'We have been fortunate beyond belief,' he whispered, 'but I feel now it will get harder.' He looked toward the gatehouse and could see the glow of a fire beneath a shelter where the night guards would take it in turn to rest.

'No easy way to do this, comrades,' said Cynan drawing his short sword, 'so let's just get it over with.'

The Welsh commander crouched and ran as fast as he could across the open space, closely followed by a dozen men. As they neared the gate an alert guard saw them and called the alarm but before he could draw his sword, Cynan's blade smashed across his face, cutting his skull in two. All around the gate defenders took to arms but it was too late and as Cynan's men charged amongst them, dozens more Welshmen started dropping from the town walls having breached the defences with little effort.

'Open the gates,' shouted Cynan as the last of the defenders fell to his blade, 'send the signal.' As many hands lifted the heavy bars across the enormous town gates, the leader looked up to see a flaming arrow pierce the stormy sky.

'There's the signal,' roared Robert Byrd, 'lancers advance.'

The fifty riders dug their heels into their horses' flanks and galloped from the copse toward the town walls. Within minutes the gate towers loomed above them and Robert could see the shapes of the houses through the archway.

They thundered across the wooden bridge and though Robert glanced toward Cynan as he galloped past, they didn't slow the pace but rode harder through the narrow streets, heading toward the slopes of the castle.

After the last rider had disappeared into the gloom, the rest of the Welsh army came running through the gates to join those who had breached the walls. Cynan knew they had been fortunate and had to seize the moment.

'Marshal,' he called, 'the town is awakening, send half of the men through the streets and suppress any acts of resistance. Spare not the blade for I would not have assassins in my shadow.'

'Aye my lord,' came the reply and within moments, hundreds of men deployed into the many tiny alleyways making up the town.

'Sergeant,' called Cynan, 'take a hundred bowmen and man the walls to guard our rear, the rest of you, follow me. If we are to succeed in taking this castle, Robert Byrd will need reinforcements before this night is done.'

Chapter Eight

Brecon Castle

'Fletcher, where are we going?' hissed Tarian, as they clambered through the heavy undergrowth. 'The path leads away from the castle walls.'

'Trust me,' said Fletcher, 'the way is true though indeed treacherous at night.'

Both men continued, accompanied by Geraint. They had waited until the hard-working townsfolk were asleep and the revelries from the taverns had fallen silent before making their way toward the castle but Fletcher had soon led them off the path and into the forest. Finally they arrived at a small door set deep into a stone wall and Fletcher paused before knocking on it gently with the hilt of his knife.

'What is this?' asked Tarian. 'Some sort of forest dwelling?'

'No,' said Fletcher, 'it is hidden entrance for the castle. Few know of its existence and of those who do, only a handful know where it leads.'

'A sally port,' said Tarian, 'if the castle is besieged, the defenders can use this to send out an armed force to circle around the attackers and fall upon them from behind.'

'Isn't that a bit risky?' asked Geraint. 'Surely if the enemy finds the sally port, they have an easy route into the fortress itself.'

'No,' said Tarian, 'these ways are often narrow and easily defended. They are usually filled with murder holes or blocked by many doors.'

'In this case, none are needed,' said Fletcher, 'for the tunnel lays below the level of the river and if the Castellan felt the sally port was a risk, by the simple lifting of a sluice gate, the passages can be flooded within minutes.'

'But it is dry now?'

'It is and has been for many years. All we need is a sympathiser to open the locks.' He turned to knock on the door again. Eventually they heard the sound of latches being drawn and the door creaked outward to reveal a young page peering out, a fearful look on his face.

'Who goes there, stranger?' he hissed into the darkness.

'It is I,' said Fletcher, 'your mother's brother.'

The look on the boy's face eased as he recognised his uncle and pushed the door wide to allow them in.

'Come,' he said, 'or I will soon be missed.'

The three men crouched low and walked into the tunnel. They waited for the boy to bolt the door before returning to lead the way up the low-ceilinged passageway. His single candle did little to light the darkness but they could feel the dampness of the walls and Geraint couldn't help but wonder about all that water being held back somewhere in the distance.

Up in the tower, Garyn paced back and forth, his mind racing. Since receiving the letter he had heard nothing and he had no idea who was responsible, or in what form the attempted release would take. Finally he sat back on one of the chairs and waited as the long evening hours dragged themselves toward midnight. Finally he heard keys in the door and jumped up to face whoever it was coming through.

'Oh,' he said eventually, 'it's you.'

'And who else did you expect?' asked Gerald of Essex as he removed his gloves and sat upon a chair. Behind him stood two guards to ensure Garyn didn't try anything stupid.

'No one,' said Garyn, 'but I thought perhaps there may have been some food sent up.'

'You have been fed once today, Welshman, don't push your luck.'

'What do you want, Essex?' asked Garyn.

'I want your part of the bargain,' said Gerald. 'You do intend to honour our agreement I assume?'

'I do,' sighed Garyn, 'even though the boy wasn't my son.'

'Hmm, that was an unfortunate outcome,' said Gerald, 'and to be honest, I'm not convinced. Still, I upheld my part of the bargain. If you are a man of your word, it is time for you to do the same.'

'What do you want to know?'

'I want to know the importance of the Macsen sword,' said Gerald. 'Why it is so important to the Welsh and what would be its value. After that, you will tell me the exact location of the corpse of Macsen and don't even think about lying or that woman and her family will suffer the full weight of my anger.'

'So be it,' sighed Garyn and leaned back in the chair. 'The sword of Macsen is the sword of Macsen Wledig, a legendary leader of the Welsh and Britain in general. It is said he was a Roman Emperor who travelled from Rome to be with his dream bride, Helen of the Hosts. When they were together, he swore that as long as his sword was in the hands of a Welshman, then the country would be free. Any man who wields the sword will unite the country behind him.'

'And is that why this Madog wants the sword, to add credence to his claim?'

'It is.'

'And what about the tomb of this Roman Emperor? Where lays his body?'

'It is within a crypt below an old church near Caern–arfon. The ruins are upon an old Roman fort known as Segontium. After the Romans left it seems the locals built a church which has now fallen into disrepair and little remains of it. Within the crypt you will find a stone coffin bearing his remains.'

'And you are adamant there are no treasures there?'

'None that I saw, though I did not unwrap his shroud and know little of the burial rituals of that strange people.'

Gerald nodded but stayed silent. Finally he took a deep breath and stood up.

'I will test this story of yours, Garyn, and see if you speak the truth for even if there are no trinkets to attract my eye, I think the bones of a heralded Welsh leader will hold value of a different sort.'

'In what way?' asked Garyn.

'Who knows but if the whole Welsh nation worships the memory of this Macsen Wledig, then perhaps his body has a ransom value. Anyway, time will tell, in the meantime I suggest you make peace with god.'

'Why?'

'Because the abbot has regained his strength and summons you to his presence. I wish I could be there to see the outcome but alas I will be gone.'

'Gone where?'

'To Caernarfon of course,' said Essex, 'this is an opportunity too good to miss. The fighting is done and I have no doubt that Longshanks will soon ride into the north to re-impose his rule on those who have challenged him. When he does, he will find me waiting to present him with the bones of a Welsh legend and the famed sword of his enemies. If I'm not mistaken, he will be impressed enough to grant me an earldom, or at least a prominent place at court.'

'Is that all you're interested in Essex, fortune and self-advancement?'

'Yes,' replied the knight simply, 'is that a problem?'

'In your eyes I guess not but most men would settle for happiness and a family.'

'Money makes me happy,' said Gerald, 'and family is overrated. As long as there's a wench between my covers then I go to sleep a happy man and let me tell you, Garyn, wenches are easily come by, whether willing or not.'

'You disgust me,' said Garyn, 'and one day you will meet your match.'

'Perhaps so but you won't be there to witness it, Father Williams will see to that. Anyway, I waste time. Enjoy your last night of life, Garyn ap Thomas, I have an appointment to keep.' He stood up and left the room, locking the door tightly behind him.

Down in the depths of the castle cellars a door creaked open no more than a hand's width and a page peered through into the gloom.

'All clear,' he whispered and the three men followed him past the kitchens before following him up a stairway to emerge into the courtyard.

'The prisoner is in that tower,' said the boy pointing across the ward. 'He is on the second level. A guard sits upon a chair at the base of the stairway in case someone tries to free him.'

'And my daughter?' asked Fletcher.

'In the same tower but two levels higher.'

'Thank you, boy,' said Tarian, 'now get away to safety, your work here is done.'

'Thank you,' said the page and he disappeared into the darkness.

'So what now?' asked Geraint.

'We'll stay in the shadows at the base of the walls,' said Fletcher. 'The guards are minimal but we don't want to alert them so be careful.'

They made their way around the courtyard until they reached the base of the curved tower. Tarian leaned slowly forward and peered through an arrow slit before whispering to his comrades.

'He is asleep and his pike lays against the wall out of arm's reach,' said Tarian. 'I'll try the door and see if I can kill him before he wakes.'

'No,' said Geraint, 'there must be no killing if we can avoid it, for it will be the villagers who pay the price. I will go and see if I can overcome him.'

Tarian nodded and stood to one side.

Geraint crouched as he went past the arrow slit and took a deep breath before turning the wrought iron handle. Luckily it opened and he pushed the door slowly inward, grimacing as it creaked upon its hinges.

Tarian watched through the narrow arrow slit as Geraint crept slowly toward the sleeping guard and worked his way behind him. Finally he pulled his knife and rested it against the man's throat while placing his other hand over his mouth.

Instantly the guard was awake and his eyes widened in horror as he realised his predicament.

'Careful, friend,' hissed Geraint applying pressure on the knife. 'Hold your silence and you may just live, cry out and you will die right here. Understand?'

The man nodded silently.

'Good,' said Geraint looking up as Tarian and Fletcher entered the tower. Tarian drew his sword and placed the point over the man's heart.

'Right, listen to me,' he said quietly, 'I want some answers and if you value your life, you will answer truly. Trust me, I am not as compassionate as my friend here and will not hesitate to run you through. Do you understand me?'

The man nodded, the look of fear still on his face.

'Good,' said Tarian, and looked at Geraint, 'uncover his mouth.'

'Don't forget,' continued Tarian, returning his attention to the prisoner, 'apart from answering my questions, the slightest sound and my blade gets bloodied. So, first question, are there any other guards in this tower?'

'Not in here,' said the man, 'but the top level opens out onto the battlements. There is one sentry there and another sleeps in the guard room alongside.'

'Good. Where are the prisoners kept?'

'There are prisoners on every level,' came the reply.

'Who holds the keys?'

The man didn't answer but when Tarian applied pressure to the sword, he looked over to a niche in the wall where a candle flickered in the draught.

'Over there,' he said.

Fletcher walked over and picked up the bunch of four keys.

'Good,' said Tarian. 'Geraint, you go to the top of the tower and ensure we are not surprised from that direction. Fletcher, you release the prisoners while I stay with our friend here and watch our rear.'

The two men ran up the stairs while Tarian sat on a small stool opposite the guard.

Ten minutes later, Fletcher reappeared closely followed by Elspeth and her son. Other prisoners followed but when Geraint returned alone, Tarian realised something was wrong.

'Where's your brother?' he asked.

'I don't know,' replied Geraint, 'he wasn't there.'

Tarian spun around and pinned the guard back against the wall, his knife pressed firmly against his throat.

'Where is he?' he snarled. 'And no more messing about. Where is the prisoner known as Garyn ap Thomas?'

'He was taken by the Castellan not an hour since,' gasped the man, 'I know not where.'

'Not good enough,' said Tarian and pressed the knife harder until a drop of blood ran down the terrified guard's neck.

'I don't know, I swear,' cried the guard and closed his eyes as he awaited the cut that would end his life.

Tarian hesitated and then withdrew the knife.

'We need to tie him up,' he said, 'perhaps he won't be missed and it will give us a little more time.'

'Time for what?' asked Geraint.

'To find your brother of course,' said Tarian, 'and from what I can gather about your past, there's only one place Gerald has taken him.'

'To the abbot,' said Geraint.

'Exactly,' replied Tarian and turned to Fletcher.

'You lead these people out of here, while we go and find Geraint's brother.'

'I'll come with you,' said Fletcher.

'No, we have to get these people out of the castle or it will all be in vain. Go back the way we came and make good your escape. If we manage to escape this place with our lives, I feel none of us will be welcome in Brycheniog.'

'So be it,' said Fletcher, 'just be careful.' He peered through the door and led the released captives back toward the kitchen block.

'What now?' asked Geraint looking at Tarian.

'Now we find out from our friend here where the abbot's quarters are.'

Father Williams sat in a high-backed chair with a sheep-skin cover over his legs. To either side of him stood a castle guard and at the rear of the room, another two guarded the exit into a rear corridor. In the centre of the windowless cell, Garyn lay on the floor, bleeding from the beating he had just received from the soldiers.

'Well,' said the abbot, staring down at the wounded man, 'at long last you lay where you belong, Garyn ap Thomas, below my feet in a pool of blood. Long have I dreamed of this day and though I may not be long for this world, I shall go to my grave a happy man.'

'Get it over with, Williams,' gasped Garyn, 'but rest assured that there will be judgement before god.'

'God? Who are you to preach to me about God? You are but a mere commoner while I control an entire abbey filled with people devoted to his service. I think I know more about him in the circumstances.'

'A habit and a cross does not a holy man make,' said Garyn, 'and you are surely begat from the devil himself.'

'A simple matter of perspective,' said the abbot. 'You have lived a life of crime and poverty while I have lived a life of plenty and worship. Who do you think our lord will see as the most godly?'

'I have no idea,' said Garyn, 'but I know this, I have never set out to hurt an innocent man for the sake of personal gain while you have made a lifetime of such actions.'

'All in a good cause,' said the abbot, 'the glorification of God's name.'

'If that is the case, then what sort of god is it that accepts the gains stolen from the poor?'

'A rich one,' sneered the abbot. He paused before continuing. 'So, master Garyn, what are we to do with you? Shall I have you beaten to death as we speak, or just have my men run you through and have done with it?'

'Do what you will, Satan, for I will not give you the satisfaction of seeing me plead for my life. Wield your blade or unleash your thugs, my heart is settled and even as the last of my blood stains your floor, I will pity your darkened soul.'

'Do not pity me,' roared Father Williams, 'for I am above you in station, morals and holiness. Save your pity for your family who now burn within the fires of hell, your own kin who died because of your failure to meet my expectations. They are the ones who need your pity, Garyn, the parents who died at the hand of an assassin's blade and your little sister who screamed as the assassin used her as a whore before cutting her throat.'

Garyn gasped as the image sunk in and staggered to his feet.

'What's the matter, Garyn?' asked the abbot. 'Didn't you know? Oh, it may have been another man's hand that wielded the blade but the coins in his pocket were from my purse and when he told me how much the girl struggled, I made him recount every sordid detail. So don't you dare pity me for I am your superior and you are not fit to clean the filth from beneath my shoes.'

Garyn roared in anger and lunged forward but before he reached the abbot he was pounced upon by the guards and forced to the floor. For several minutes he fought as hard as he could but was eventually overwhelmed and lay on the stone slabs, gasping for breath as he sobbed at the memory of the little girl who had suffered so much because of him.

'That's it, Garyn,' sneered the abbot, 'wallow in your own wretchedness, for you see, I may have arranged to kill your family all those years ago but their fate was set by you, a stubborn boy at the time who thought he could defy his betters. How does it feel, Garyn ap Thomas, how does it feel to have the death of your family on your hands?'

'No,' gasped Garyn eventually, 'you are wrong. You can twist the words whichever way you want, monk, but I will not accept this guilt. The choices I made were for the right reasons and though they led to tragedy, no one could foresee where your twisted mind would lead. Yes, my heart breaks for my family but even out of that there came good, for if I hadn't have taken the path I did, then my brother would also be dead and I would have nothing.'

'But your brother is dead,' said the abbot, 'drowned at sea while fleeing the mess you caused. You have nothing, Garyn, and lay before me stripped of honour, dignity and conscience. My work is done and I can now send you to where you truly belong, the unending pain of Satan's fires.' He got slowly to his feet and withdrew a thin blade knife from within his sleeve. 'Hold him tight,' he said, 'this moment has been far too long in the coming.'

The abbot limped over to Garyn and held the knife before his victim's eyes, the blade glinting in the firelight.

'Behold your demise, Garyn. In a few moments this steel will ever so slowly enter your body and pierce your innards but don't wish for the swift yet fleeting pain of a wound to your heart, for I would prolong the agony. Your lungs will be punctured and I will watch with great mirth as you die gasping for breath, slowly drowning in your own blood.'

'Just do it, monk,' said Garyn and stared defiantly into his would-be killer's eyes.

The abbot walked slowly around his prisoner, softly dragging the flat of the blade around the flesh of Garyn's throat.

'One more thing before you go, blacksmith,' he said, 'one more tale to tell, so your humiliation is complete. You may think that your bones will tomorrow lie in peace alongside the remains of your family but you are wrong. Before the first rays of the sun have bested the morning mist, the dogs will already be fighting over your carcass and whatever is left will be scattered amongst the forests of Brycheniog, quite appropriate really as that is what happened to your family.'

'I don't know what you are saying, monk, my kin lie in consecrated ground by the church.'

'Oh no they don't, Garyn. I admit that they once did but after you fled my custody the last time, my frustration knew no bounds and I had them dug up and displayed in the village square as the bloodline of a brigand. Don't worry for they didn't stay there long; the dogs saw to that but suffice to say their remains ended up as no more than a stain on the shoes of beggars.'

'I don't believe you,' said Garyn quietly, 'not even you would stoop so low.'

'On the contrary,' said Williams, 'I have reached depths you can't even imagine.' He returned to face Garyn once more. 'Lay him down and hold his arms and legs.'

Garyn was stretched out upon the cold slabs of the room and the monk lowered himself to sit across his stomach.

'This is it, blacksmith,' he said, 'the time for talking is done.' He placed the point of the knife against Garyn's chest. 'When you get to hell, save me a seat at Satan's

table and tell him I'll be there shortly.' The abbot took a
deep breath and leaned forward to plunge the knife into
his victim's body.

Chapter Nine

The Walled Town of Denbigh

'Faster,' roared Robert Byrd as they galloped through the narrow streets, 'the alarm has been raised and we must secure the well before they launch a counterattack.'

The riders spurred their horses harder and raced up the slopes toward the castle walls.

'What's that?' shouted Robert as a circular enclosure came into view. He raced over and slid from his horse to peer down into the depths. 'This is it, dismount and secure a perimeter.'

The men climbed from the horses and five of the riders took the reins before leading them back down the hill and into the town. Whichever way went the battle, there was no point in losing valuable steeds.

'Line of twenty facing the castle,' shouted Robert, 'another line in support. The rest, place yourself on a flank and plug any holes in the line should they appear. We need hold out for only a short while for with God's aid, Cynan follows us with the infantry.'

'Something's happening,' came a shout and all eyes turned to see the giant gates of the castle swing open and a troop of horses come galloping out.

'Look to your weapons,' shouted Robert, 'front rank take the horses' legs from beneath them, second rank, kill the riders as soon as they hit the floor. Take no prisoners, we do not have the strength to keep them.'

'Here they come,' shouted a voice and Robert drew his own sword to face the English cavalry racing toward the well.

Down below, Cynan was breathing hard as he ran through the streets, leading his detachment toward the hill, knowing it was pivotal to the defence of the castle. Any commander worth his salt would risk everything to protect the precious water source and although he had sent fifty riders to secure the prize, nobody actually knew how many defenders were still within the castle and if it held a strong garrison, then Robert Byrd and his men could be easily cut from the field within minutes. It was important they had the support of the infantry as soon as possible.

Onward they ran, pushing away any civilians venturing outside their homes to see what was happening. Random soldiers or over-zealous citizens who took to arms to defend their town were dealt with ruthlessly, cut down where they stood without question of quarter. Fires raged where other detachments were torching the buildings and as the streets began to fill with smoke, more and more people appeared from the gloom, crying in fear at the sight of the enemy soldiers rampaging through the town. Screams of the wounded echoed eerily amongst the swirling smoke and rivulets of blood mingled with rainwater, sending probing fingers of scarlet along the drainage channels.

'My lord, the advance party is under attack,' shouted one of his men and Cynan looked up to see the small cavalry troop about to engage Robert's command.

'Faster,' roared Cynan, 'get up the hill as quickly as you can, if Robert's men fall, the enemy will hold the high ground.'

The men doubled their efforts and clambered over the low walls at the base of the hill. Cynan knew that sending a small party deep into an enemy held fortification was risky but if the gamble paid off, it would be a massive blow to the castle and one which the English defenders would be unlikely to recover from.

—

'Brace!' roared Robert and seconds later he staggered backward as the line took the full force of ten horses, line abreast. Bodies flew everywhere and unearthly screams filled the night sky as some of the animals suffered deep wounds and fell to the ground in agony.

As their riders tried to recover, Robert's second line of defence ran forward with axes and clubs, smashing them against the armoured helms of those too slow to defend themselves, sending plate steel through skulls and into the soft tissue beneath.

Those still able, jumped to their feet and drew their swords before wading into Robert's line, delivering deep cutting blows through the flesh and bone of the Welsh attackers. Metal crashed on metal and each man fought frantically, hardly able to breathe or think such was the ferocity of the battle.

Eventually there came a pause as men gathered their breath and the English retreated a few paces to regroup. All were now unhorsed and though they were well armoured, the extra weight meant they tired quickly.

'My lord, more men approach,' shouted a voice and Robert's heart sank when he saw at least fifty armed men racing from the castle to aid their cavalry.

'Retire to the well,' he shouted, 'place your backs to the wall and defend only the space to your front.'

Slowly the men in the cordon walked backward until they were shoulder to shoulder around the well.

'Steady your hearts men,' shouted Robert, 'for though we lay outnumbered, they fight for coin while we fight for freedom, a value unmatched by all the gold in Christendom.'

The remaining men roared their support and banged their swords against their shields, shouting defiantly toward the oncoming enemy. Within seconds the English infantry crashed into them and once more steel cleaved flesh in a maelstrom of pain and blood.

For several minutes the battle swung in both directions but the tiredness of the Welsh told until finally they numbered little more than a dozen.

'To the last, men,' gasped Robert, 'to the last.'

Wearily they lifted their swords to defend the final assault but just as it looked like they would be overwhelmed, a man smashed into the English line's rear, taking a soldier's head from his shoulders with a swipe of an axe.

He was the first of many and within seconds, the rest of the Welsh infantry swarmed over the brow and engulfed the enemy in a sea of steel. Those defenders fortunate enough to be on the outer edges of the English lines quickly abandoned their heavy weapons and ran for the castle while the remainder died where they stood, slaughtered by Cynan's ferocious assault.

The Welsh numbers increased as they poured up the hill and Cynan's sergeants set about forming defensive lines. Pointed stakes were planted into the ground, each braced in a lethal defence against further horse charges while archers located themselves amongst the loose boulders across the slope. As soon as the second detachment finished clearing the streets, they made their way up the road to the gates and set up even more lines, just out of reach of the castle's crossbows.

Robert Byrd sat with his back against the well, grimacing as one of his comrades tried to remove his chainmail. As soon as Cynan knew they were safe from counterattack, he returned to the well and knelt alongside his second in command.

'Robert,' he said, 'how is your wound?'

'It hurts like nothing I have ever experienced,' he grimaced.

As soon as the chainmail was off, Cynan lifted up the woollen undershirt to see what damage had been done. Robert's side was black and it was obvious there were several broken ribs.

'A mere scratch,' said Cynan, 'I expect you to be galloping alongside me on the morrow.'

Robert started to laugh but gasped in pain at the effort.

'Perhaps tomorrow is a bit ambitious,' he replied, 'though if I am favoured by fortune, I suspect that I will one day soon be able to beat you in the gallop.'

'I have a horn of the best wine that says you won't,' said Cynan with a smile and turned to one of his men.

'Go into the town and find a physician. I want Robert bandaged and sent in a cart to the nearest village with proven Welsh allegiance.'

'Just lay me in one of the houses below,' said Robert.

'No, it's not safe,' said Cynan. 'If we are attacked by the Earl of Lincoln we may have to move quickly and that, my friend, is something you are not capable of at this moment.'

'Do you think he will return?' asked Robert.

'Oh yes, he will return but hopefully, by the time he does, there will be a new castellan within Denbigh.'

'I'm sure there will,' came the reply.

'The siege will be the simple part,' said Cynan, 'but without water it is only a matter of days before they feel the strain. The hardest part was securing the well and the actions of you and your men have ensured a successful outcome. All we have to do now is be patient.'

'What if de-Lacey comes back?'

'We will be waiting and we won't give up the town walls as easily as he relinquished them, I can promise you that.'

'Good,' said Robert and grimaced again as pain shot through his entire body.

'Tie him upon a board,' said Cynan, 'and get him off this hill. Once he has been seen by the physician, get him to safety.'

'Aye my lord,' said a sergeant and set about making the arrangements.

The following morning the rain had stopped, and Cynan's men set about preparing the town's defences against any counterattack that may come from de-Lacey's column still somewhere out in the Welsh hills. Cynan found himself in the unusual position of forming two defensive lines, one facing inward toward the castle in case of any breakout and one facing outward, expecting the English cavalry at any moment. The Welsh warlord sent word to all the outlying villages demanding that any fletchers send all stocks of arrows immediately as well as any man fit enough to hold a sword and within two days, the defending garrison had increased significantly. On the third day a sentry sounded the alarm and every defender on the town wall looked to their weapons, suspecting the long-awaited counterattack had started.

Cynan ran up the steps of one of the towers and peered out over the plain on the other side of the river. Finally he turned to the soldier at his side.

'Stand the men down, sergeant, the column carries the standard of Madog. Open the gates and make our brothers welcome, their arrival could be most opportune.'

'Aye, my lord,' said the sergeant and descended the steps, closely followed by Cynan.

Minutes later the Welsh column rode in, led by Madog himself. As the Prince dismounted, the rest of the patrol were led into the narrow streets to seek shelter and rest after the arduous ride.

'Madog,' said Cynan walking up to him, 'well met. Your presence is unexpected though welcome.'

'Cynan,' said Madog removing his gauntlets as a boy took away his horse to be watered, 'I see you have been busy.'

'The castle will be in Welsh hands within the month,' replied Cynan. 'The defenders are without water and I have a strong line outside the gates to prevent a breakout.'

Madog looked up at the town walls.

'Your wall is well defended,' he said.

'I suspect when word reaches de-Lacey that his beloved town has fallen, he will return with all haste but we will not be found wanting.'

'You have good reason to be so careful,' said Madog, 'for he was indeed on his way back here not two days ago. You were betrayed by an informer and de-Lacey set about falling upon your flanks while you were engaged with the siege.'

'So, where is he?'

'Licking his wounds amongst the hills. We found out about the threat and rode to engage him.'

'You defeated de-Lacey's column?' asked Cynan.

'No, complete victory was not forthcoming for the ground hindered my lancers but my infantry held him up long enough to inflict heavy casualties and send them racing to the cover of the forests. We may have gained you a few days, Cynan, but do not underestimate this man. He has fought alongside Longshanks in many campaigns over many years and is an astute tactician.'

'Yet he came off second best to your men?'

'On this occasion,' said Madog, 'but I think the last few years has put fat about his belly and arrogance behind his eyes. I'm sure he won't underestimate us again, so ensure your men are alert and prepared to display a mettle such as they have not needed before.'

'I can assure you my men are ready,' said Cynan, 'but nevertheless, you have my gratitude for your intervention.

Come, we have had a pig killed this very day and though it is intended for the cauldrons to feed the men, the cooks have saved a slice of belly for my trencher. We will share the meat together as comrades.'

'Your invitation is gratefully received,' said Madog, 'and I am happy to accept, assuming my men are also fed.'

'They will be well cared for,' said Cynan, 'as will your mounts.'

'Then lead the way, for it has been many a day since I relished the taste of pig.'

The two men walked to a nearby stone cottage and past the two guards before ducking into a firelit room. A servant girl sat on a stool near the fire, cooking the meat while another stirred a pot she had just placed upon the table.

'Make another place,' said Cynan as he approached the table, 'my guest will share my fayre.' He poured a jug of ale into two wooden tankards and both men sat at the table to wait for the food.

'So,' said Cynan eventually, 'what brings you away from Caernarfon?'

'It became obvious that it was too difficult to defend should a well-trained army approach,' said Madog, 'and we needed to take the fight to the English. We have already taken the castles at Howarden and Dolwyddelan. Along with the skirmish with de-Lacey, we are making ourselves known to the English barons.'

'An impressive haul considering the short time span.'

'Perhaps, but we caught Howarden sleeping and Dolwyddelan was undefended, the bigger prizes lay before us.'

'And they are?'

'Once we have consolidated at Dolwyddelan, we ride on Criccieth and Harlech.'

'Tell me,' said Cynan, 'I admire what it is you have done but your strategy evades me. Do you really think you can defeat Longshanks?'

'At the moment, if we were to meet on the field of battle, probably not,' replied Madog, 'but this is not about a clash of swords it is about a clash of cultures. The people of Wales have accepted the English yoke for too long and have become accustomed to the weight. The main battle we face is not against English knights but the complacency of our own people. Even now, although many have flocked to our banners, ten times that have stayed in their beds, happy to accept the English tyranny in return for a quiet life. Well that has to change, Cynan, there is only so much that people like you and I can do. Yes, we can besiege a castle but what happens when we move on? Unless the people refuse to don the yoke once more it will all be for naught. I am not the provider of freedom for Wales but what I am is the ember that starts the fire. Every castle we take or manor we burn sends a message not only to Longshanks but to those still abed. The English are not unbeatable, they are not untouchable and do not have a God given right to walk these lands as master, they are skin and bone and bleed the same as us. All it takes is the mettle to make a stand. Longshanks may be able to defeat an army, but he will never defeat a cause.'

'A pretty speech,' said Cynan, 'but our young men die in the same flames.'

'Then what of you, Cynan. You fight as strongly as any, what is the cause that makes your heart race?'

'I too desire a free Wales,' said Cynan, 'but have to confess my reasons are born of frustration rather than nationalistic pride. For generations my family ruled large swathes of land throughout Mid Wales. They were fair lords and the people were happy under our tenure but when Longshanks defeated Llewellyn twelve years ago, Edward confiscated most of our lands and bestowed them on those traitors who knelt to his banner. My father died a broken man closely followed by my mother, her heart torn in two by the way she saw her husband fall from grace to die in shame. To see a once great man give up to despair is a terrible thing, Madog, a death crueller than the cut of any blade.'

'I am sorry fate took your family down that path,' said Madog.

'Fate had nothing to do with it,' said Cynan, 'it was all the hand of Longshanks and that is why I fight, to pay back the debt of heartbreak on behalf of my family. Yes, the prize has changed and indeed if the freedom of our country is the outcome, then I will pray at my parents' memorial but that is secondary. At the moment, I seek only the destruction of all things English, after that, well, we will see what happens.'

'A sad tale,' said Madog, 'but I have been told you seek the crown of Wales for yourself.'

'I have never sought the title, Madog, but for many years I carried the burden of resistance alone. In the beginning our numbers were few, but as our ranks grew, we became a thorn in the side of the English. Eventually we had an army and the English left whole swathes of land lest we water the soil with their blood. At last people could see that there was another option to servitude and we have formed cantrefs where the English fear to tread. The movement increased and eventually the flames fed themselves culminating in the siege of Castell du Bere. I knew then the advance would only be stopped by death or victory and intended continuing the resistance but imagine my surprise when I found out about some lord in the north claiming the crown of Wales, someone who was yet to swing a sword in anger.'

'A fair observation,' said Madog.

'And a great concern,' said Cynan, 'one which I was not about to leave unaddressed. The movement was too important to have it ruined by someone playing at kingship.' He paused to take a drink while staring into Madog's eyes. 'However,' he continued, placing the tankard on the table, 'I am man enough to confess that I might have been hasty with my judgement. Your results so far are indeed impressive though truth be told, fortune has indeed been your bedfellow. I do not seek kingship, Madog, but if my hand is forced then I will take it if there is no other option. To have a weak king is worse than to have no king for it invites infighting and that way leads to self-destruction. So, continue along the path you have chosen and if you turn out to be the man you appear to be, then I will be the first to kneel before your banner, if not, then I will just as easily wipe your men from the field of battle and claim the throne for myself.'

Madog was silent for a few moments before replying.

'In the circumstances, I feel that is the best I can expect.' He picked up his own tankard and held it up toward Cynan. 'Let us continue in this manner, Cynan,' he said, 'on different paths toward a shared goal and at the end of the journey, what will be will be.'

Cynan picked up his own tankard again.

'So be it,' he said and both tankards clashed together in a toast, spilling ale upon the table.

—

One of the servants brought over the chunk of pork and cut it in half before adding boiled vegetables to the platters. Both men ate hungrily but were only half done when the door barged open and a soldier burst into the room before removing his helm.

'Owain,' said Cynan, standing up, 'what brings you with such angst.'

'My lord, the flag of parley flies above the castle, they want to talk terms.'

Cynan turned to stare at Madog in surprise.

'Well,' he said, 'it would seem they are in a worse state than I thought. Come, join me in the negotiations.'

The two men donned their chainmail and helms before adding their side weapons. On the way out, Madog picked up the last of the pork to eat on the way up to the castle. Meat was too valuable a commodity to leave lying in waste.

—

Ten minutes later, Cynan and Madog sat upon their horses before the castle. On either side were two heavily armed sergeants, each weighed down with heavy plate armour and both known as ferocious warriors. Before them lay the drawbridge covering the spike lined ditch surrounding the fortress. The sound of the portcullis being raised echoed from within and eventually the double gates opened to reveal four riders waiting within. As soon as the way was clear, the English party rode out to meet the Welsh, reining their horses in when they were no more than ten paces apart.

The leader was dressed in full ceremonial armour covered with a white tabard bearing the colours of Edward.

'My name is Phillip of Lincoln,' he said, 'Castellan of Denbigh in the absence of our lord, Sir Henry de-Lacey. Who speaks on behalf of the Welsh?'

'That would be me,' came the reply, 'Cynan ap Mare-dudd, knight of Llewellyn and soldier of Wales.'

'Llewellyn?' repeated Phillip in surprise. 'A man long dead as far as I am aware.'

'Dead in the flesh but not in the memory. What do you want, Phillip of Lincoln?'

'I seek compassion,' said Phillip. 'The people within the castle thirst and whilst it is the duty of men such as us to suffer such deprivations, it is a sad day when civilians die due to actions out of their control.'

'Is that not the way of all wars?'

'Perhaps, but they were out of our control. I have influence in this situation only and if you are a man of honour, then you will allow the most basic of human needs to those who do not choose the life of a soldier.'

'How many civilians do you have?'

'About a hundred. If you can let us have access to the well under a flag of truce then we will need no more than a day to fill our barrels and your conscience will be clear.'

'Phillip of Lincoln,' replied Cynan, 'just in case it has escaped your notice, your castle is besieged by a superior army with the sole intent of wresting it from your hands. Why would we give succour to those charged with blocking that path?'

'Because the civilians bear no fault for situations out of their control. If you were a man of compassion, you could avoid the suffering of the many for the actions of a few.'

'You speak pretty words, my lord,' said Cynan, 'but this is not a game we play. Men will bleed, people will die, this is the way of such things but your compassion does you merit. Any man, woman or child, needing access to the well will be granted passage. However, upon leaving the castle gates they will not be allowed to return. Civilians will go to their kin within the town but should armed men leave, then they will be detained under guard until the castle falls, then to be released to return whence you came.'

'If this is the case then you condemn men to die of thirst, where is the chivalry in this?'

'Where is the chivalry in enslaving an entire nation?' responded Cynan. 'And I am confused at your request. This is a siege, sir knight, an assault upon the servitude you have imposed upon the people of Wales. We have already both lost many men and before this task is done, many more will die, whether from thirst or by the sword. Either you are stupid or you stall for time thinking your master will soon return to aid your plight. I suspect the latter so let me say this, the man alongside me has already routed the Earl of Lincoln and his army not ten leagues hence. His command lays scattered across the battlefield, already carrion for the crows and the head of Henry de-Lacey is on its way to Caernarfon to be displayed upon the gate towers of the town. Do not play games with me,

Phillip of Lincoln, I am here to take this castle at all costs and if that is over your rotting corpse then so be it.'

'You insult me, sir,' shouted the Castellan, struggling to control his horse, 'and I would have redress.'

'In the name of god,' roared Cynan, 'this is not some petty tournament to be fought for the favour of ladies, it is a war. Men will die and walls will fall, such is the way of things. You have had my response, Englishman, your civilians may leave, your garrison cannot, unless it is under a flag of surrender. You have until noon tomorrow and then the offer is withdrawn.'

'It is not enough,' said Phillip, 'I need more time.'

'It is all you have,' said Cynan, 'the lives of many now lie in your hands, both English and Welsh. You talk of a chivalric code so why not display that which you preach, surrender the castle and there will be no more bloodshed for the sake of mere masonry.'

Phillip considered Cynan's words for several moments before answering.

'If we cede the castle,' he said, 'what guarantee do I have that your men will not fall upon us as wolves?'

'You have my word,' said Cynan, 'and what's more, you will be allowed to leave under your own colours carrying full arms, however, I promise you this. If there is any sign of trickery on your part and any blade is drawn in anger, then I swear by almighty God we will fall upon you with a ferocity the likes of which has never been known and no quarter will be given until the last of your English blood stains the Welsh soil beneath our feet.'

'I will think upon it,' said Phillip, 'in the meantime, I will send out the women and children.'

'So be it,' said Cynan. 'My herald will be waiting here at dawn for your final decision.'

The English knight nodded and turned to ride back into the castle. Cynan also turned and rode back down the hill.

'Cynan,' said Madog quietly, 'De-Lacey yet lives and still heads a strong force.'

'The Castellan doesn't know that,' said Cynan, 'and the thought that there is no possibility of relief will aid his thought process.'

'Is victory using untruths as a weapon acceptable?'

'Is war acceptable, Madog? I suggest that whatever weapon can bring conclusion to the conflict is a good one. Lies are just another weapon in our arsenal.'

'Interesting perspective,' said Madog. 'What makes you think he will accept your terms?'

'My sources have told me the well inside the castle dried up weeks ago and they rely on the one outside its walls for their water. Now it is in our hands, and strongly defended, there is no way they can hold out. I believe there is a strong garrison within the castle and ordinarily it would be an impossible task, but in this instance their strength is also their weakness.'

'In what way?'

'The larger their number, the more resources they use. A man can live without many things, Madog, water is not one of them. If I were him, I would save the lives of my command, give up the castle and return to fight another day.'

The following dawn saw Madog and Cynan standing upon the town perimeter wall, a good viewing platform to see the triple towers of the castle gates on the hill above. For a while they thought that the Castellan had decided to wait out the siege and hope for relief but eventually Madog pointed at the flag of Edward, slowly descending the flagpole above the gate.

'They are lowering the colours,' he said, 'it looks like your terms have been accepted.'

'The man has more sense than I credited him with,' said Cynan. 'Come, we should prepare to accept the handover.'

An hour later a column of English cavalry rode slowly out of the gates followed by a hundred foot soldiers. Each was heavily armed and wore whatever armour they possessed. As the Castellan reached the far end of the drawbridge, one of Cynan's men rode to meet him.

'My lord,' said the Welshman, 'my master sends his regards and has asked me to accept the flag of the castle on his behalf.'

'Where is your master?' asked Phillip. 'Tradition demands a surrender is accepted by the victor in person. His absence places doubt into my heart regarding my men's safety.'

'Cynan ap Maredudd is not known for following tradition, my lord, but rest assured his word is his bond and as long as your command keep their weapons sheathed then there will be no blood shed this day.'

'So be it,' said Phillip and gestured for his second in command to approach. The flag was handed over without ceremony and the column continued down the hill. As they rode through the town, the people came to the windows to watch them go. Many were glad to see them leave but those of English descent quickly packed a few belongings and ran out into the street to join the exodus, fearing the rule of the Welsh.

The main road through the town was lined with Welsh infantry, each bearing their own weapons from pike and billhooks to swords and clubs. There were even those bearing scythes and pitchforks amongst their number, such was the diversity of the army's composition. As they passed, an old man spat toward the Castellan and though his second in command's hand flew to his sword, Phillip snapped out a command.

'Hold,' he said, 'do not be drawn into conflict by the action of a peasant, it is beneath you.'

'But my lord, he should pay the price of such an insult.'

'He will pay soon enough, Fredrick, they all will.'

As they reached the town walls the column halted before the closed gates. Phillip pulled his horse aside and looked up at Cynan on the gate tower above.

'Well, sir,' he called, 'you have my congratulations, the castle is yours. However, it is worth pointing out that it fell not to force of arms but to unfortunate circumstance.'

'A victory, nevertheless,' said Cynan.

'Granted,' said Phillip before adding, 'of course, you do realise this is but a temporary set of affairs and if I have my way, we will meet again in the near future, and the situation will bear little resemblance to that which we now share?'

'I expected nothing else,' said Cynan.

'When that day comes, Welshman, I assure you there will be no fancy negotiation or deals to be made, it will be battle without quarter until one of us lies dead upon the ground.'

'A meeting to relish,' said Cynan, 'but until that day dawns, I bid you farewell. Ride out, Phillip of Lincoln, go back to England and leave Wales to the Welsh.'

'This is not over, Cynan,' snarled Phillip, 'and I swear by all that is holy, I will have retribution.'

'Open the gates,' roared Cynan and watched as the English column left Denbigh town. He turned to face Madog at his side.

'Well,' he said, 'thus another castle falls in Edward's ring of steel, which, including Dolwyddelan makes four in total.'

'A tally to be proud of,' said Madog, 'but I think we have probably ridden the wave of good fortune as far as we can.'

'Why say you that?'

'Because by now word will be spreading like a forest fire amongst the English strongholds. They can no longer ignore us, Cynan, and will realise we are a force to be reckoned with. As we speak, I expect every outpost to be stocking their stores and sharpening steel. No, something inside me says that from here on in, it is going to get a lot harder.'

'A fair judgement,' said Cynan, 'and the truth of the matter will soon be found out.'

'In what way?'

'The taking of Denbigh has raised the spirits of my men and I would take it in harness while the fires burn bright.'

'To what end?'

'I hear the people of Mold have suffered extensively at the hands of the constable there. It is said he has people flogged in the stocks for the slightest of crimes and hunger is a bedfellow to all.'

'Mold is low on the list of priorities,' said Madog, 'and lacks any strategic importance.'

'The size of the castle matters not; it is the effect of the ruling classes within. Surely the people of Mold are no less deserving of our attention than those of the town below us?'

'Accepted,' said Madog, 'and I do not deem to question your path.'

He looked down as the last of the English infantry marched out through the town gates. Within seconds the sound of the oaken gates symbolically slamming into place roused the previously quiet Welsh army and the air erupted into deafening cheers of victory.

'Come,' said Cynan, 'I have a castle to inspect.'

'No,' said Madog, 'you carry on. I will rally my command and ride out within the hour. There is much to do, Cynan, but in the meantime enjoy your victory and let's hope there are many more to follow.'

'The path is clear before us, my friend,' said Cynan, 'all we need to do is find the courage to tread it.'

The men grasped wrists in comradeship before Cynan descended from the walls to lead his cheering army up to the castle. As he went, Madog turned to the man alongside him.

'Sergeant, muster our command, we have work to do.'

Chapter Ten

Brecon Castle

Garyn stared into the emotionless eyes of the abbot. The old man's face was just above his own and as it slowly eased into an evil smile, a trickle of spittle ran down from the corner of his mouth to drip onto Garyn's chin. The rotten stumps where the teeth had once been contributed to the fetid smell of the monk's breath and Garyn gagged at the overwhelming stench.

Father Williams pushed harder on the knife and Garyn gasped as the blade pierced his skin.

'Ready for hell?' snarled the abbot.

'Do it,' screamed Garyn and held his breath as he awaited the killing thrust but before the abbot could drive home the blade, the door crashed open and two men burst into the room. For half a second, everyone paused as they took in the scene and one of the English guards released his hold on Garyn to reach for his sword.

Garyn instantly took advantage and used his free hand to punch the priest, knocking him and the knife to one side. This spurred the other men to action and Geraint swung his sword in a wide arc to smash into the first man's head, lodging halfway through the skull while Tarian kicked the second kneeling guard as hard as he could in the jaw sending him sprawling across the floor.

The two other guards at the end of the room sprang into action and drawing their swords, ran at the two intruders.

'Kill them,' screeched the abbot from the corner of the room where he lay sprawled on the floor.

Geraint tried to release his sword from his victim's skull by driving the heel of his boot down onto the man's face but it was no good, the blade was lodged tight. He drew his knife and faced one of the other attackers. The English soldier swung the two-handed sword in a sideways arc, hoping to cut Geraint in half but the Welshman saw it coming and dropped to the floor, the blade passing within a whisker above his head. For a moment the soldier was unbalanced and Geraint took advantage to thrust his knife upward into his attacker's groin.

The guard screamed in agony but retained control of his sword. He lifted it up to drive the point downward into the man at his feet but as he raised his hands above his head, Garyn smashed a stool into his face, knocking him backward to land on the floor. Instantly Geraint threw himself upon the fallen man and drove his dagger over and over again into his chest.

'Garyn,' he shouted as he caught his breath, 'help Tarian.'

Garyn looked around and saw the older man struggling with the other guard. Tarian had lost his knife and his sword and the younger man was getting the upper hand. Garyn ran forward and jumped upon the Englishman's back, throwing his hand around his head and as he yanked it back, Tarian took the opportunity to do something none of them expected, he leaned forward and tore his attacker's throat apart with his teeth. The Englishman staggered backward with arterial blood spraying every-where, his hands clawing uselessly at the gaping wound as he fell to the floor. Garyn stared in horror and turned to face Tarian, not knowing what to say. The white-haired man spat out a piece of flesh from his blood-stained mouth and wiped his sleeve across his face.

'Don't judge me, Garyn,' said Tarian quietly, 'there are many ways to kill a man. He now lays dead while I am still here. The end justifies the means.'

Across the room, Geraint bent to cut the throat of the man Tarian had kicked when he first entered. When he was done, he stood up and all three Welshmen looked at each other in silence.

'Is that it?' asked Tarian. 'Are there any more?'

'Not that I know of,' said Garyn, 'except for the monk.' He looked around but was shocked to see the cell was empty.

'He's gone,' gasped Garyn, looking toward the open door at the other end of the room. 'He must have taken the opportunity during the fight.' He started forward toward the door but Tarian grabbed his arm.

'Where are you going?' asked Tarian.

'I need to catch him,' said Garyn, 'there are outstanding matters to resolve.'

'No,' said Tarian, 'it is too risky. We need to get out of here, for all we know he could have already raised the alarm.'

'Look,' said Garyn, pulling his arm away, 'I don't know who you are and I am grateful for your aid but there are things here you don't understand. That man is responsible for killing my family and I will have redress even if it costs me my life.'

'I understand your grief,' said Tarian, 'but revenge is not worth your life. Let it go, there will be other opportunities.'

'Why wait?' asked Garyn. 'I have just found out that man is responsible for my family's murder, he paid for my sister to be raped and then he desecrated their graves. The burden is too great and I need to end this once and for all.'

'What about your family?'

'I have no family,' said Garyn.

'You have a brother,' said Tarian quietly.

'My brother died fleeing a situation of my making,' said Garyn. 'I even have his blood on my hands.'

'No you don't,' said a voice from across the room.

'What do you mean?' asked Garyn. 'He died on a ship trying to cross the western sea.'

Geraint stepped forward into the circle of candlelight.

'Your brother didn't die, Garyn,' said Geraint. 'He survived to live a fruitful life in the north and for the last twelve years thought you dead from a hangman's noose.'

'How do you know this?' asked Garyn but instead of answering, Geraint took another step forward until he was within touching distance of his brother.

Garyn's eyes narrowed as he focused on the features of the stranger.

'How do you...' he started but fell silent as he recognised the features of the man before him.

'You look like my father,' he said slowly, 'I don't understand.'

'Garyn,' said Geraint, 'it is me, your brother.'

Garyn raised his hand up to touch the side of Geraint's face and for a few moments they stared at each other in silence. Slowly, the doubt on Garyn's face eased as he realised the man was telling the truth.

'It can't be true,' whispered Garyn, unable to take it in, 'I thought you long dead.'

'As I did you,' said Geraint.

Garyn grabbed both of his brother's shoulders and without another word, dragged him into his embrace as tears fell from his eyes.

'Lord be praised,' he gasped, 'I thought I was truly forsaken and all my family were dead.'

'It is a strange world we live in,' said Geraint pulling away, 'and there is much to discuss but Tarian is right, we have to get away from here before it is too late.'

'Geraint, you heard what I just said, that monk is the devil in disguise and has the blood of our family on his hands. We must seek redress.'

'And we will,' said Geraint, 'but now is not the time, there is too much at stake.'

'If we leave it, he will escape and many more will suffer at his hands.'

'I think not, Garyn,' said Geraint. 'He is at death's door but I swear, once this has all been sorted out, we will seek steps to lay our retribution upon him and clear our family's name. Now come, we have to go.'

Garyn followed the men out and through the passages, heading toward the courtyard. On the way they passed the bodies of two more English soldiers, the handiwork of Tarian and Geraint less than ten minutes earlier. Soon they were moving quietly through the shadows toward the kitchens but just as Geraint thought they would make it unseen; a cry arose from one of the tower windows.

'*Alarm!* Intruders in the castle!'

Within seconds a bell started ringing and they could hear voices from all around as the garrison responded to the call.

'Quickly,' shouted Geraint, all thoughts of subterfuge gone, 'the time for stealth is done.' He turned to the side and ran straight across the courtyard, making a beeline for the kitchen block. The others followed but though their speed was quick, an alert guard spotted them and called out through the darkness.

'Halt strangers,' he called.

'Where are they?' came another voice.

'Heading to the north wall,' shouted the guard.

Confusion reigned for a few moments which gave the Welshmen time to gain access to the kitchens unhindered and they ran through the corridor toward the cellar. As they passed the kitchen door a large man stepped out with a meat cleaver, wondering what all the noise was about but before he could react, Geraint barged him out of the way and the cook fell to the floor, losing his blade into the bargain.

'Come on,' cried Geraint, 'this way.'

'What about him?' asked Garyn as he passed the cook.

'Leave him, they know we are here anyway.'

They ran down to the cellar and ducked into the passageway leading from the castle. Minutes later they emerged into the forest and ran as fast as they could through the foliage.

'What do you mean intruders?' roared Gerald at the messenger. 'Who dares breach my walls.'

'We don't know who they were, my lord, but it would seem they have released the prisoners from the tower and assaulted the abbot.'

'Is the outlaw gone?'

'He is.'

Gerald threw a gauntlet against the wall in temper.

'I am surrounded by imbeciles,' he roared, 'and swear somebody will hang this day for their incompetence. How did they get in? Where was the guard?'

'They entered by the old sally port and were gone before we knew they were here.'

'Have you stood the garrison to?'

'Aye, my lord, and a mounted unit is set to ride out to scour the forest, they can't have got far on foot and if they have mounts waiting, they will leave a trail.'

'Do it,' said Gerald pulling on his jerkin, 'and assemble a unit of foot soldiers to accompany me within the hour.'

'To where, my lord?'

'To Brycheniog,' said Gerald, 'if the woman and her son have been set free then you can guarantee that they will have headed back to their own people. I intend to find them and have them hung for aiding the escape of a brigand. Tell me, is the abbot still alive?'

'He is, my lord, and sits within his chambers attended by the apothecary.'

'Good, I will have words and when I am finished, ensure the men are ready. I will have my revenge before daybreak.'

'Aye,' said the soldier and left the room.

Gerald strapped on his sword and headed through the passageways within the castle walls toward the abbot's quarters. Without knocking, he barged in to see a servant girl bathing some scratches on the old man's face. Beside her the apothecary was mixing a draft to ease the abbot's pain.

'Oh, there you are,' sneered Father Williams. 'I thought you would be fast asleep, safe in the confines of your royal bedchamber while all about are threatened by brigands.'

'Cease the jibes, monk,' said Gerald, 'it would seem you have escaped the worse end of the deal.'

'There are four men lying dead not a stone's throw from here,' said the abbot angrily, 'and it is only by good fortune that my body does not lay alongside them. What sort of garrison do you run where it is so easy to gain access to a castle of Edward? How did they even get in?'

'I know not the detail yet,' said Gerald, 'but rest assured the truth will be forthcoming and anyone found wanting in their responsibilities will be dealt with accordingly.'

'You do that,' growled the monk, 'and in the process, make sure that the blacksmith is captured. His escape angers me beyond belief and I swear to you by almighty God that my fortune will remain hidden from all men forever more unless his head is placed before me before I die. Is that clear, Gerald? If you want to know the locations of the graves then I want that man dead at my feet within days.'

Gerald turned to the serving girl and the apothecary.

'Get out,' he said.

'But my lord,' started the apothecary.

'You heard me,' said Gerald, 'get out and shut the door.' The man packed his bag and along with the girl, left the room, slamming the door behind them. Gerald turned to face the abbot.

'Now you listen to me, monk,' he snarled, 'we had a deal. In return for delivering him into your hands you promised to give me the list of graves. I delivered my half of the bargain so pay up, give me the information.'

'Look around you, sir knight,' shouted the abbot, 'where is he? Do you see him for I don't?'

'I did what we agreed,' shouted Gerald. 'I placed him within your very hands. It is no fault of mine that you let him slip through.'

'Really?' sneered the abbot. 'It was your castle his comrades managed to breach, your sentries they evaded, your guard who told them where to find me and your so-called soldiers who fell to their blades. You are solely responsible for this disaster, Gerald, and I will not pay a single coin for your absolute incompetence.'

Gerald drew his knife and ran across to the monk, pushing his chair against the far wall and resting his blade upon the abbot's throat.

'Careful what you say, monk,' he hissed, 'for I have had just about enough of your continued demands. I could kill you right now and not one eyebrow would be raised.'

'You won't kill me, Gerald,' said the monk with a sneer. 'I am too valuable. My knowledge is worth a fortune and the greed is too great within you. You need me alive and you will do anything to secure the knowledge.'

Gerald stared deep into the man's eyes before pulling back and allowing Father Williams to sit upright once more.

'Don't presume to know what it is I want, monk, this whole thing is getting wearisome and I could just as soon kill you now and have my men dig up every grave in every churchyard.'

'Do that and you will turn every village against you from here to London,' said Williams. 'They may be weak individually but give the Welsh a cause to support and they can turn as nasty as any rabid dog. The air is already ripe with talks of revolution and any such action from you will be the catalyst to tear these walls from around you. No, just accept it, Gerald, you fell short but there is yet time. My strength is returning and I feel I may yet have a few months. All you need to do is bring me his head, forget about trying to capture or trick him into returning, that gateway is now closed. All I want is proof his pathetic life is at an end.'

'Well, monk,' said Gerald, 'I will say one thing for you, once you get a quest in mind you go after it as true as an arrow. Never have I seen any man so obsessed with retribution as you.' He paused before taking a deep sigh. 'So be it,' he said, 'I will hunt him down with a passion to match your own but if there is any more stalling upon my return, then I will personally gouge out your eyes and watch the dogs tear you apart.'

Father Williams grinned, his blackened stumps visible in his diseased mouth.

'If your actions match the braveness of your words, sir knight, then it won't come to that, for I will have my revenge and you will become the richest man in Christendom. Now, if that isn't worth one more effort, then I don't know what is. Be gone and do whatever it is you need to do, but bring it to me, Gerald, bring me the head of Garyn ap Thomas before the opportunity is lost.'

Out in the forest, Garyn, Geraint and Tarian ran as fast as they could through the trees, eventually stumbling out onto the northern road.

'Where are they?' gasped Tarian.

'This way,' said Geraint and ran along the track. Within minutes they came across the horses they had left there hours earlier.

'Right,' said Geraint, turning to Garyn, 'we have to get away from here as quickly as we can. I expect Gerald will send his horsemen after us but if we ride light, then we can stay ahead of him.'

'To where?' asked Garyn.

'Back to the north,' said Geraint. 'I hear Madog and Cynan are carving their way through the country like a farmer's scythe and we will be safe amongst their number.'

'What about Elspeth and her family? Surely the Castellan will learn of Fletcher's involvement and make them pay the price?'

'They will have already left,' said Geraint. 'Yesterday we made arrangements for them to seek refuge at a farm amongst the hills, they will be safe there for now and will already be on their way. I fully expect Madog's allies will lay siege to Brecon in the near future and when that happens, God willing, we can all return and live in peace.'

'And what of us?' asked Garyn. 'What path is ours?'

'I know not,' said Geraint, 'but first we must flee this place, come on there is no time to waste.'

The three men spurred their horses and took the north road toward Builth.

Chapter Eleven

North Wales — Three Weeks Later

Madog stood at the table in his command tent. His officers stared at the map before them, fascinated at the picture it portrayed. For a while he let the men talk amongst themselves but as the last man entered, the Prince called for silence.

'Gentlemen,' he said, 'thank you for coming. Upon this table there is a map of Wales, drawn up at my request showing the current situation. All our comrades have sent the intelligence in response to my requests and for the first time we have a complete picture of the uprising. Please, bear with me as I explain and I will take questions at the end.'

He picked up a knife and pointed to the north coast.

'First of all,' he said, 'the northern coast lies in our hands as does Ynys Mon.' He swept the blade from the English border across to the west coast. 'All this ground is in our control except for here and here. He pointed at Rhuddlan and Flint castles. Rhuddlan is well forti-fied and holds a garrison in excess of five thousand well trained men under the command of Reginald De-Grey. He patrols Flint and offers support to the castle which is locked down for siege conditions. I see no benefit in pursuing any of these at this time so have focused our attention elsewhere.'

He pointed further down the map.

'As you know, we have ransacked Caernarfon and Howarden castles and made Dolwyddelan our base. In addition, we currently lay siege to Criccieth and Harlech and though they are well defended, we expect a break-through in a matter of days. After that we will march immediately to Aberystwyth to oust the castellan there.

'Further South, Cynan has already taken Castell du Bere, Denbigh and Mold, and is laying siege to Builth as we speak. His cavalry also controls the main roadway between the north and south.

'To the west, Maelgwyn ap Rhys lays siege to the castle at Cardigan and marches upon Pembroke while in the south, Morgan ap Maredudd is laying waste to English fortresses at a rate hard to follow. Already he has captured Abergavenny and Morlais, and I believe has Caerphilly in his sights. The English control Cardiff and use the docks there to resupply their forces in the south but overall, they fear venturing forth in case they encounter Morgan's men.' He stood up and looked around the table.

'As you can see,' he said, 'over the last few months we have made great headway and by focusing on this so-called ring of steel, we are denying the English secure places to rest and resupply their men. Edward's whole strategy for keeping Wales subdued depends on this ring being unbroken with each fortress supporting the next, as do the links in a chain, but I am here to tell you, the ring is broken and lays in pieces at our feet.'

The men erupted in cheers and Madog allowed the celebration for a few moments before calling for silence.

'Yes there is much to rejoice,' he continued, 'but let it be tempered with caution. So far, we have caught the English unawares and though their castles fall faster than winter rain, the harder path lies before us. Already Edward has sent ships from Bristol and Ireland to resupply those fortresses upon the coast and the whole of Flint is denied us by De-Grey and his forces. It is now, as we descend into the depths of winter, that our men's fervour will dampen and we must guard against losing the fire in their bellies.'

He turned back to the map.

'My sources tell me that Edward has delayed his campaign to France and musters his barons around him in Worcester. It is said he is recruiting infantry from the north and has disembarked his fleet in the south to join with the Earl of Gloucester while the Earl of Warwick musters his considerable forces to support the King.'

'It sounds as if he is at last taking us seriously,' said Meirion, 'and amasses a serious force.'

'Indeed he does,' said Madog, 'but what is more concerning is the fact that five thousand Welshmen had already answered his call to arms for the French campaign and were stationed in Bristol waiting to embark on the troop ships. I have heard disturbing rumours that these men have been re-tasked to march north and we face the prospect of Welshman facing Welshman across the battle-field, a prospect that leaves a bitter taste in my mouth.'

'Do you know anything about his strategy?' asked one of the warlords.

'No, but if I was him, I would stay close to positions of strength as much as possible. Rhuddlan is well fortified and Conwy is unassailable. I believe he will bring his forces into Wales here,' he indicated a position high on the English–Welsh border, 'and campaign west through Flint, drawing on De-Grey's forces if needed.'

'To what end?' asked Meirion.

'I think he will head west to reclaim Caernarfon,' said Madog. 'It is the most majestic of all his castles and its fall must have hurt him a lot. By retaking Caernarfon, it will give him a base to consolidate and then launch his counterattack southward.'

'So am I right in saying, your strategy is to defend Caernarfon and deny him the castle?'

'On the contrary,' said Madog, 'I have no intention of wasting men defending a pile of stones. I have said it before and I will say it again, our strength lays not in fixed defences, but in the flexibility of our tactics and the knowledge of our own lands. Our men have grown up in this environment and the steep slopes of the hills are nothing to them whereas the English groan at the mere sight. What I propose is this, let him amass his forces and plot his assaults. He will expect formal lines and desperate defence but what he will find is an enemy as fluid as a mountain stream, appearing like the morning mist and fading away just as quick. We will harass his lines, draining their life blood as silently as a leech yet when opportunity affords, fall upon them like a mountain wolf. His frustration will know no bounds.'

'Madog,' said a voice, 'the tactics you describe are all very well but hold little difference to those already employed by warlords across Wales. Surely this campaign is about ending the English presence once and for all and I suggest that hit-and-run tactics will not defeat an English army the size that Edward holds under his command.'

'I agree, Walter,' said Madog, 'but there is a purpose to my thinking. At the moment we are vastly outnumbered by the enemy and any pitched battle will have only one possible outcome, however, there is a way to address the imbalance. We need to increase the size of our own armies with immediate effect and until our numbers increase, we cannot risk the field against Edward.'

'And where do you intend to find these men at such short notice, especially men who are trained in the way of war?'

'Oh that part is easy,' said Madog. 'All I need to do is convince them.'

Across the border, Longshanks also stood at a briefing table though this one was in far more comfortable circumstances, the main hall in Worcester castle. Beside him stood Gilbert De-Claire, the eighth Earl of Gloucester and William De-Beauchamp, the ninth Earl of Warwick. Alongside them were several of the most senior knights as well as Nicholas Fermbaud, Castellan of Bristol Castle. Their own map adorned the table though it was far more detailed and contained the representation of every castle in Wales, both Welsh and English.

'Report,' said Longshanks and all eyes turned to Fermbaud.

'My lord,' said Fermbaud, 'the north of Wales is effectively under the control of the Welsh, led by this minor lord of Ynys Mon who lays claim to the title Prince of Wales. Despite the audacity of such a claim, many are flocking to his banner, no doubt encouraged by the success of his campaign so far. The catalyst was the taking of Caernarfon, a disaster aided by the fact the castellan was away from the fortress at the time. After that, Madog split his force and took Howarden and Dolwyddelan. In addition there are reports that Criccieth and Harlech are under siege, though information is sketchy at best. We have sent resupply ships to aid their cause and though their garrisons are small, their design makes them a formidable task for any deeming them a prize. We hold the northwest of the country and Reginald De-Grey has a force in excess of five thousand men under his command. There are a few hundred infantry based in Flint castle but such is their strength and levels of supplies already in store, the constable there is confident of repelling any siege.'

'Excellent,' said Longshanks, 'when this campaign is done, bring this situation back to my attention. Any man who prepares so thoroughly will be rewarded. What about the west?'

'Not good, my lord. A warlord by the name of Maelgwyn ap Rhys lays waste to the English estates from Pembrokeshire down and several castles have already fallen. There are stories of unprecedented brutality inflicted on any of English birth and it is said thousands have already died. Our castle at Cardigan has fallen and Pembroke is under siege as we speak, hanging on only due to our supply ships being able to dock within the port. His columns raid inland especially down toward Carmarthen and no man is safe from their untrained soldiers, many of whom are interested in only whatever bounty they can steal from English properties.

'Along the southern coastline,' he continued, 'Morgan ap Maredudd terrorises Gwent and Morgannwg. Ogmore

Castle has been utterly destroyed along with Morlais and Abergavenny.'

'I know of this man called Morgan,' interjected the Earl of Gloucester, 'and for many years he has been a thorn in my side. These latest revelations about his assault on the great manors of south Wales come as no great surprise for his influence makes the running of such estates difficult and I suspect he is using the uprising as an excuse to increase his efforts against my interests.'

'Surely you mean the interests of the crown?' said Longshanks.

'My lord, I do not mean to be rude and of course, all such estates ultimately belong to you but if you examine the list of manors and castles he has attacked you will see he targets property that I hold under my direct influence.'

'Do you have a grudge between your families?' asked Longshanks.

'We do. Many of the lands gifted to me by your gracious hands once belonged to his family and he has sworn to oppose me at every step. He has burned farms and burgages right across Gwent. The man is a nuisance and needs putting in his place once and for all.'

'You may have your chance,' said Longshanks and turned to face Fermbaud once more.

'So tell me of this Cynan,' he said.

'Cynan ap Maredudd is a law unto himself,' said Fermbaud, 'and although he seems to follow the lead of Madog, his name was known to us long before the young upstart set sights upon the title. Indeed, it was he who was responsible for the cowardly ambush that slaughtered my patrol into Wales a few months ago. He seems to be on a personal crusade against anything English and gives no quarter on the field. He has already taken Castell du Bere and Denbigh. It is rumoured Builth lies in ruins as does Mold, and there is no place safe from his reach. He rampages through Wales like a wildfire and one would be forgiven for thinking it is he that leads the revolt yet Madog has captured the people's hearts and they jostle for position.'

'Can this be used against them?' asked Longshanks. 'Perhaps we can turn brother against brother?'

'If hatred of all things English didn't burn so fiercely in his breast I would agree, but while our countrymen still live and toil on their side of the border then there is an uneasy truce between them.'

'Is there anything else?' asked Longshanks.

'Not as far as the situation goes but it may be useful to know that they have no ships in support of their cause and no single base of operations. Essentially, they are a fragmented army, and always on the move.'

'This in itself is a problem,' said Longshanks, 'yet unsustainable when dealing with a large body of men. If there was a single command structure based in one castle, no matter how strong be the walls I would have no hesitation in descending upon them with the full force of the English army and wiping them out once and for all. However, fate has seen fit to deny me that opportunity so we have to adopt different tactics. It would seem that though this uprising prevails across most of the country, it revolves around four men, those you have just named. It is my strong belief that if we take out the figureheads, there is no strong dynastic line to replace them and once the head of each army is removed, the body will collapse.'

He looked around at the nobles present.

'I have today received word from Henry de-Lacey. As we speak, he is encamped within sight of Rhuddlan and enjoys the hospitality of Reginald De-Grey. His castle at Denbigh lies in the hands of the Welsh and it also seems he suffered a defeat in open combat against a column of Madog's. Despite this he assures me his command is still strong and honour demands he is allowed to redress his shame. I am inclined to allow his request though not as a solitary strike. This is what I intend to do.

'Two days from now, our men will march out to put down this uprising. In the meantime I will send word to Henry de-Lacey to engage Madog at the earliest opportunity but I will send my cousin, Sir Edmund, to aid him with a heavily armed column. They will campaign south and west to engage Maelgwyn ap Rhys. He will relieve the sieges of our castles there but keep the pressure on the Welsh along the entire coast, giving them no opportunity to rest. This will give us a chance to establish a foothold in Wales without having to needlessly worry about any threat of ambush from Madog's army. The order of advance will be as so.'

He turned to face the Earl of Gloucester.

'Gilbert, you will have your chance to put paid to the meddling of this Morgan ap Maredudd. You will cross into Wales with your full command and ride south to engage him with all haste. I suspect he will engage in tactics of evasion but you are to give him no chance to rest. We have a garrison at Cardiff you can draw on and may engage with the fleet at Bristol to keep you resupplied. You are to pursue him relentlessly until he surrenders or has fallen. Leave no stone unturned and when you are successful, as you must be, then turn your attentions upon the people of the south and leave them no room for misunderstanding about what happens to those who stand against the English crown. Do I make myself clear?'

'Aye, Majesty, you do.'

'Good,' said Longshanks and turned to the Earl of Warwick.

'To you, William, lies the greater task. You are to take your army into Mid Wales and seek the one called Cynan. Your forces are formidable and I have no doubt that your command will be a match for him. In addition you will keep a substantial force in reserve ready to ride north or south to support the other columns should the need arise. In particular I want you to establish a strong standing force in Mid Wales, ready to intercept any Welsh taking the north–south road in any direction. Make Mid Wales your own and ensure none can travel through without you knowing. I want the country cut in half.'

'Understood,' said William.

'Finally, I will lead a column into Wrexham and march through Flint to consolidate our safe base there before linking up with Reginald De-Grey. Once done, the rest of my army will follow and we will campaign eastward, via Conwy, putting pressure on this Welsh prince to meet us in open warfare. In addition, we will take the island of Ynys Mon as we did against Llewellyn and deny them the support of the many farmsteads there. If he refuses to fight, we will force him southward into Mid Wales and subsequently into the waiting arms of William's standing force.'

He looked up again.

'Gentlemen, I will admit to initially dismissing this revolt as the actions of mere troublemakers leaning against their local lords but in the past few weeks it has become apparent that it has grown into a serious movement and unless we deal with it immediately, it could become a serious threat to our rule in Wales. I want you to address this with every resource at your disposal. Show these people that we have had enough of their pathetic attempts at self-rule and they will bend a knee to the English crown once and for all. During your campaign, don't withhold the sword arm for the sake of doubt for every Welshman is deemed to be part of this revolt unless they can prove otherwise. If you come across the enemy, strike with all the ferocity you can muster and spare no man the blade. Already they have heaped embarrassment untold upon my house by capturing these castles and I would have them pay the ultimate price for their audacity, do I make myself clear?'

'Aye, Majesty,' came the response.

'Gentlemen, therein lay the plans. I will not demean your intelligence by outlining the detail of each campaign for that is your job. Suffice to say, the path to victory lays in finding their leaders. Remove the head from the beast and the body will fall. Be gone, my lords, and let fortune guide your way.'

Every man acknowledged the King and bowed their heads slightly as he left the room, leaving them to study the map in their own time.

'Fermbaud,' said the King as he left, 'attend me.'

Nicholas Fermbaud followed Edward and walked alongside him as he received his instructions.

'You will pass word to my command,' said Longshanks, 'we ride out at dawn. Tell them they have this night to prepare and expect a hard ride, I want to be in Rhuddlan as soon as possible. When I have gone, you will ride to Chester to meet Orland and the men from the north. When they arrive, march them west with all haste and muster at Flint castle, there to await my further orders.'

'Aye, Majesty,' said Fermbaud. 'Is there anything else?'

'Yes,' said Longshanks, stopping and turning to face him. 'This forthcoming campaign will demand courage from every man in the field, whether pike man or knight. I expect you to step up to the mark and display a mettle deserving of your title. Whispers abound in the passages of the court belittling your last foray against the Welsh and many would have me remove you from this campaign and send you back to manage the treasuries. However, I see more in you than that, Fermbaud, and feel it is no fault of your own that I have allowed you to grow fat within the castle of Bristol. You were knighted for a reason and over the next few weeks, I expect to be reminded of that reason on a daily basis. Do I make myself clear?'

'You do, my lord.'

'Good, this is another chance to redeem yourself, Fermbaud, don't waste it.'

Without another word he strode down the passageway and into a side room, slamming the door behind him.

The next day saw over three thousand armed men muster on the fields outside the castle as Edward's column prepared for the march. The frosty morning air stung the lungs of the soldiers and the fields resounded with the sounds of the sergeants checking their men. Impatient horses, excited at the activity pawed at the ground, their breath forming small clouds of steam about their heads and servants ran in every direction, carrying out the whims of their masters. Soldiers took the opportunity to kiss goodbye to those loved ones who had followed the column thus far but now they were actually going into battle, they knew Edward would contemplate no followers about his army, whether family or otherwise. He needed the men to be focused on one thing and one thing only, the campaign. Other men sat on their packs, waiting in silence for the march to begin while others played dice with their comrades, laughing or cursing depending on their luck. In an adjacent field the supply wagons were going through the final checks, sacks of grain were rammed tightly into every available space and barrels of ale fastened securely against the sides of the carts. Butchers wagons were piled high with salted meat and barrels of dried fish, while sacks of hard biscuit and dried fruit filled other wagons, the staple diet of the main army should fresh supplies be difficult to come by.

Further carts carried tens of thousands of bolts for the crossbows and there were even several dismantled mangonels amongst the stores, available for relatively quick assembly should the need arise. Spare swords and knives were few for it was expected that should they engage the enemy and be victorious then the availability of side weapons would not be a problem, they would just take them from the dead. Similarly, every hundred archers had a young boy assigned to their unit tasked with collecting what arrows they could when any battle was over.

Every man carried a blanket and enough dried food for one week in his pack and wore whatever clothing they could afford. The lucky ones had gambesons, the quilted jackets that were fairly effective against glancing blows or an arrow at the end of its range, while the older heads even went as far as to have thin steel plate stitched to the protective jackets for although it made them heavier to carry, the extra protection they afforded may just save the wearer's life. By far the most important piece of clothing for each man was their cloak, a long garment of waxed leather, essential not only against the notoriously wet Welsh weather, but also as a waterproof shelter when they camped between towns. Some units had communal tents and as many men as possible would squash inside but those new to campaign only had their cloaks to fall back on.

Already, heavily armed patrols had been sent onward to those castles still in English hands to warn them the King was on campaign and they would be expected to offer him and his command whatever resources necessary to maintain the offensive, whether it be shelter, supplies or manpower.

—

Although the sight of so many men at arms was impressive, it was nothing compared to the full strength that waited to join them as they campaigned across the border. Another two thousand would join them in Wrexham and combined with the infantry from the north and Reginald De-Grey's garrison at Rhuddlan, Longshanks would be leading an English column almost ten thousand strong. His cousin Edmund would soon join up with Henry de-Lacey in the west making a second column of over three thousand while the Earls of Warwick and Gloucester added another ten thousand each. Combined with the supply wagons and the sailors of the fleet, it meant that

Edward commanded an army of over thirty-five thousand men, a force never heard of before in any of the Welsh uprisings across the years.

The constant shouting and endless noise generated by the waiting column fell silent as a horn echoed out across the fields and people turned to see the gates of Worcester castle swing slowly open. For a few moments, nothing happened but to a fanfare blasted from the castle walls, Edward rode out resplendent in his full ceremonial armour. Behind him came two standard bearers flying the flag of the King's house and behind them came fifty fully armoured knights, each resplendent in the colours of Edward.

Soldiers and civilians alike threw themselves back off the road as the riders galloped past, the horses' hooves throwing up the mud as the people cheered their king. Edward rode to the head of the column a full half a mile away and as he approached, the sergeants made the men stand either side in regular ranks, tribute to the fact their monarch was amongst them.

'Marshal,' he called, reining in his horse, 'are we ready to move?'

'We are, my lord,' replied the officer, 'and only await your command.'

'Then as soon as my knights have passed, set the men about the march. The day is young, marshal, and I want to see at least ten leagues behind us before we set up camp. At that speed we can be in Wrexham within three days.'

'Aye, my lord,' shouted the marshal and as the King galloped away, he turned to his command.

'*Men of England*!' he roared. 'Column of three, prepare to march!'

The men ran forward and arranged themselves into the common marching formation, adjusting their kit as they did so. Those who had heard the King giving his orders passed the word down the lines and soon the army was ready for the march.

As the last of the knights galloped past, the marshal roared out his order.

'By royal command, men at arms, advance.'

Like an enormous uncoiling snake, the army started to move along the road, the ground beneath them already a muddy bog from those in front. The fight back had begun, Edward the First of England was heading back into Wales and this time, he was going to stay.

Chapter Twelve

Brycheniog

Gerald of Essex rode into the town with ten mounted lancers and fifty infantry. The sound of their passing did not go unnoticed but though many eyes peered from between closed shutters, everyone knew that for a patrol to be out in the hours of darkness, there must be something wrong and when that was the case, it was essential to keep as low a profile as possible. As they reached the town square, Gerald dismounted and walked into the tavern, closely followed by a dozen of his men at arms.

Instantly the noise fell away as the people inside stopped talking and turned to see what the stranger wanted. Gerald looked around and slowly drew his knife, causing murmurs of consternation throughout the tavern.

'Can I help you, sir?' said a portly man, coming forward to greet the knight.

'Who are you?' asked Gerald.

'I am the innkeeper, sir, and I run a good house. No whores or bawds here, my lord, it is a good business and I pay my taxes on time.'

'I doubt that,' said Gerald with a sneer. 'Bring me ale and quick about it.'

'Of course, sir,' said the man and waved over at the servant near the barrel. 'Ale for our lord and make sure the tankard is clean.'

Gerald walked over to the nearest board, the trestle table common to such places, and looked down at the two men staring intensely at their leather jacks of ale.

'You,' said Gerald, placing the blade of his knife under the man's chin, 'look at me.'

The man looked up at the knight and though there was a knife against his throat, his eyes held barely concealed contempt.

'What is your name?' asked Gerald.

'Tom of Brecon, sir,' said the young man.

'And what is your trade?'

'Farm labourer, sir.'

'There is a fire in your eyes, Tom of Brecon, do you know who I am?'

'You are the Castellan, sir, lord of this manor and Constable of Brycheniog.'

'I am,' said Gerald, 'so tell me, you seem to have a goodly number of friends here, can I assume that you are a popular man?'

'I don't know about that, sir, I am just enjoying an ale after a hard day at the plough.'

The innkeeper appeared and handed Gerald a wooden tankard, filled with frothing beer. Gerald sniffed at it before taking a sip and swilling it around his mouth.

'I've tasted worse,' he said and took a deep drink before throwing the tankard into a corner.

'Let me put it another way,' said Gerald, returning his attention to the farm labourer, 'I assume a young man as popular as you will know most of the people in Brycheniog?'

'I know a fair share,' said Tom.

'I thought so,' said Gerald, 'in that case you won't mind telling me where I can find the house of the fletcher.'

Tom's eyes darted toward the others in the room but they had all found interest in different directions, none keen to get involved with the situation.

'I don't know of such a man,' said Tom.

Gerald leaned over and whispered.

'Wrong answer,' he said quietly and without warning, swung his knife downward to cut off the man's ear.

Tom screamed and tried to rise but Gerald grabbed the back of his head and smashed it down against the board, knocking over the containers of ale. All around the room men rose from their benches but fell silent as the soldiers drew their swords. Gerald's voice resounded off the tavern walls.

'Silence,' he roared and as the noise fell away, he leaned forward and spoke into his victim's other ear.

'Right,' said Gerald, 'let's start again but this time I want you to consider two things. Firstly, I am not known as a man of patience but I suspect you know that already. Secondly, I don't know if labourers can count but just in case you can't, let me inform you, there is only one ear currently attached to your head. Now, it would be a great shame to lose that one as well but in case there is any doubt, just be aware that I will ask this question one more time only. After that, my questioning will be pointless as you won't be able to hear me. Do you understand what I am saying?'

'Yes sir,' gasped Tom, his eyes watching the blood from his wound mingling with the spilled ale.

'Good, then let's start again. Where can I find the house of the fletcher?'

'Sir,' said Tom, 'I beg mercy for I truly do not know.'

Gerald grimaced in disappointment but as he moved the knife to sever the other ear, a voice called out across the room.

'Sir Gerald, hold your arm. The boy speaks truly for it is unlikely he knows of the house of which you speak.'

Gerald turned his head slowly and stared at the man on his feet.

'And who are you, may I ask?'

'My name is Father Michael and I am the priest of this village.'

'Ah, a holy man,' said Gerald. 'Why does that not fill me with confidence?'

'I speak the truth, my lord, I know this boy and his family. They farm one of your burgages not two leagues from here and rarely venture into the town.'

Gerald released his victim and walked toward the priest. Behind him two of the serving girls ran to help the young man, taking him into the only other room in the building.

'So, priest,' said Gerald, 'am I to understand that you know the whereabouts of this dwelling?'

'I do, my lord, but am concerned on their behalf for it is obvious your need to find the family upsets your temper.'

'A very astute observation,' said Gerald, 'however, that is no business of yours. Now, furnish me with directions and I will be on my way.'

'The directions are difficult to explain, my lord, for the streets are many and they hold no signage as to their names. It would be better if I took you there myself.'

'Agreed,' said Gerald and pointed toward the man's tankard. 'Finish your ale, priest, for I am a fair man and would not separate a holy man from his beer. Be quick and then join me outside.'

As the soldiers left, the tavern broke into activity, many angry about the treatment of the labourer.

'Who does he think he is?' hissed a voice. 'Surely he is not above the law. Tom is disfigured for life.'

'You know as well as I,' said the priest, 'Essex is the law around here and answers to no man except the King. He could have us all hung as brigands and not a brow would be raised in question.'

'Why did you agree to help him?'

'I had no other option. If I hadn't intervened then Tom would now be minus both ears. I have bought Fletcher some time but someone needs to warn him. Who here knows his house?'

'Most of us,' said a voice, 'but we will never outrun those horses.'

'I know a shortcut, sir,' said a voice and Father Michael turned to face the young boy who had spoken, 'and if I go by way of Dead-Sheep Stream, I can be there before you.'

'Good idea,' said the priest, 'go now and tell the fletcher to leave immediately. They have no time to pack anything, just get out and into the forest. I will delay them as much as possible.'

'Yes sir,' said the boy and ran out of the rear door.

The priest turned to the rest of the men in the tavern.

'The rest of you, wait until we have gone and then I suggest you return to your families and think about your safety. The constable seems in a foul mood and you can wager that when he finds the fletcher missing, he will unleash his anger against the first poor soul who crosses his path.'

'What about Tom?' asked the innkeeper.

'Take him to the church and summon the apothecary. The wound needs to be cleaned and seared before infection takes hold.'

After the priest had left and the sound of the horses' hooves on the cobbles had died away, the talk in the tavern turned to the ongoing oppression by the English and the up-swell of resistance in the north. Finally one man stood and banged his tankard on the table. The men fell silent and looked toward him in anticipation. Edwyn was a farmer who tilled the soil on behalf of Gerald's estate and though he was a man of few words, when he spoke, people listened. His huge frame seemed to dominate the room and the large leather jerkin trimmed with an enormous ruff of sheepskin added to his striking appearance.

'Enough,' he called, looking around the room, 'you speak like washerwomen with the latest gossip. All around me I hear boasts of what each of you want to do to the Castellan yet when the opportunity lay before you, not one man raised his voice in anger. Poor Tom suffered a grievous injury through no fault of his own and though we all knew it was unjust, what did we do about it? Nothing. Not a sword, not a knife, not a fist, not a word. We sat back and averted our eyes. Is this what we have become, sheep to the wolves that live behind their walls of stone? I remember sitting at my father's knee and hearing the stories about how the men from these parts fought alongside the Welsh kings from the days of Hywel Dda right up to our own Llewellyn ap Gruffydd, not ten years since. Brycheniog men have always been known across Wales and beyond as men of honour, brutal in battle, yet magnanimous in victory.' He looked around again. 'Where are those men he spoke of? Those heroes of Welsh descent who would rather die than bend a knee to a tyrant for I see none before me, despite their ale fuelled empty words.'

'You too were silent, Edwyn,' said the innkeeper.

'Aye, that I was,' said Edwyn, 'and the shame lies upon me like the heaviest cloak. But I am no longer going to turn the other way as that tyrant places unreasonable tallies upon my farm. Every day I work harder yet every day we eat less, taxed to starvation by men who gather wealth like we gather hay.'

'We have always served a lord,' said another, 'it is the way it has always been.'

'Granted, but at least in the days of Cadwallader there was a fairness about the system. Yes, there were taxes and in all honesty the family probably grew rich off our backs but at least they never pushed us to the point of starvation. Although there was poverty, every man could spare a crust for his neighbour and the lash was a sight unseen. Well, enough is enough and I for one will bear it no longer. Our brothers across Wales are making a stand and I say we join them, stand up to avarice and cruelty and once more make this town the honourable place it once was.'

'We cannot take on the entire English army, Edwyn.'

'Perhaps not, but do not giant oaks from small acorns grow? All we need to do is to look after our own corner and should every town do that, these flames of revolution can become a raging fire.'

'What do you intend to do?'

'I intend to pay my dues, Tylor, I intend to join the fight and stop cowering like a frightened knave.'

For a few seconds there was silence but eventually another man stood to speak.

'Your words are wounding, Edwyn, yet truthful. We are treated thus because we allow it. It is time for that to stop and if there is indeed a Welsh army sweeping across the country, then there is no better time than now. What do you want us to do?'

'I do not have detail about me,' said Edwyn, 'but propose meeting up away from the effects of ale and boastful talk to discuss what action we can take. There is a disused barn not two leagues hence, deep in the valley of Deer Fall. Let us all pledge to meet there at sunset on the morrow and agree our path.'

'You realise you talk treason,' said a voice, 'and that is punishable by hanging.'

'Treason or freedom, Selwyn?' asked Edwyn, 'which is your point of view?'

'I only say that which is on many minds, Edwyn, these things have to be faced.'

'Granted, but let us open them up to discussion when the rest of the townsmen are present.'

He looked around the room one last time.

'So be it. Tomorrow at dusk bring an open mind and any fellows who harbour similar feelings of unrest but let it also be known that any man, woman or child who brings this meeting to the attention of the Castellan or his garrison, then that family will be exiled forever from Brycheniog.'

'If anyone takes that path, Edwyn, then the harsh kiss of a knife on their necks will be the reward, not exile.'

'Aye,' shouted the men and Edwyn nodded in gratitude. For an age longer the men talked amongst themselves and Edwyn finally stood to leave.

'Until the morrow,' he said but as he donned his cloak, the door burst open and a young man came running in.

'Alarm,' he shouted, 'look to your buckets and carts, the Fletcher house is ablaze.'

—

By the time the men reached the fletcher's house it was obvious there was nothing they could do. The flames from the thatched roof lit up the night sky and the sound of cracking stone pierced the night, such was the intensity of the blaze.

Fire was one of the most feared disasters in the village and the call to help had already been heeded by many townsfolk but they now stood back in resignation, their buckets discarded as useless by their sides.

At the far end of the road, Gerald sat upon his horse alongside his soldiers, having enjoyed witnessing the fruitless attempts at extinguishing the fire. Edwyn approached the priest, breathing hard from the run.

'Father Michael,' he said, 'is there anything we can do?'

'No,' said the priest quietly, 'the building is beyond any intervention we can bring to bear. All we can do is watch the sparks do not set fire to those on either side.'

Edwyn looked at the groups of men already dousing the thatch of nearby houses.

'What of the family?' asked Edwyn. 'Are they still inside?'

'No, luckily they had already gone but Gerald still saw fit to leave his mark.' He looked down the road towards the English knight.

'He did this?' asked Edwyn.

'He did,' said the priest, 'but it's not the fact that he has fired a house that hurts so, it's the look on his face that says he knows he can get away with it.'

'Does he?' replied Edwyn. 'We'll soon see about that.'

—

Deep in the heart of Wales, Garyn, Tarian and Geraint rode hard through the night, finally seeking shelter amongst the rocks of a craggy hill. Tarian set about making a fire while Garyn and his brother sorted out the horses.

'This is still like a dream to me,' said Garyn as they worked, 'how can you now be alive when I thought you dead for so long?'

'It is a strange story, Garyn, and one long in the telling but suffice to say I survived the sea voyage and settled in the north to fulfil a vow that now comes to fruition, but you have to believe me, I only did so when I was told you had died as a brigand. Otherwise I would have scoured these lands from peak to vale in search of you.'

'I believe you,' said Garyn, 'and truth be told, I too oft heard rumours of my death and did not seek to correct those who spoke in error. To be a corpse was a good defence against those who sought the bounty upon my head.'

'So it is true, you are an outlaw?'

Garyn paused and considered his answer.

'If you mean the words exactly, then yes we live outside the law of the King but we are not brigands and have our own morals to which we adhere.'

'You talk of the Blaidd?'

'I do and am honoured to name them as comrades.'

'They are often cursed amongst the people, Garyn, I struggle to balance your argument that you are not a brigand.'

'It is a commonly held view, brother, and one gladly spread by the English, or those who feel the sharpness of our blades. The facts are we have never taken as much as a morsel from the hands of the poor and indeed, oft distribute any spare we have to those in dire need, especially any who have suffered the loss of a husband or brother to an English rope for resisting their tyranny. But raiding the English supply lines was not our only means of survival and oft we sold our swords to the highest bidder as mercenaries.'

'A role that could be viewed as dishonourable,' suggested Geraint.

'Perhaps so but don't forget, the title of mercenary was also a mantle once worn by our father and though I am my own man, I would be doing him an injustice if I thought he was anything less than honourable.'

'A point well made,' said Geraint. 'Come, we are almost done here, let's get ourselves to Tarian's fire.'

They finished seeing to the horses and returned to join Tarian who had a small pot on the flames, already filled with water to make a stew.

'It is no feast but will be hot and adequate,' said Tarian, adding dried meat to the stock.

'Tarian,' said Garyn walking over, 'we have ridden many leagues together this night and you fought on my behalf back in the castle, yet I know nothing of you and have not had a chance to express my gratitude.' He held out his hand and grabbed the man's wrist.

'If your brother's description of you is true,' replied Tarian, 'then I suspect you would have done a similar thing for me had the situation been different.'

'I hope you never have to suffer such an injustice,' said Garyn, 'but if so, and until such a day comes, I can only pledge my blade in your name should it be required.'

'Appreciated,' said Tarian sitting down upon a rock. 'So,' he said looking up at the two men, 'have you two been getting acquainted?'

'To an extent,' said Geraint, taking his own seat, 'but there is so much to tell, I fear we may need a scribe to record it all.'

'A scribe I can't provide,' said Tarian, 'but we do have a hot drink, a welcoming fire and a long night before us, so if that doesn't warrant the telling of tales, I don't know what does.'

Garyn joined them and looked across at his brother.

'Well?' he asked. 'Who's first?'

Chapter Thirteen

Howarden

Longshanks walked through the abandoned ruins of the castle; his rage silent within him as he witnessed for himself the devastation Madog's army had wrought. Accompanying him was the Constable of Howarden, the nearby town that had looked upon the castle as a refuge and focus of trade.

Most of the dead had been buried but evidence of the massacre still lay all around, a memory of the thriving community that had once graced the castle both in and outside of its walls. Clothing, weapons, cooking pots and even the occasional piece of burnt furniture lay scattered throughout the castle's ward, all having been ransacked from rooms throughout the buildings and seemingly discarded when they were judged as having little or no value.

Winter had finally arrived and though there was a thin layer of snow upon the ground, the clean white blanket didn't quite cover the destruction that the sacking of the castle had brought, and even now the occasional gust of wind was laced with the smell of ash from the torched wooden buildings. He looked up at a corpse hanging from one of the windows of the castle keep.

163

'Who is he?' asked Longshanks. 'One of the Welsh?'

'He was indeed Welsh, my lord,' replied the constable, 'but not one of the rebels. He was a local man found looting the dead, days after the battle. My decision was to make an example of him to avoid others following his lead.'

'I concur with your judgement,' said Longshanks. 'How many were killed?'

'The castle had a garrison of thirty, my lord, but the slaughter did not end there. Madog sent a detachment into the town seeking any of English birth. Those not quick enough to hide were despatched without mercy. Many were hung but as the rebels ran out of rope, they simply slaughtered their victims with blade or axe and though the men rallied against them, they were no match, for the blood lust was high amongst the enemy and they were like rabid dogs. Over a hundred were buried over the following few days and never has this town suffered such devastation.'

'Why did he take out his anger on the villagers?' asked Longshanks, kicking away a pile of snow to reveal the corpse of a dead dog.

'I know not,' said the constable, 'and though there is talk that it was not by his command, it is a weak justification, the people were slain by those under his banner. As far as I am concerned the blood is on his hands and no other, but my lord, that is only half of the problem. They emptied our granaries and meat stores to feed their armies. As well as burying those who fell by the blade, we will soon be burying their children from hunger unless we get succour from those who can help.'

'Have you sent word to Reginald De-Grey?'

'We have but though he sent a cart of bread, he houses a vast army himself and needs every mouthful for his own soldiers.'

'What about Wrexham?'

'We have sent messages, but winter is upon us and everyone is nervous about lowering their stocks, especially as there is war all about us.'

Longshanks stopped walking and looked around.

'I have seen enough,' he said. 'I will arrange a scribe to attend you before this day is out. Tell him what it is you need to survive the winter and we will send a message to Wrexham under my royal seal, to provide the supplies you need.'

'Thank you, my lord,' said the constable.

'One more thing,' said Longshanks, 'do you have word where this army now resides?'

'No, though I know they oft use Dolwyddelan as a base. An army would do well to take a closer look.'

'Noted,' said Longshanks and turned to leave the castle. Outside, a patrol of four knights awaited him and as soon as he emerged through the damaged gateway he climbed astride his horse. 'Tell the people of Howarden their loss is acknowledged,' he said, 'and rest assured, the deaths of their loved ones will be avenged.'

'Thank you, my lord,' said the constable as he watched the King ride away.

—

When Longshanks reached his encamped army he rode between the hundreds of tents before dismounting and walking into the farmhouse he had commandeered for the past few days. Around him were two and a half thousand men at arms and though at first glance the strength seemed modest for a king on campaign, everyone knew he had sent another fourteen thousand to Rhuddlan to set up a garrison from which to foray further into Wales.

'Summon my officers,' he said, discarding his riding cloak, 'and bring me watered wine, I thirst from the ride.'

The servants scurried away to do his bidding and soon, two knights entered the room and bowed slightly before joining him at the table.

'Sir Giles, Sir Warren,' said Longshanks, 'I have today witnessed the brutality of the man we pursue and I do not like what I have seen.'

'I had heard rumours,' said Sir Giles, 'but like all such stories, I thought they may be embellished in the telling.'

'Well these ones are not,' said Longshanks. 'The man's heart is obviously poisoned against all things English and he will not stop until there are none left this side of the border. He has to be stopped and stopped soon for every day we hesitate, more English blood stains his hands.'

'Do you know where he lies, my lord?' asked Sir Warren. 'For our spies have not yet reported back and we only await confirmation.'

'There is nothing more solid than that which we already know,' said Longshanks. 'He uses Dolwyddelan as a base but rampages from town to town across the north seeking out our brethren, pulling them from their beds and opening their throats for nothing more than the nature of their birth.'

'Then what would you have us do, my lord, for we cannot pursue shadows?'

'We will wait no more and take the fight to him. You will ride upon Dolwyddelan immediately and if it is in

Welsh hands, lay siege upon it. Use every resource you can and if your numbers are found wanting, draw upon the garrison at Rhuddlan. Rip it from their hands, Warren, and garrison it with a strong force of our own. Once done, send patrols to dominate the country thereabouts and deny them succour from any of similar allegiance.'

'Aye, my lord,' said Sir Warren.

'Sir Giles,' continued Longshanks, 'ride to Chester with all haste. There you will obtain a fleet of ships and task them with sailing to Flint castle. Crew them with your command and sail along the coast to Ynys Mon. Your task is to assault the bridge there and secure a bridge-head for our army. Once done, defend it at all costs until I arrive. I will bring the rest of my column along the coast and will ride into Ynys Mon as we did when Llewellyn was the enemy. The island is a main source of Madog's supplies and most of the burgages there are allied to his colours. In addition there is rumour that he receives supplies via the port in the north of the island, possibly from Ireland though this is not confirmed. Whatever the truth, if Ynys Mon is denied him then his movement is severely wounded.'

'Aye, my lord,' said Giles. 'When is this strategy to commence?'

'You are to ride immediately and I expect your assault to be made before the month is out.'

For the next hour they discussed the tactics in detail before the knights left and the King summoned his aid.

'Prepare the men,' he said, 'we have wasted too much time. Tomorrow morning, we seek this Madog out and test the mettle of his claim.'

Two weeks later, three men sat at the side of a road, waiting for confirmation they could continue. Before them a guard of twenty blocked their path for though Geraint's name was known to them, none knew him in person and they needed proof of his identity. Eventually a rider approached and gave orders to the soldiers at the roadblock.

'Let them through,' he shouted from his horse, 'the prince will see them.'

Geraint, Garyn and Tarian remounted their horses and rode past the sentries toward the wooded slopes of the hills before them.

'Follow me,' said the rider and before long, the signs of a large body of men started to appear in the fields alongside the path. The evening was dark and as they reached the outskirts of the forest, the pace slowed as the going became more treacherous underfoot. Often branches whipped across their faces in the darkness but eventually they dropped into a valley and could see many trees had been cut down and tents erected amongst the stumps and debris of the fallen wood.

'Wait here,' said the rider and crossed a bridge over a swollen stream. Tarian looked around the clearing and though the night was now dark, he could see hundreds of fires just beyond the forest edge, a sign of a strong army taking shelter from the winter weather. Across the stream, the guide emerged from a tent followed by another man and Geraint grinned to see it was his old friend, Madog.

'Hail, Geraint,' called the Prince, 'well met. Get yourselves over here so we can celebrate your home-coming in the manner of men.'

The three riders dismounted and handed their horses over to the grooms sent from the command tents.

'Geraint,' said Madog, grabbing the man's shoulders as they met on the bridge, 'I feared you had fallen in your quest. You too, Tarian.'

'We are both well, Madog,' said Geraint, 'though for a while I was unsure whether we would emerge with our lives. This is Garyn, the brother I thought dead but not only is he alive and well, it seems he also leads the Blaidd.'

'So I have heard,' said Madog and held out his arm. 'It is good to meet you at last, Garyn, the exploits of you and your men raise you to the ranks of fable in these parts. They say you have slain more Englishmen than Llewellyn ever did.'

Garyn grasped the Prince's wrist to seal the friendship.

'Tales are for the children, my lord, and I would doubt most of what you hear, but it is true that we have managed to severely disrupt the English supply lines these past few years.'

'A service I hope you will continue now you are freed,' said Madog.

'I have not ridden alongside my men for many weeks, my lord, but I am confident that they continue without me for the Blaidd are bigger than one man.'

'That's good to hear, Garyn, but I am being a poor host. Please, join me to eat and drink. We can discuss further at the warmth of the fire.'

—

Once the wet cloaks had been discarded and the offered food consumed with great relish, the three travellers sat around the central fire with the Prince and discussed what had happened over the past few weeks. The fire smoke snaked upward to disappear through the hole in the apex as Madog told them of the astounding successes of the Welsh campaign so far. Geraint and Tarian were particularly pleased as they realised the boy who they had feared may struggle with the burden of leadership had embraced all it entailed and become a successful leader of men.

'So what is next?' asked Geraint. 'Will the army retire to their villages until the winter is over?'

'No,' said Madog, 'we dare not. As we speak, Edward rides his columns into Wales. If we disband now, it is possible that he will gain the advantage and there is no guarantee my men at arms will return in the spring. If that happens then all this will have been in vain.'

'So where lies your path?'

'A few days ago, I was encamped before the walls of Harlech castle,' said Madog, 'but though we have had it under siege for several weeks, its ramparts remain unbreached, as do the walls at Criccieth. The weather has been against us but nevertheless, it's completely isolated and it is only a matter of time until they must open the gates.'

'Can you not assault it with trebuchets and fire?'

'I fear our casualties will be too great, Geraint, apart from the cavalry, my men are mainly farmers and serfs and though we have been successful thus far, against a fortress such as Harlech their efforts may not be enough. In this case, it will be starvation that breaks the castle walls, not fire or stone.'

'And Criccieth?'

'The same situation, though I fear it may be supplied from the sea. If that is so, then we will just keep a holding position to deny the enemy access or to allow the garrison to ride out seeking retribution against any villagers loyal to our cause.'

'You can't maintain that forever.'

'Perhaps not but if we can achieve independence in the meantime, then the walls may not have to fall, perhaps we can negotiate their handover in any talks.'

'Do you think we can win this war, Madog?' asked Tarian.

'I have long said that if we were to face the forces of Longshanks head on then we would come off second best, however, those are not our tactics. We will continue to harass him at every turn, disrupting the English occupation wherever we can, and disappear into the mountains before he has the chance to chase us down. If we can continue to do this, then eventually he knows he will have to come to the bargaining table to sue for peace.'

'Why would he do that?' asked Garyn.

'Because his greater focus is upon Gascony. Every day he stays in Wales is a day that the French reinforce their defences. I suspect it is only a matter of time before he must choose which is the bigger risk and he will turn his attention to Gascony. To do that, he has to have peace in Wales.'

'But what's to stop him suing for peace and then turning his army on us upon his return?'

'Oh, I have no doubt that will be his intention,' said Madog, 'but that could be months or even years from now but by then we will be organised and will have gathered the support of those Welsh barons yet to declare in our favour. Even if Edward is successful in Gascony, his treasuries will be empty and his men weary. I doubt he would have the support of his barons for yet another Welsh war.'

'So this is your strategy?'

'It is. To harass his every step and make any Englishman who lives this side of the border rue the day they were born. This way we will become a drain on his resources and his hand will be forced.'

'So why are you encamped here?'

'A transit camp only,' said Madog, 'my spies will report back tomorrow as to the position and strength of Edward's forces. Once I know that, we will make the next move.'

'So,' said Tarian, 'it seems that everything goes as well as we could have hoped?'

'It does, so tonight we can rest in safety and I would hear more about your adventure in the south. Tell me your story, Garyn, for I am intrigued by your tale.'

For the next hour or so, Garyn recounted how he had sought the Sword of Macsen and how he ultimately ended up in the dungeon of Brecon castle before being rescued by Tarian and Geraint. Finally he fell silent and Madog leaned forward in fascination.

'So,' said Madog, 'the sword of Macsen, it actually exists?'

'It does,' said Garyn, 'but lays in the hands of Gerald of Essex.'

'That is a shame,' said Madog, 'as although we seem to be making great strides without it, there is no doubt its influence as a unifying force could still have a positive impact upon our cause. Tell me, do you think it possible to locate and perhaps steal this sword from the castle?'

'No, my lord. I have no idea where it is kept and though we have managed to breach the walls of Brecon castle once, I suspect the defences will be strengthened with immediate effect. Essex is a brutal man but he is not stupid.'

'And what about the corpse of Macsen Wledig, does it still lay in Segontium?'

'As far as I am aware, it lies there still.'

Madog looked at Garyn for several moments before replying.

'I think we need to obtain this body,' he said eventually.

'But why?' asked Geraint.

'Because with or without the sword, the body of someone held in such high esteem by the people of Wales can be seen as a sacred object. If it was to fall into the hands of the English, they could use it against the people.'

'In what way?'

'Even possession of something so holy can be a powerful weapon,' said Madog, 'and those of a simple mind may see Edward's claim to the throne of Wales as justified by the possession of such a holy relic.'

'But Edward doesn't know about Macsen Wledig,' said Geraint.

'Gerald does,' said Garyn quietly.

'Yes, but not the location.'

'He knows exactly where the body lies for I told him myself. It was in return for the chance to see my son before I was to be put to death and I am ashamed to say my tongue was loosened by the promise.'

'There is no shame in such a thing,' said Geraint. 'A man's allegiance to his son is far greater than to any flag.'

'I would agree,' said Garyn, 'but my shame lies in the fact that the boy was no kin of mine and was fathered by another. I was tricked by Gerald and he now knows everything there is about Macsen including the location of his tomb.'

'We cannot allow him to get the corpse as well as the sword,' said Tarian. 'Together they would present too strong an omen to those who follow our banner. We have to retrieve the remains of Macsen and secrete them away until we have a chance to bury them with honour.'

'Agreed,' said Madog, 'and we have no time to waste.' He turned to face Garyn. 'My friend, I know you have only just arrived from a long ride but I must ask you to set forth on this quest in my name. Take fifty lancers and ride to Caernarfon with all haste and once there, remove Macsen from his tomb.'

'What would you have us do with the remains?' asked Garyn.

'That is not important at the moment, the main thing is to just keep them out of English hands.'

'I am settled with the request, my lord, but will not need the support of your lancers. Sometimes strength is also a weakness and though the north is in our hands, it is no secret that Edward has his own spies amongst the towns and upon the road. An armed force even fifty strong will attract attention and have no chance against an English column. It is better I ride alone for at least that way my passage may be seen as a simple traveller.'

'I will go with you,' said Geraint.

'No,' said Garyn, 'but I have a request to make of you. My comrades in the Blaidd lay encamped in a valley two days from here. So far, our influence has been minor in this conflict but I feel now is the time to show our hand. Ride there and pass them a message on my behalf, tell them to meet me at Caernarfon seven days hence and to prepare for conflict.'

'I will not lose you again, brother, my path lies with you.'

'I will seek the Blaidd on your behalf,' interrupted Tarian. 'I know the area of which you speak but will need the final directions. Geraint can ride with you, brother alongside brother, as it should be.'

Geraint turned to Garyn.

'Well?'

'So be it,' said Garyn. 'Tarian, do you know the rocky valley to the south of Black Cairn ridge?'

'I do.'

'Then just follow the river south through the valley and into the forest. Do not worry about finding the Blaidd, they will find you. Pass them my message, it is time to declare our stance.'

'Consider it done,' said Tarian.

'Good,' said Madog eventually, 'now that is agreed, let us drink and rest. Who knows when we will have the chance once more?'

As he poured ale from a jug, the flap of the tent opened and a guard ducked into the firelit gloom.

'My lord, Gerwyn ap Tomas has ridden in and demands audience.'

'Granted,' said Madog and turned to the rest of the men in the tent. 'Gerwyn is one of the men sent out to spy upon Edward's movements, he may have news.'

Moments later a man ducked into the tent and looked around. His face was gaunt and his cloak sodden from many hours riding through the rain.

'Gerwyn, you look exhausted,' said Madog, 'come closer to the fire. Geraint, get the man a stool.'

The scout discarded his heavy cloak and reached out to the flames, desperate for the warmth it promised. Garyn handed him a chunk of meat and a tankard of ale, watching in silence as the man rammed the food into his mouth as if he hadn't eaten for days. Eventually the messenger drank deeply before belching and wiping his bearded face with the back of his sleeve.

'Thank you, my lord,' he said. 'I have ridden for two nights without rest for I bear grave news.'

'Then share it, Gerwyn, for these men are our allies.'

'My lord, Edward pushes across the north with renewed vigour. As we speak, he sends patrols into the mountains, but two days ago I saw something that warranted my immediate return, a force many hundreds strong camped at the port at Flint castle.'

'I expected no less, Gerwyn,' said Madog. 'Flint is a stronghold for the English, it makes sense to have forces in reserve.'

'These are not reserves, my lord, for they lie a league to the east; these were men waiting on the shore. I asked questions of the locals and they have been told to provide supplies ready for a number of ships due to dock in a matter of days. Apparently, there is a fleet due to arrive from Wrexham within days and the men at Flint intend to board the ships and sail west.'

'How many ships?' asked Madog.

'I don't know exactly but there are over a thousand men waiting to embark and that doesn't include any that boarded in Wrexham.'

'To what end?' asked Garyn. 'For wherever lays their target, even a force of two thousand in the heart of enemy-held territory is a tempting target and Edward is too good a leader to risk his men needlessly.'

'I agree,' said Madog, 'and there must be a prize worth the risk.'

'Do we have any held castles along the coast?' asked Geraint.

'No, even Caernarfon lays empty, it has to be something else.'

'The bridge,' said Tarian quietly.

All eyes turned to face the old man.

'He did it before,' explained Tarian, 'when he defeated Llewellyn, the first thing he did was deny Ynys Mon to the Welsh army, therein cutting the Prince's supply lines by half. He must see the island has a similar role to play and repeats his tactics from twelve years ago.'

'That's it,' said Madog, 'it has to be. There is nothing else of value along that stretch of coast.'

'Is there a defending force on the bridge?' asked Geraint.

'There is,' said Madog, 'but few in number, against two thousand they will soon fall.' He turned to the guard at the tent flap. 'Summon the officers, I want the army on the march before dawn. If God is with us, we may just have enough time to avoid the same mistakes as before.'

The sergeant nodded and left the tent.

'Well, gentlemen,' said Madog, 'it seems that we all have our paths laid out and though we now have no chance to relax, I suggest one more drink to whatever lays before us.' He raised his tankard, 'To freedom,' he said.

'To freedom,' replied those in the tent and they drank their tankards dry.

Chapter Fourteen

The Menai Straits – January 1295

Madog peered down to the water's edge from his position between the trees. He had chosen the location of the ambush carefully for though the muddy shoreline would offer no solid ground for a cavalry charge, it also prevented any quick disembarking should the English decide to attack them head on.

'Are the men ready?' he asked.

'Aye my lord,' said Meirion, 'and our sentries say the ships are just around the headland.'

'Good,' said Madog, 'tell them to lay low until the last moment. We may only have the one chance.' He retreated into the trees and waited patiently for the enemy ships to come into view. Less than an hour later, the first vessel appeared; a large galley propelled by two rows of oarsmen on either side. Upon its decks, Madog could see row upon row of armed men, waiting for the chance to disembark and take the wooden bridge joining Ynys Mon to the mainland. Within minutes, another twelve troop barges appeared and though these didn't have the impressive sails or masts of the galley, their low profile and single rows of oars made them ideal as troop carriers and again Madog could see their decks massed with English soldiers. Slowly they entered the straits and Madog knew his plan would work, they were sailing straight into a trap.

He looked down at the archer crouching behind a mound near the bank. The archer stared back up at him in concentration, waiting for the signal that would surely come. Finally Madog raised his hand before dropping it in a sharp downward action. The archer dipped the head of his arrow into the fire pot at his feet and as soon as the tightly wrapped cloth was well alight, shot it high into the air, the black trailing smoke visible for leagues around.

—

'My lord,' shouted a soldier on the ship, 'look.'

Sir Giles looked into the air and watched the graceful arc of the arrow as it sailed over the top of the ship. For a few seconds its importance was lost on him but suddenly he snapped to his senses and spun around to face the shoreline.

'Shields,' he roared, realising the danger but even as the men reached for their shields, the first wave of arrows fell upon them like the heaviest rain.

Those soldiers who were too slow suffered grievous injuries and many died where they sat as flight after flight of arrows fell amongst them. Behind them, the troop ships were suffering the same assault and for a few minutes the deadly hail of steel-tipped arrows fell amongst them without response.

'Archers to arms,' screamed Giles. 'Captain, take us in to the shore.'

'My lord, that is not a good idea,' answered the experienced captain.

'Do as you are told, man,' shouted Sir Giles, 'or we will be picked off as easy as rats in a barrel.'

'Sire you do not understand,' shouted the captain from behind the protective shelter of the mast. 'The bank along there is deep mud and your men will be trapped within its embrace. Go that way and every man aboard these ships will be dead within minutes.'

'Can you turn us around?' asked Sir Giles.

'I can but it is a slow process which will take us even closer to the enemy position.'

'We have to do something,' shouted Giles, 'my men are dying as we speak.'

'What about the far shore?' asked the captain. 'We can ground the galleys there and be out of arrow range from the mainland. The ground is hard and you can still attack the bridge from the island side.'

'Do it,' said Giles and moments later the ship lurched to the right as the captain roared out his orders.

Back on the mainland Madog gave the order to cease firing and watched as the ships headed for the far shore.

'Ready mangonels,' he shouted and gangs of men carried a dozen small catapults from within the trees, placing them upon the bank. Though they were intended for use against the wooden walls that often topped the stone buttresses of many castles, they could easily reach the galleys now turning mid channel.

'Ready,' shouted Madog, 'release!'

Carefully selected rocks flew through the air toward the ships and though the entire volley missed, the operators quickly adjusted the elevations to better their aim. Within minutes, more rocks followed and Madog's men broke into wild cheering as two scored direct hits, one amongst the men of the ship, while the second smashed a hole in the side of a barge.

The men aboard the second vessel panicked and though the gaping hole lay just above the water line, the panic on the deck caused the boat to list and the seawater poured into the hold.

All around the boats the air filled with rocks and each captain urged their rowers to greater efforts to escape the bombardment. Within minutes most were out of range except for the one that had been damaged in the earlier barrage. By now it listed severely and it was obvious it was sinking. Many of the men aboard fought each other as they sought places of perceived safety, clinging on to the rails in panic and even the men ashore could hear the screams of those below decks as they struggled to escape through the tiny hatchway. Within moments the galley totally capsized and as it sank slowly below the water, the survivors jumped into the sea to try and swim to shore. Those adorned with chainmail disappeared immediately below the waves, never to surface again and even those without armour were dragged down by the weight of their sodden gambesons. Only a few reached the safety of the shoreline, the sailors savvy enough to discard their heavy clothing before abandoning the ship.

By now the mangonels lay idle and Madog's army watched in silence as hundreds of men drowned before their eyes but even though it was a terrible way to die, there was little remorse from the Welsh, for those who now sank beneath the waves had been intent on burning the homes of those who had administered the defeat.

Madog looked up and saw the rest of the barges unloading the men on the far bank, knowing the initial assault had been as successful as he could have hoped but the battle wasn't over yet. There were still almost a thousand infantry disembarking on the far shore and unless he acted swiftly, they could still prove a threat to Ynys Mon.

Once again, he gave a signal and another flaming arrow pierced the morning air. This time nobody in Madog's army moved except for turning their gaze to a small hill on the other side of the strait. For a few seconds nothing happened but as the sound of a horn echoed across the water, the far green hill seemed to turn black as hundreds of cavalry galloped over the crest and down toward the panicking English.

The result was slaughter, for though the English were well armed, the attackers did not give them time to form any defensive formations and the cavalry smashed into them, creating carnage with lance and sword.

Giles knew the day was already lost but there was no way he could withdraw for their backs were against the sea and to continue to fight against cavalry would end up in only one outcome. Behind him, the captains of the barges screamed their commands, the oarsmen pulling heavily to take the ships back into the relative safety of the strait and though many men were still on board, the ships pulled away and headed back the way they had come, hugging the shore of the island to stay out of range of Madog's archers.

'My lord,' shouted a voice amongst the English still fighting on the shore, 'we are undone, the enemy regroups for another assault.'

Sir Giles looked toward the Welsh cavalry a few hundred paces away, already forming up for another charge. Without archers, he knew they were helpless against the cavalry and there could only be one outcome. Since landing on the shore they had already lost hundreds of men and he knew he had to do something or what was left of his command would be wiped out.

'Sergeant, order our men to lay down their weapons,' he said, 'and hold their arms aloft, I will seek terms for our surrender. It is a sad day but we have been out-thought and I will not send more men to their deaths needlessly.'

'Aye sir,' said the sergeant and gave the command to the two hundred or so Englishmen who still lived.

Across the water, Madog could see there was a pause in the battle and correctly assumed the English had surrendered. It made complete sense as otherwise the remainder of their army would be wiped out to a man.

'The day is yours, my lord,' said Meirion beside him, 'your tactics were sound.'

'A deadly blow indeed,' said Madog, 'but it leaves me with more questions than answers.'

'In what way?'

'What did they think they were going to achieve?' asked Madog. 'Even if they had taken the bridge, surely they realised we would just take it straight back, their numbers were too small to defend it for any length of time.'

'Unless they were just an advance party,' said Meirion, 'and the main force follows behind.'

Madog spun around to face his comrade.

'Of course,' he said, 'that's it. Even as we speak there could be ten thousand Englishmen just leagues away. Sound the withdrawal, Meirion, get our men out of here.'

'What about you, my lord?'

'I'll ride across to Ynys Mon and extract our forces.'

'If we withdraw, then Edward can still take the bridge.'

'Burn it,' said Madog, 'I would rather lose the island than one more of my men.'

'That means we will lose the support of the farms.'

'As will he,' said Madog. 'Don't forget, Meirion, winter is upon us and the supply of food from the island is minimal. Unlike Llewellyn we have most of Wales behind us and we can draw on the many villages on the mainland to help support the cause. The effect of losing the bridge will be minimal and we can rebuild it in the spring. Take the army to the hills and we will rendezvous by the lake at Snowdon.'

'So be it,' said Meirion as Madog mounted his horse.

—

An hour later, the Prince and a patrol of thirty lancers rode up to his force on Ynys Mon having crossed the wooden bridge. The Welsh infantry stood in a giant circle facing inward toward the English captives now sat upon the floor minus their weapons. The commander of the infantry guard strode up to Madog and saluted the Prince.

'My lord, the action was successful. Many escaped but these were taken prisoner.'

'A task well done, Emrys,' said Madog. 'Did their commander survive?'

'Indeed he did, my lord,' came the reply. 'He is over there.'

Madog looked over to see a group of men kept isolated from the rest of the prisoners. Madog rode over and as he approached, a man clad in full chainmail stepped forward to meet him.

'Are you the master of these men?' asked Madog.

'I am, my name is Sir Giles Thornton of Bath. To whom am I speaking?'

'I am Madog ap Llewellyn,' came the reply, 'Prince of Wales.'

'Prince of Wales?' sneered Giles. 'I think my king will have a say in that.'

'What your king thinks is irrelevant in the matters of today,' said Madog. 'The fact is you are my prisoner and have been well defeated by a superior force.'

'You are to be commended for your tactics, that much is true,' said Giles, 'but it is a mere skirmish in a greater war, the outcome is irrelevant.'

'Think what you will, Englishman, but guard your words for I have yet to decide your fate. Insult me or my countrymen and this day could see your corpse swinging from the nearest tree.'

'It would not surprise me, Madog, for I hear tales of your brutality. It seems the rules of war are not something that you are familiar with.'

'War is war, Giles, and if some Englishmen have died needlessly, then that is unfortunate but put their deaths against the many thousands of innocent Welsh women and children who have died over the generations at the hands of your ancestors. I think the scales tip heavy in your favour.'

'So what do you intend to do Madog, kill us all in cold blood? For if that is the case, at least have the grace to do it quickly. These men are paid soldiers who follow orders given by the likes of me. You should give them the honour of a quick death, irrespective of my own fate.'

Madog looked across at the men under guard.

'No,' he said finally, 'they will not die at my hand, at least not today. They will be released unharmed to return to your fellows, as will you.'

Giles stared at Madog before answering.

'What trickery is this?' he asked. 'You are the victor and the spoils are yours. If you release us you must know we will probably meet again across a battlefield.'

'I do,' said Madog, 'but there has been enough killing this day. Get your men to discard their armour and any weapons still about their person. Once done, you are free to cross to the mainland and return to Rhuddlan. My men will escort you part way but after that you are on your own.'

'I am confused,' said Sir Giles. 'You must know that Edward will pay a ransom for the return of me and my officers.'

'I do,' said Madog, 'but this is not about money, it is about freedom. All I ask is that if you ever have any of my men in a similar situation, then consider clemency in return. Now, I have to go but be assured, you and your men will live to fight another day. Until that time, fare ye well, Sir Giles.'

Without waiting for an answer Madog turned and galloped away leaving the bemused English knight behind him. As he reached the bridge, he shouted over to the infantry commander.

'Sergeant, strip them of any armour or weapons and redistribute it amongst our own men. Escort them a few leagues back toward Rhuddlan and release them unharmed. Once done, meet me at Snowdon on the morrow, there is much yet to do and if my suspicions are correct, we may have an opportunity undreamed of in the next few days.'

'Aye, my lord,' said the sergeant, 'anything else?'

'There is. Before you go, fire the bridge. If we can't have Ynys Mon, then no one will.'

–

A few leagues away, Garyn and Geraint stood amongst the trees of a copse and looked over to the deserted village on the site of the old Roman fortress. The houses were now no more than burned-out shells, a result of the battle to take Caernarfon a few months earlier, but despite this there were still signs that people remained on the derelict site.

'It's pointless waiting anymore,' said Garyn, 'come on, let's get it done.'

'What about her?' asked Geraint pointing at an old woman searching amongst the rubble of a collapsed building.

'She seems harmless enough,' said Garyn and left the treeline to walk up the slope. Before long they reached the old fort and headed straight for the derelict church where Garyn had found the cross weeks earlier.

'Here it is,' he said, kneeling down alongside a clearly defined slab. He took out his knife and cleared the dirt before lifting the slab up to reveal the entrance of the tomb. 'You stay here,' said Garyn, 'and if the remains are still there, I'll pass them up.' He lowered himself down and sat against a wall as he used his flint to get a flame on a handful of fine dry wood shavings from his pouch. Within minutes the tinder had caught and he lit the wick of a candle from his pocket.

'Is he still there?' called Geraint from above.

'He is,' said Garyn, peering into the sarcophagus, 'pass down the bag.'

The empty turnip sack landed on the tomb floor, raising a cloud of ancient dust and Garyn lost no time placing the dishevelled pile of bones inside.

'Sorry, Macsen,' he said quietly as he worked, 'it's not the best of places for a Welsh legend but in the circumstances, it's the best I can do.'

Minutes later, Geraint pulled him out of the tomb and into the open air. For a few seconds they sat on the grass to catch their breath before replacing the slab and returning the way they had come but as they reached the clearing where they had left their horses, they stopped in surprise, staring at the six riders waiting for them.

'So we meet again, Welshman,' said Gerald of Essex from his horse. 'You really didn't think you could escape me, did you?'

'How did you find me?' asked Garyn.

'Oh it wasn't difficult,' said Gerald. 'It seemed obvious to me that once you had escaped you would head back to retrieve the body and as there is an enormous price on your head, I thought it time well spent to wait here until you showed up. An astute investment if I say so myself.'

'So what do you want, Essex?'

'The same as last time,' said Gerald. 'The abbot wants you back though this time he is more flexible on the terms.'

'In what way?'

'He will accept just your head.'

'What payment could he possibly offer you that makes you ride the length of a country in my pursuit?' asked Garyn. 'Surely there are better things for a knight of the King to be engaged in, especially as we are at war?'

'Indeed there are,' said Essex, 'and even though war can be profitable, the riches offered by the abbot are far more substantial and I have to say, easier obtained.'

Geraint looked around the armed men, calculating their chances of escape but realising there were few options.

'So,' continued Gerald, 'it seems you have come to the end of the road, Welshman, while I will have it all. Not only do I get the money from the priest but it would seem that fortune indeed smiles upon me for when I present the sword of Macsen to Longshanks, along with what I suspect you hold in that bag, I fully expect his royal recognition and my place in the King's court will be secured.'

'You are like an open sore that refuses to heal, Gerald,' snarled Garyn, 'and I swear that even though I may die this day, I will sell my life dearly so look to your sword, our business is not done.'

'Oh I don't intend getting my blade bloody, Welshman, the time for such nonsense is over.' He turned to the five soldiers alongside him. 'Kill him,' he said coldly, 'kill them both.'

Garyn discarded the sack and drew his sword as the men dismounted. Geraint drew his own blade and though they knew they were outnumbered, they realised that attack was the better form of defence and both ran forward into the fray.

Within an instant, one of the soldiers fell to Geraint's blade but though he was skilled in the way of the sword, the horsemen were also well drilled and within moments the brothers were forced back toward the trees. Another horseman retrieved a crossbow from the pack upon his horse and as the fight continued, he drew the lever back to arm the bow. Finally he added the bolt and lifting it up to his shoulder, took aim at Garyn's chest.

Seconds later an arrow sped through the air, smashing through the chainmail to pierce deep into the flesh beneath, shattering bone and piercing the heart of the victim.

For a moment Gerald stared in disbelief but as the crossbowman fell dead to the floor, his weapon still unfired, the knight screamed a warning.

'Archers,' he screamed, 'it's a trap.'

The four soldiers attacking Geraint and Garyn hesitated and looked around in confusion, the action costing one his life as a second arrow pierced the air to smash into his chest.

The two brothers watched with relief as the three remaining men ran back to mount their horses, though not before one received an arrow in his shoulder. For a second, Gerald of Essex hesitated but in spite of the risk, he spurred his mount forward and galloped straight toward Garyn. The Welshman took hold of his sword in two hands, ready to defend against the charging knight but at the last moment, Gerald swerved his horse and as he passed the brothers, leaned down and plucked the sack containing the remains of Macsen from the rock upon which it lay.

'Stop him,' shouted Garyn but it was too late and they watched in vain as his horse galloped down the slope.

'What just happened?' gasped Geraint. 'Who shot those arrows?'

'I don't know,' said Garyn, 'but I think we are about to find out.'

Both men turned toward the sound of someone coming through the undergrowth and Geraint stared in astonishment as he recognised the man carrying a longbow in his hands.

'Fletcher?' he exclaimed. 'What are you doing here?'

'Paying back a debt,' said Fletcher and turned to face Garyn. 'Garyn ap Thomas,' he said, 'for many years I stood by and let others sully your name in return for a quiet life for my family. I know now that I was wrong and should have had more honour. I cannot regain those years on your behalf but when I heard Gerald of Essex had set out to find you, I knew I had to do something. Luckily I managed to pick up his trail and have shadowed him these past few weeks.'

'Lucky for us you did,' said Geraint.

Garyn stepped forward and grabbed the Fletcher's wrist.

'There is no debt to repay, Fletcher,' he said, 'for my love for your daughter was real and I would carry the burden of shame a thousand lifetimes if it meant she lived one moment of happiness.'

'Then you will be pleased to know she has indeed had a happy life and her husband is a good man.'

'Then it has been worth it,' said Garyn, 'but this conversation must continue another day, I have to go.'

'To where?' asked Geraint.

'I have to go after Gerald of Essex,' said Garyn, 'he has both the relics and I cannot allow that to happen. You take Fletcher back to Madog and tell him I have failed in my task but will do everything in my power to reclaim that which belongs to Wales.'

'No Garyn,' said Geraint, 'like I said, henceforth my place is at your side and I will ride with you.'

Both men turned to Fletcher.

'These are momentous days around us,' said Fletcher, 'and for too long my bones have grown lazy with old age. My house has been burned to the ground, my family hides in exile, and all around us Welshmen die in a common cause. This is a chance to right a lot of wrongs and though I will be no good in a fight of swords, my aim is still sharp with a longbow so if you will have me, I will also ride alongside you.'

'That's good enough for me,' said Garyn, 'get your horse, we have no time to lose.'

Chapter Fifteen

The Western Road

Walter Mallory walked alongside the cart being drawn by two oxen and driven by his friend, Huw de Griffin. They had been on the road for several days, following a road parallel to the northern coast albeit several leagues inland. The going was slow, as the column of similar carts disappearing into the distance had churned the road into an endless sea of mud and was often stationary as beasts were cajoled or beaten into the extra effort necessary to pull them free of the cloying filth.

Behind them the supply column stretched a similar distance and frustrations were high at the continued delays on the road.

'I tell you,' said Huw, 'at this rate it will be spring before we make camp.'

'I've said it before,' said Walter, 'we pile these carts with too much weight. With less load we would not lay so heavy upon the road and we would make better time.'

'Ours is not to question,' said Huw. 'Those who make the laws think they know better than us, and who am I to tell them otherwise. I have enough lash marks on my back for one life, thank you very much. All I want to do is get this over with and get back to my village.'

'The way this campaign goes, that could be years from now,' moaned Walter. 'We've followed Longshanks from Chester and still he hasn't bloodied his sword.'

'They say this Madog is like a spirit,' said Huw, 'and no man can catch sight of him.'

'Well, he may be a spirit,' said Walter, 'but he is a spirit with bite. They say he has already captured over a hundred castles throughout Wales and sets his sights on London.'

'Nah, he isn't interested in England, just wants his home back, that's all and who can blame him?'

'Careful, Huw, that's treason talk, if one of the soldiers hears you, you'd be strung up before nightfall. Best keep our mouths shut and just keep plodding on. We have to stop soon and when we do, I for one intend to find a dry space amongst the barrels for some sleep.'

'Me too,' said Huw.

The two men fell silent for a while until the column once more ground to a halt. Huw stood up on the cart and peered over those in front to see what caused the stoppage but the light was failing and all he could see were soldiers arguing with the cart masters. Finally a horseman came riding back down the column with news.

'Listen to me,' he shouted, 'a cart has lost its wheel on the road before us. Its position makes it difficult to repair before dark so we will go firm here tonight. See to your animals and secure your carts, we will move out at dawn.'

'What about the supplies?' asked Walter. 'Doesn't Edward need them for his own men?'

'They will manage for one night,' said the rider, 'for they each carry field rations, besides, even if we could move, we couldn't catch them up. I hear they have made good ground and are almost three leagues ahead.' The rider rode on to pass on the message and Huw guided the oxen team off the road to what little shelter the nearby trees offered.

'You get them some water,' said Walter, 'I'll see about getting a fire started.'

Huw looked up at the sky.

'Better raise a shelter as well,' he said, 'that sky looks full of rain.'

'Hey,' said Walter looking around him furtively, 'do you think we could sneak a piece of dried fish from one of those barrels? I've noticed the lid is loose.'

'If we are caught, we'd be put to the lash,' said Huw.

'I know, but I'm fed up with the water they call soup. One piece of fish to add taste won't be missed, besides, most of the guards are up at the broken cart. Nobody will be the wiser.'

'Alright but be quick and if you're caught, you're on your own.'

Five minutes later Walter returned and opened his jerkin, revealing the two pieces of salted fish beneath.

'What do you think you're doing?' hissed Huw. 'Hide them over there before you are seen. Once we get the soup bubbling, we'll drop them in.'

'Why can't we roast them?' asked Walter.

'Because the smell will bring the guards,' said Huw. 'Now come on, it's almost dark.'

'Soup time,' called a soldier, walking along the path with a sack of root vegetables. As he passed each wagon, he handed over two large onions and a small loaf of bread.

'No meat again?' whined Huw.

'Meat is for the fighting men,' came the reply, 'just be grateful for what you've got.'

'Wait till he goes back the way he came,' said Huw, 'and then drop the fish in the pot. I'll get these onions chopped.'

An hour later the entire coast was in darkness except for the hundreds of small fires along the length of the supply column. Men talked quietly amongst themselves, most bemoaning the hardship of the campaign and the awful weather but while most of the civilians could see no further than their own discomfort, the more experienced guards looked nervously toward the hills, painfully aware that being so far behind the main column meant they were dangerously exposed to attack.

The night drew close to midnight and though most men were fast asleep, Huw and Walter sat in their small tent stirring the thick broth of onions and fish. They had added some of the bread and waited patiently as the liquid thickened nicely.

'Almost ready,' said Huw, sipping some off a spoon, 'it's a meal fit for Longshanks himself, that is.'

'It'll do for me,' said Walter, handing over his wooden bowl, 'get some in there for I can wait no longer.'

Huw dipped the ladle into the pot but before he could pour any into Walter's bowl, he looked up in alarm as the flap was throw open and an unknown man stepped into the tent. His face was blackened beneath a hooded cloak and he grinned menacingly at the two men.

'Who are you?' started Huw but before he could finish, the man thrust a lance through Huw's chest, bursting through his back in a mess of flesh and bone.

Walter turned in panic and started to call out before a mace caved in his skull, splattering his brains over the inside of the tent. As the fire went out, doused by the long-awaited fish soup, the forests along the path echoed with the sounds of screaming men as two thousand Welsh men at arms descended from the forest to unleash their fury on the undefended supply column.

–

Without substantial numbers of soldiers to defend the column, the result was slaughter. Many were killed as they slept and those who managed to escape the initial assault were chased down in the darkness and put to the sword. People begged for mercy but the blood lust was high and the massacre went unabated until everyone travelling with the carts was either dead or had escaped into the night.

Within half an hour, the only sign of life was the Welsh army swarming amongst the wagons, taking everything they could carry back up into the hills. Over and over again they did the trip until finally, as dawn broke, anything left was torched or damaged beyond repair. Oxen were slaughtered as well as any horses not deemed fit enough to use as mounts and by the time the sun had cleared the horizon, the west road was a scene of desolation, filled with smoke and the smell of death. Up on a nearby ridge, Madog looked down with quiet satisfaction. He had taken the King's supply column and he knew that without it, Longshanks was vulnerable. An unexpected opportunity had presented itself and the Prince knew he held the upper hand. Edward Longshanks, King of England was at his mercy.

Chapter Sixteen

The Northern Coast

'Where has he gone?' shouted Garyn, reining in his horse and staring down into the lowlands. All three men scanned the valley, looking for the fleeing knight.

'I don't know,' said Geraint, 'but he heads eastward. I think he knows he can't run all the way back to Brycheniog so I suspect he'll seek refuge at the nearest English stronghold. Conwy lies ten leagues in that direction but even he won't be able to continue this pace through the night. Come on, I know a shortcut through the mountains and if we ride the night through, we may just cut him off.' He turned his horse and headed toward the nearby hills.

The following morning they crouched amongst some rocks near the road and looked westward. Fletcher handed around some dried beef and they each gnawed on it gratefully, glad to get something after their slow but difficult ride through the mountains. The morning was half gone when suddenly Geraint's arm shot out and shook Garyn by the shoulder, waking him up from his exhausted sleep.

'Someone's coming,' he hissed and Garyn climbed up beside his brother to stare up the road.

'That's Gerald of Essex,' he said eventually, 'though he has two comrades only. The wounded man must have died in the night.' He turned to Fletcher. 'How many arrows do you have left?'

'Four,' he replied, 'but they will need to be a lot closer to guarantee success.'

'Don't worry,' said Garyn, 'I don't intend to slay them from the shadows, we are not brigands but I do intend to try and reason with him. If he does not agree I suspect it will come to blows.' He turned to Geraint. 'Brother, if he demands close combat, you are to let the fight take its course, even unto my death. This is personal and though the remains of Macsen are a prize, the grudge goes far deeper.'

'I will not let him kill you, Garyn.'

'If that is my fate then I will gladly accept it. I have caused too much pain and this is my chance to put it right or pay the price, either way is acceptable to me.'

'But Garyn…'

'Geraint, you must trust me on this. If he betters me in fair combat and you intervene, I will never forgive myself or indeed you. The path has been long but one way or another, at least one destiny will end today. Will you promise that you will allow this to be the way I say?'

Geraint paused before nodding.

'You have my word,' he said, 'but I swear if there is any sign of treachery from him or his men then my promise is cancelled and I will add my arm to yours.'

'Agreed,' said Garyn. 'Fletcher, you stay here amongst the rocks and watch the riders like a hawk. They may chance their arm irrespective of Gerald's orders. If they do, drop them as you would a deer.'

'It will give me great pleasure,' said Fletcher.

'Right,' said Garyn, 'let's get this done.' He and Geraint mounted their horses and rode out onto the road before stopping a hundred paces before the approaching Gerald of Essex.

—

Gerald slowed the pace of his horse and eventually stopped, staring at the two men before him.

'This is getting annoying, Welshman,' he growled, 'and my patience is about to run out. Cede the path, or suffer my anger!'

'I will not give you the path, Essex, but I do have something to offer you instead.'

'What could you possibly have that holds any interest to me?'

'What about my head?'

Gerald sat upright and stared at Garyn in confusion.

'I don't understand,' he said, 'what are you saying?'

'I am offering you the chance to claim your prize,' said Garyn, 'to meet me man against man on the field of conflict. Isn't that what you knights train for, the opportunity to battle an equal without quarter?'

'The chivalric code is not for the likes of you, Welshman, so don't deem to understand the ways of your betters. First let me say this, we are not equals nor ever will be. I am a landed knight of King Edward while you are the serf son of a blacksmith. To grant your request would be to justify your claim and I see no reason to do so, especially as you lay outnumbered.'

'You forget about my archer in the rocks,' said Garyn.

'Ah, a typical Welsh trick,' sneered Gerald. 'Fight from the shadows where there is little chance of injury.'

'On the contrary,' said Garyn, 'he has been instructed to hold back unless there is trickery on your part, as has my brother.'

'Your brother,' said Gerald in surprise, 'so I have both sons of Thomas Ruthin before me. I suspect the abbot may dig up the graves with his own hands were I to return both your heads.'

'Dig up graves?' repeated Garyn. 'Your words have no meaning.'

'Perhaps not to you,' said Gerald. He paused, still staring at Garyn. 'So tell me,' he said eventually, 'why should I lower my standards and fight you as an equal, what is in it for you?'

'If you win,' said Garyn, 'you will be allowed to take my head but my brother will take my body to be buried amongst the trees.'

'And if by some twist of fate you are the victor?'

'Then you will return the body of Macsen to me, as well as the sword.'

'What makes you think I have the sword with me?'

'Because you stated that it is intended for the hands of Longshanks and I don't believe you would have ridden the length of Wales without it.'

'Very astute of you,' said Gerald, 'and quite correct, it lays in my saddle pack but you will never witness the new form it takes, Welshman, because I accept your challenge and will take great pleasure in removing your head.' He slid from his saddle and removed his cloak before withdrawing his double-handed sword from the scabbard attached to his saddle.

Garyn did the same and though he held a similar sized sword, his armour was no more than chainmail compared to the plate that adorned his opponent. Both men walked toward each other and stopped ten paces apart.

'I take it you require no terms for quarter?' said Gerald.

'None,' said Garyn, 'we fight to the death by whatever means necessary.'

'So be it, Welshman, look to your weapons and be on your guard for today you join your family in hell.'

Without further warning, Gerald swung his sword toward Garyn, catching his opponent by surprise and Garyn had to throw himself backward to avoid an early wound. Gerald followed up the impetus with swift and skilful swings, each administered so fast that Garyn had no time to counter with blows of his own. The assault was furious and testament to the skill and fitness of the English knight but despite his ferocity, the continued exertion and weight of the armour took its toll and he soon paused to gather his breath.

'I thought you were here to fight, peasant,' gasped Gerald, 'or is this the way of all Welshmen, to run and hide when faced with an uncertain outcome?'

'There is more than one way to fight, Essex,' said Garyn, 'and sometimes discretion has its place.'

'Some would call that cowardice.'

'Only the stupid,' snarled Garyn and launched a coun-terattack toward the knight. This time the impetus was with the Welshman, and though the few blows to land were easily deflected by the heavy plate armour, within moments they both stood apart once more, drawing deep breaths of cold morning air. Over and over again, each man took the initiative, both struggling to find an opening in his opponent's defence.

Geraint watched with concern as the fight ebbed back and fore and though Garyn landed fewer blows, he could see the English knight grew increasingly weary, weighed down by his armour and fatigued by the constant manoeuvring of the lightly adorned Welshman.

'You tire, sir knight,' shouted Garyn between deep breaths, 'and your armour becomes a burden. I suggest such finery is more suited to the tournament fields of London rather than the tilled fields of common men. Cast it off and fight as equals.'

'Like I said before,' gasped Gerald, 'you are not my equal.' He stepped forward again with surprising speed and though Garyn had anticipated the move, he tripped over a rock and fell backward to the floor. The knight also fell, getting entangled in Garyn's flailing legs and as they grappled in the mud, the momentum took them over the bank to roll down the slope to the marshland below.

Geraint ran to the edge and stared down as did the two English soldiers but as the struggle continued, he failed to notice the two Englishmen talking quietly between themselves, planning an intervention on behalf of their tired master.

Down in the marsh, both men staggered to their feet, and stood knee deep in dirty water. Both blades had been lost and the knight retrieved a spiked mace from his belt. Garyn reached for his knife but was dismayed to find he had lost it in the fall. He turned to seek refuge and though there was no way out, there was a single boulder protruding from the bank no more than shoulder high.

Gerald staggered through the water, determined to end the fight once and for all. His armour was now covered in mud and tangles of weed hung from his closed helmet, obscuring his vision. He looked around quickly, the sound of his own heavy breathing echoing around the inside of his helm and failing to see his quarry, lifted his visor to get a better view.

For a few seconds he could see no one but looked up in alarm as Garyn jumped off the rock to send the knight sprawling backward. The impact knocked the breath from both men and they landed in a heap amongst the mud and water. Gerald tried to get to his feet but the cloying mud held him fast, clinging onto the heavy steel plate.

Exhausted, Garyn dragged himself on top of the knight's body and for several moments, gasped for breath as he stared down into the man's eyes through the open visor.

'So it ends, Essex,' he panted, 'your time in our country is done.'

'Wait,' gasped the knight, an edge of panic in his voice, 'we can make a bargain. You let me go and I will make you the richest Welshman in the country. I have access to gold and jewels beyond compare.'

Garyn shook his head in disbelief.

'You really have no idea do you,' he said, 'even now after all this you think you can buy our allegiance with petty baubles. Well, let this be your last thought in this life Gerald, all the gold in the world is but poison compared to the sweetness of liberty.'

Before Gerald could answer, Garyn's hand shot up beneath his opponent's helm and forced his head back into the mud.

For almost a minute the knight thrashed in panic, the mud and water splashing around the two men and it took all of Garyn's remaining strength to keep him down but finally the struggle died away and the body lay silent beneath Garyn's hands.

Gerald of Essex was dead, choked by the very mud of the country he once stalked with brutal arrogance.

—

Up above, Geraint sighed with relief but as he was about to descend to help his brother climb up the bank, a shout echoed from the rocks and he turned to see one of the English descend upon him with drawn sword. Instantly he knew it was too late, there was no way he could defend himself but as he raised his chainmailed arm in a futile gesture of defence, an arrow flew through the air and thudded into the attacker's chest. Despite the wound the English soldier staggered the last two paces and landed the blow but all strength had gone and the blade glanced harmlessly off Geraint's arm. The man fell dying to the floor and Geraint turned to face the threat of the second soldier but the man remained where he was, by the horses, his attention totally focused on Garyn below.

Even as Geraint called out a warning, the sickening thud of the crossbow bolt being released echoed down the road and the lethal arrow embedded itself deep into Garyn's back.

'No!' screamed Geraint as Garyn fell forward into the mud, and as Fletcher's second arrow flew through the air to strike down the bowman, Geraint bounded down the slope to reach his wounded brother below.

'Garyn,' he gasped, lifting him from the water and laying his brother's head upon his own lap, 'by the love of God, this is not just.'

'What was it?' gasped Garyn. 'An arrow?'

Geraint nodded and lifted his brother higher to see the wound. The main force of the bolt had been absorbed by the chainmail but it still had enough force to pierce deep into the flesh beneath.

'How bad is it?' gasped Garyn.

'It's missed your lungs,' said Geraint, 'but I don't know how deep it lies. We have to get you out of here, brother, but I will not lie to you, this is going to hurt like the fires of hell.'

'Just do it, Geraint,' said Garyn with another gasp of pain, 'I am done here.'

Geraint looked at the face of the dead knight peering coldly upward beneath the rapidly clearing water.

'Yes,' he said eventually, 'I think you are.'

An hour later, Geraint and Fletcher carried the semi-conscious body of Garyn between them and entered the low doorway of a nearby church. The priest came forward to see what was happening and quickly ushered them through into the back room when he saw the extent of Garyn's injuries.

'Father, we need refuge for a few days,' said Geraint. 'I need to see to my brother's wound but I know this place is alive with the English. I have to know; do you owe allegiance to Madog or Longshanks?'

'My allegiance is to God only,' said the priest, 'and all men are equal in his eyes. You will be safe here.'

'Good,' said Geraint, 'we need fire and hot water. Is there a village nearby where I can find an apothecary?'

The priest looked at Garyn's fevered face.

'There is but it is too far and his arrival will be too late. I studied under a monk with similar skills many years ago and though I cannot promise anything, if you require, I will try to ease his plight.'

'That would be a boon indeed,' said Geraint. 'Tell us what to do.'

The priest swept the few eating implements from the table.

'Strip his clothes,' said the priest, 'and lay him on here.'

'Garyn,' said Geraint into his brother's ear, 'I have to break the arrow.' He looked around and was handed a candle by the priest. 'Here, bite on this.' He placed the wax candle between his brother's teeth and took a deep breath.

'Ready?' he asked and without further warning, snapped the crossbow bolt tight to the chainmail shirt.

Despite the candle, Garyn screamed in pain before passing out and collapsing onto the table.

'Quick,' said Geraint, 'help me with the rest before he wakes.' Removing the chainmail was difficult for some links were pressed into the flesh and Garyn groaned in agony several times before he lay on his side upon the table, stripped to his waist.

The priest picked up the broken shaft of the arrow and placed it against Garyn's chest, calculating how deep the wound must be.

'How long were these arrows?' he asked.

Geraint gave him his best estimate.

'And are they usually barbed?'

'No, but the head may be ridged and is definitely wider than the shaft.'

'Then there is danger in pulling it out the way it went in,' said the priest, 'for it will drag the flesh within and tear at the already damaged muscle. I think we have to drive it through. It lays nearer the front wall and I believe its route misses the ribs. Any further damage will be to the muscle only.'

'Are you sure?'

'Of course not, but it is the best I can do.'

Geraint looked at Fletcher.

'The priest is right,' said the fletcher, 'I have seen such injuries before and often withdrawing the bodkin causes more damage than the initial wound.'

'So be it,' said Geraint and turned to the priest. 'Do it.'

Five minutes later they were ready. Fletcher provided a narrow shaft from one of his own arrows and dipped it in the pan of water now boiling on the fire. The priest dropped a thin strip of clean linen into the pot and they all waited a few moments while the hot water cleaned the implements within. Finally the priest retrieved the cloth and tied it to the short end of the crossbow bolt still sticking out of Garyn's back.

'Quickly,' said the priest, 'while the cloth is yet hot for it will clean the wound.'

Fletcher held his own arrow shaft against the end of the bolt and with a final look to Geraint, nodded he was ready.

'Forgive me brother,' said Geraint and using the hilt of his sword as a hammer, drove the shaft deeper into Garyn's back.

The unconscious man screamed in pain as the arrow-head burst out of his shoulder and as Geraint held him tightly, the priest grabbed the arrow and pulled it completely through Garyn's body, along with the long strip of hot, wet fabric.

The priest checked the shaft of the crossbow bolt for any missing pieces and probed the wound with his fingers.

'As far as I can see there is no major bleeding apart from that already caused by the first impact,' he said. 'Of course, there may be a fragment of chainmail in the wound but I don't think so. Anyway, there is nothing I can do about that. The wound is as clean as I can make it, now we have to sew him up and pray to God.'

'Is there anything else you can do, Father?'

'I have some poultices to keep away infections but apart from rest, that's all we can do. He is in God's hands now.'

Chapter Seventeen

South of Caernarfon

'What do you mean the supply line has gone?' asked Longshanks. 'That's impossible.'

'My lord, the rebels fell upon it during the night and slaughtered every living soul. All the supplies have been stolen or burned and there remains nothing that may be of use.'

'How can he have known where we were?' asked Longshanks. 'I accept that our movements may attract the interests of spies but to have an army so close capable of destroying a well-defended supply column suggests he knew our plans.'

'Whatever the reason, my lord, it seems they must have watched as your main army passed and waited until they knew their target was beyond the relief of our men. The devastation is total and there is not so much as a loaf of bread left that can be used.'

'This is a serious setback,' said Longshanks walking back and fore, wringing his hands in concern. 'We are only a day away from Caernarfon but if the castle still lays in the hands of Madog, then any battle will see us fight on empty stomachs with little chance of resupply. Though our army is stronger I fear any sustained fight would result in a victory for the enemy.'

He looked over at the messenger.

'Instruct the sergeants to prepare the men for the march. We will retrace our steps immediately and return to Rhuddlan. There we will assemble a new supply column and this time, support them with an army of guards. We will return in a few weeks but in the meantime, we will seek shelter and supplies from Reginald De-Grey.'

'Aye, my lord,' said the messenger and ducked out of the tent.

Two days later, Edward's army crawled eastward, their morale shattered. The going had been hard and the weather a constant struggle. Some fell by the wayside and many suffered from dysentery or similar campaign diseases that beset all such armies on the march. Apart from the discomfort and hunger, the English were constantly on edge from the intermittent attacks from small groups of Welshmen who would appear from nowhere, unleash a hail of arrows amongst the column and then disappear as quickly as they had come. The two nights since they had turned back had been sleepless and fraught with danger as the Welsh took advantage of the darkness to probe the English defences and by the time they approached Conwy, the column was riddled with disease, frustration and exhaustion.

Despite the dire state of the enemy, their numbers were strong and Madog, watching from the trees on the mountains above, still held back from committing any full-scale attack.

'Their cavalry outnumber ours four to one,' whispered Madog to Meirion, 'and their infantry is twice ours. All we can do is keep picking away at their lines but be assured, before they lay sight on Rhuddlan castle, we will take the opportunity. Another day or so and I feel they will be ripe for the taking. Send message to our reserves, Meirion, muster in the eastern hills, our destiny may well be decided in the next few days.'

Both men crawled back from the brow and returned to their horses.

Down below, Peter Grant, one of Edward's officers rode up to meet the column. He had been forward on a scouting mission and returned to brief the King.

Edward held up his hand to halt the column as Peter reined in his horse.

'My lord, I have grave news,' he said. 'The river ahead is swollen and the bridge has washed away. To travel inland would add two days on our journey to reach a suitable passing place and even then, we don't know if the rebels have burned them. My best estimate is that the nearest guaranteed crossing place lies three days south and then the return leg is through rough territory without any clear paths. It also lays in the hands of Cynan.'

Longshanks looked up at the cloud-filled sky, the constant rain running down his face and into his sodden clothing.

'We can't last another three days,' said Edward, 'let alone battle a fresh Welsh army, the men are on their last legs. We need shelter now.'

'My lord, if I can suggest something, there is nothing we can do regarding the river or the weather but Conwy still lies in our hands and is only two leagues in that direction. Your castle there is a formidable fortress and though we may be cornered on the headland until the weather eases, at least we will have English walls about us.'

Edward looked at the men around him, all freezing, hungry and exhausted. Even Peter's face was gaunt from the strain and he knew they couldn't go on much further.

'Your suggestion is well made, Peter,' said the King, 'and a welcome resolution. Instruct the van to change course and head to Conwy. In the meantime, gather what provisions we have left and furnish it to the ten strongest riders we have. They will be tasked with riding to Flint via the long route, even though the risks are great, but should they get through, they will instruct Reginald De-Grey to send relief with all urgency on my behalf.'

'Aye my lord,' said Peter and turned to gallop back into the face of the storm.

—

Two leagues away, another man rode through the rain with news for his commander.

'My lord,' shouted the Welsh scout, reining in his horse before Madog, 'the English column has turned north.'

'Are you sure?' asked Madog.

'As certain as I can be,' said the rider. 'Already the lead elements near the town's walls and the rest follow like half-drowned dogs. We reckon he seeks the shelter of the castle for the river is too high to cross.'

Madog turned to Meirion.

'Where is the bulk of his army?' he asked.

'Most are at Flint though many still encamp at Rhuddlan.'

'That means he is isolated,' said Madog, the excitement evident in his voice. 'There is no way he can ford the river until he reaches Llanrwst and that is at least two days away. If we can dominate the open ground he will be cut off from his main army until the weather breaks and that could be weeks.'

'This is it,' said Meirion, 'the opportunity you craved. Unleash your army against Conwy and lay siege to the castle. If we can take its walls as we have done so many others, Longshanks himself will be beneath your blade.'

'Conwy is a formidable fortress, Meirion, and we have no trebuchets close enough to get here in time, they lay siege to Harlech even as we speak.'

'You do not need trebuchets, my lord,' said Meirion. 'Hunger and disease will bring death just as fast as any missile we throw over its walls. Don't you see? Although he has lost many men, his army is still over a thousand strong and to feed that amount of mouths within the confines of a castle even as large as Conwy will take huge amounts of provisions and that, my lord, is something they don't have. All we need to do is cut off their supply lines and hope the weather stays bad. After that, the fall of Conwy will take care of itself.'

'I agree,' said Madog, 'muster the men, Meirion, and lead us out onto the slopes. Let them see for the first time the strength of our fist so they will add speed to their flight. The quicker they are cornered in Conwy the better.'

'Sergeants in arms,' shouted Longshanks as he rode through the town walls of Conwy, 'send men into every building within this town, strip them of any food or drink and have it sent up to the castle.'

'What about the citizens, my lord?'

'Tell them to leave the town immediately and seek refuge amongst the villages hereabouts. If Madog comes, as he will, there will be no hiding place for them anyway and it is better their supplies feed our men than those who follow Madog.'

'Aye, my lord,' came the reply.

'You there,' shouted Longshanks, pointing at another sergeant, 'gather what archers we have left and man the town walls while we consolidate our position. If they come, hold them off as long as possible before withdrawing to the castle.'

'Aye, sir,' shouted the soldier in reply and as the army spread throughout the walled town, Edward rode to the steep ramp leading up to the high entrance of the castle.

The Castellan was waiting, having been warned by his sentries and as the King approached, he bowed deeply.

'Majesty, welcome to Conwy, your castle awaits.'

'Your welcome is noted, Hugh De Norm,' said Longshanks. 'Make it known to your garrison that before this day is out, we expect to be besieged by the Welsh. My army will camp within these walls and will protect them with all our might. Space will be wanting but I feel there is room enough. In the meantime, set whatever men you have spare to joining mine and moving any resources of value from the town to inside the walls, though quick about it for Madog is on our heels.'

'Yes, my lord,' stuttered the Castellan, 'of course.'

Longshanks spurred his horse and rode into the castle followed by his knights, leaving the shocked Castellan in his wake.

—

The English sentry stood atop one of the many towers along Conwy's fortified town walls and though they were excellent against the raids of brigands, everyone knew they would be little use against a full-scale siege. A comrade walked past, handing out chunks of bread obtained from the castle stores, the first such food he had received for three days and as he bit gratefully into the hardened crust, his eyes widened as they focused on the slopes not half a league distant from the town.

'In the name of god,' he gasped, dropping the bread and reaching for his crossbow, 'to arms! Here they come.'

All along the walls the cry was repeated and archers loaded their crossbows as quickly as they could. The screams of the attacking army could be heard clearly through the early evening air and as the defenders crossed themselves in fear, they could see the enemy numbered in their thousands.

'Shut the gates,' shouted a sergeant, 'apply the barriers.' He turned to the men in his command. 'Listen to me,' he shouted, 'we are in no shape to fight these men so this is what you are going to do. As soon as they are in range, await no orders from me, just loose as fast as you can. Keep firing as long as you are able for every dead Welshman is a good Welshman, but as soon as their ladders hit the walls, as they will, retreat with all haste to the castle. Run like you never have before for if the castle bridge is threatened, it will be raised even though you may be outside. Is that understood?'

'Aye my lord,' shouted his command.

'Good. Then look to your front, men, the enemy are but moments away.'

The first battle of Conwy went exactly as planned for Madog and his army and their siege ladders were against the town walls within minutes of the assault starting. His bowmen sent flaming arrows high above the walls to fall amongst the town buildings and soon palls of black smoke rose high into the evening air, signs that although the rain was still heavy, the oil sodden arrows had penetrated deep into the drier layers of thatch on many buildings. Some men in the front ranks were felled by the bolts from the English crossbows but as the walls were so thinly defended it wasn't long before Welshmen could be seen running along the battlements and soon the city gates were opened from the inside allowing Madog's cavalry to gallop through.

As soon as it was obvious the walls were lost, the defenders ran down the stone steps and through the streets, desperate to reach the castle but though they could see the gates still lay open, those civilians who had not fled the town also sought the safety the walls offered and the streets were crowded with desperate people.

'Out of the way,' shouted the archers, but their words fell on deaf ears as desperate people fought each other to reach the ramp. Up on the battlements, Longshanks could see the Welsh pouring over the town walls and knew he only had moments left to secure the castle.

'They can't get through,' said the Castellan beside him, 'the crowd is too big.'

For a few moments Edward hesitated but as the first of Madog's army appeared at the end of the streets before the castle, he knew he had no option.

'Close the gates,' he said.

'Majesty, by far the majority of your archers still fight to get through the crowd.'

'There is nothing more we can do,' said Longshanks, 'raise the bridge and lock us down, from this moment on, this castle is under siege conditions.'

–

For the rest of the evening and deep into the night Madog's army rampaged through the town seeking anyone of English descent before putting them to the blade or hurling them alive into burning houses. Despite the need for shelter, most buildings were fired and soon the entire walled town of Conwy was ablaze, the fires lighting up the dark winter's sky and screams echoed through the night.

Edward watched from above as the town was systematically taken apart by the Welsh army and though none threatened the walls of the castle, he knew his own forces' predicament was dire. He lifted a goblet of honeyed water to his mouth but stopped halfway and stared down to the end of the nearest street. In amongst the clouds of black smoke yet illuminated by a nearby blaze, a man sat silently on his horse looking up at the castle, ignoring the carnage being wreaked all around him.

Edward stared back, realising this must be the commander of the Welsh army and as both men's eyes met, for the first time in history, Edward the First of England gazed into the face of Madog ap Llewellyn, Prince of Wales.

Chapter Eighteen

Rhuddlan

Orland rode into Rhuddlan at the head of five hundred cavalry, recruited from the mid counties across England. Fermbaud was already there, commanding another thousand infantry from the north and as far as the eyes could see, there stretched a canvas city housing thousands more men controlled by Reginald De-Grey and the remainder of Edward's own army. Orland dismounted in the castle courtyard and walked to the hall to seek Reginald De-Grey.

A servant served him wine and meat while he waited and ten minutes later the Castellan of Rhuddlan strode into the hall. Orland stood up and greeted the knight.

'My lord, I am Orland of York, personal bodyguard and confidant of the King. I have arrived from the north where I have raised an army of cavalry at the King's behest.'

'Welcome, Orland,' said Reginald, pouring his own tankard of wine. 'You come at an opportune time for fortune does not favour us.'

'In what way?' asked Orland.

'Where do I start?' asked De-Grey. 'The King is besieged within Conwy castle without chance of relief, Cynan ap Maredudd burns his way across the country and to top it all, we are under threat from another of Madog's armies coming from the south. It seems we are on the back foot.'

'Wait,' said Orland, placing his tankard back on the table, 'did you just say the King is besieged within Conwy?'

'I did and it is indeed a terrible thing but there is nothing I can do to help him. The river is in flood and this cursed storm holds my hand from any attempt at relief.'

Orland walked around the room as he absorbed the information. Within seconds he returned to stand before De-Grey who now sat in his court chair.

'My lord,' said Orland, struggling to control his temper, 'I have not had the pleasure of meeting you before though your name has come up in conversation. The King speaks highly of you and assured me you are a fine knight yet from the evidence around me I am beginning to doubt his words.'

De-Grey placed his tankard down on the table and stared at Orland.

'Choose your words carefully, sir,' he said, 'for you are in my castle and subject to my hospitality.'

'And fine hospitality it is,' said Orland, 'but while we converse politely over wine and sweetmeats, our king probably lives on dirty water and horse flesh. Why haven't you launched a relief mission with every man under your command?'

'It is not as easy as that,' said De-Grey, his voice rising. 'I have a responsibility to defend Flint and the men in this castle are tasked with doing just that. I am the only lord in the north of Wales who has managed to hold back

Madog's advance and I will not relinquish these lands for a foolish errand.'

'You call the rescue of your king foolish?' gasped Orland in astonishment. 'I would suggest it is the only thing that should be on your mind irrespective of the safety of Flint. I have just ridden through one of the biggest armies I have seen in years encamped on your very doorstep yet you tell me you can't spare a column in aid of your sovereign. I am aghast, sir, and challenge your decision in the name of the King.'

'You don't understand,' shouted De-Grey standing up. 'The nearest ford is three days' ride south of here through territory dominated by the enemy. There is no guarantee we would make it.'

'And there is no guarantee that our king will survive this siege without our help,' replied Orland, 'whether it is three days or three months there should be a column galloping to his aid as we speak. As for the enemy forces, what did you expect? We are at war with the Welsh in the heart of their own country, of course they will defend their lands but that is why we are here. This is war, not some easy settlement in friendly lands.'

De-Grey stared at Orland with distaste, angry that he was being lectured by a man of lesser station within the walls of his own castle.

'You are full of fancy words, sir,' he said, 'but with respect, you have not been here while I have kept this county safe from the rebels.'

'How many men have you lost?' asked Orland quietly.

'Why is that relevant?'

'Tell me,' repeated Orland, 'how many men have you lost in battle to the forces of Madog?'

'Like I said, we have maintained a strong garrison and kept the rebels at bay.'

'How many?'

'We have lost not one man and that is a statement to be proud of.'

Orland shook his head and sneered at De-Grey.

'You haven't even engaged him, have you? All these months and you have steered clear of facing the rebels but pulled your forces around you like a comforting cloak.'

'You are wrong, sir,' shouted De-Grey, 'for as we speak, I have a thousand men at arms riding through Denbigh in support of Sir Henry de-Lacey, Earl of Lincoln.'

'Perhaps but there are ten times that many camped on your door while your king's life hangs in the balance not ten leagues from here. You should be ashamed.'

'There is nothing I can do. Until the weather eases, my forces are hamstrung.'

'Of course there is something you can do,' shouted Orland. 'Send half your army to reach the castle as soon as they can. Tell them to ride south to the ford within this very hour and not stop until they see the walls of Conwy. They can eat and sleep in the saddle but they must reach the castle in half the time they anticipate.'

'In addition, while they ride to Conwy's rescue, task the rest of the army growing fat within their tents to sweep south through the forests of Denbigh and engage Cynan's forces immediately. Deny him the comfort of rest and add a burden of doubt in his mind. Put him on the back foot and while he worries about his own back, the relief column will have an easier ride.

'This is a war and the best form of defence is attack. You hold the main force of the King's army within your jurisdiction yet you sit back and sip wine while the Welsh wreak havoc amongst any of English descent. Send them south to take the fight to the rebels. Madog and Cynan have had it their own way for too long.'

'I suppose I could spare some men,' started De-Grey.

'There is no suppose about it,' said Orland. 'Saddle the horses and look to their weapons. Get the infantry on the road to seek the Welsh and while they march, pack whatever ships you can get with stores and send them along the coast into the river Conwy. The castle has its own dock protected by strong walls and I am astounded there are not already ships queuing up to unload stores on the pier there.'

'But the weather?'

'To hell with the weather,' shouted Orland. 'If nine out of ten ships sink then so be it for the one that gets through may save the life of the King.'

'I'm not sure,' said De-Grey hesitantly.

'Then let me tell you this,' said Orland leaning on the table, 'while you play at soldiers in your nice safe castle, I am commandeering the King's army on his behalf. Within the hour they will be on the march and doing what it is they came here for, taking the war to the upstart prince.'

'You can't do that,' said De-Grey, 'you don't have the authority.'

'Perhaps not but when this is over, you can report me to the King, that is, if he still lives.'

Orland stood up and stared at De-Grey in disgust.

'Your actions so far have fallen short of a knight of Longshanks,' he said, 'but it is not too late. Do what you know is right, my lord, and there is still time to redeem this situation. I will leave you to your thoughts but in the meantime, I have a war to fight and a king to rescue.' Without another word he turned and marched out of the hall, leaving the Castellan staring at his back.

—

Orland marched across the field outside the castle and shouted orders across to his officers.

'Tell the men not to set up camp but just refill their food bags and water skins. Get the horses fed and watered and lose any unnecessary baggage. They will need hard rations for five days as well as their weapons.'

'What about cover, my lord?'

'Leave the tents, just bring the waterproof cloaks.' He walked over to Fermbaud who was deep in conversation with another knight.

'Fermbaud, the situation here is appalling and I have just found out our king is under attack at Conwy. I will ride immediately to raise the siege but they will need urgent supplies as soon as possible. Arrange a supply column with all haste and follow me to Conwy via the southern ford. It is a circuitous route but the only one available.'

'Leave it to me,' said Fermbaud, 'I will gather whatever I can and set out by dawn.'

'Good, do not spare the horses for I feel their situation may be dire. Ensure the column is suitably defended for the rebels' presence is heavy in the area through which you ride.'

'Understood,' said Fermbaud and watched Orland disappear amongst his men as he barked the orders needed for the relief column.

In Conwy, the fires had died down amongst the houses and the besieging army now wandered through the rubble, picking up whatever they could find. Hundreds of archers formed a ring around the castle but though the occasional arrow was fired over the walls, Madog had ordered their use only as a means to keep the inhabitants guessing. Without heavy trebuchets, he knew he couldn't breach the walls and hunger was his best weapon. Still, the occasional arrow landing in the inner wards meant the defenders had to be on their guard at all times.

—

Edward sat in his rooms talking quietly with the Castellan.

'So, update me on the situation,' he said.

'There are over twelve hundred souls now within the walls,' said the Castellan. 'With the food we secured from the town and our own stores, we reckon we can last about another week at half rations.'

'What about water?'

'The well is half full and though this rain is a curse, we have tasked every man with collecting what they can in every container available. Firewood is limited but if the siege is prolonged, we can start taking the timber from the stables.'

'Why do we need so much wood for the fires?'

'My lord, the most efficient way to feed the garrison is with stew. Meat goes a long way in a broth and is easily shared out but to do this, we have to keep the cauldrons going, besides, if we have to kill the horses for meat the flesh will have to be cooked.'

'If the timber runs low, feel free to take the furniture from the royal rooms,' said Longshanks. 'In addition, ensure my officers suffer the same rationing as the men, as will I. What about weapons?'

'The armoury has been emptied and the men are well armed. All the arrows are distributed amongst the archers along the walls and if the enemy come, we will darken the sky with shafts.'

'Good,' said Longshanks, 'I don't expect an assault but it is better to be prepared. You have done well, Castellan, but do not rest on your laurels. Tell the men to stay alert for there is no telling what this Welshman has up his sleeve. In the meantime, I hope my messengers will get through or this could be a very difficult winter.'

Chapter Nineteen

Denbigh

Cynan ap Maredudd looked down from the ridge for a few moments more before turning to face Robert Byrd.

'I have seen enough,' he said. 'I estimate we outnumber them at least three to one and rarely will we enjoy such an advantage. Muster the men and rendezvous in the valley beneath Minstrel's Crag. The ground is well suited to cavalry yet offers enough rocky protection for our archers. I estimate we have two hours before they get there so make sure our men are in place.'

'Aye, my lord,' said Robert and galloped away to give the commands.

Cynan and his army had left a minimal holding force in the captured castle and patrolled the forests of Denbigh to dominate the area and deny it to the English. At one stage they had successfully fought off a half-hearted attempt to retake the town by Henry de-Lacey but the earl had withdrawn before Cynan could do any real damage to the column.

Since then, Cynan's spies had followed the English as closely as they dared and when they saw them heading back to Denbigh for the third time, they had immediately returned to warn the warlord about the renewed threat.

Subsequently Cynan had taken the opportunity to deal with de-Lacey once and for all and despite the undeniable strength of the English column, his own forces could easily do them damage in open warfare. This was yet another opportunity and one that was too good to miss.

—

Within the hour his men spread out across the valley presenting a wall of armed Welsh infantry. Their cloaks were heavy with rain and their simple weapons consisted of anything they could make or that had been taken from the enemy after previous battles. There was little armour and what there was consisted of a mix of whatever they could find. Despite this, morale was high for they had enjoyed great success against the better-armed English for many months and what they lacked in equipment, they made up for in numbers and spirit. The plan was simple, let the enemy advance upon them until they were within range of the archers hidden amongst the rocks and when they fled the deadly onslaught, the cavalry would run them down with lance and spear. Further Welsh foot soldiers would swarm from the hills on either side to attack the English horsemen and seal off the valley for this time, Cynan would allow no mistake.

—

Gradually silence fell amongst the ranks and as the first of the English appeared over the horizon, Cynan rode his horse up onto a high ridge to see the battle unfold.

'They've seen us,' said Robert quietly, and Cynan watched as the English column spread out into line abreast. Even at this distance Cynan could see their numbers were low and he shook his head in bewilderment.

'Won't that man ever learn?' he said with a sneer.

'Every mistake he makes,' said Robert, 'adds more English bodies to feed our soil and that is surely a good thing.'

'Here they come,' said Cynan and both men watched as the English advanced down the valley.

Within minutes they reached the markers placed upon the valley floor by the Welsh archers to determine range but rather than advance, the whole line stopped as one.

'What are they doing?' asked Robert. 'It seems they are waiting for something.'

As if in answer to his question, a horn echoed throughout the valley and as the Welsh soldiers looked around nervously, the English army's change in tactics became all too apparent. Over the hill rode hundreds of previously unseen English horsemen and they fell upon the rear of the archers' lines without mercy. From across the valley, Cynan could hear the cries of battle but apart from managing to get a few arrows away, the archers stood no chance. Within minutes their numbers were decimated and another blast from the horn signalled the English cavalry to reform at the valley bottom alongside the infantry.

Cynan was aghast, the loss of his archers meant that any advantage he had was significantly reduced, and the addition of the new column of horses to the English lines meant his army was now severely compromised.

'Where did they come from?' shouted Cynan in anger. 'No one told me there was a second force.'

'They carry the banner of Rhuddlan,' said Robert, 'and must be a relieving force from Reginald De-Grey.'

'Whoever they are,' snarled Cynan, 'our fate has just taken a turn for the worse. Even if we deploy what horsemen we have, their strength is too much and we will be routed. This day cannot be salvaged, Robert, sound the retreat before it is too late.'

Robert gave the signal and one of the Welsh horns sounded across the valley but as Cynan's men looked up in confusion, the English took it as a signal to attack and as the warlord and his officers looked down in desperation, de-Lacey's army raced forward to engage the disintegrating Welsh lines.

The result of the battle was never in doubt for as the English cavalry crashed into the Welsh lines, the defenders immediately broke in panic and any cohesive defensive strategy was lost. Well-armed horsemen raced amongst the fleeing men cutting them down almost at will and though some of the more seasoned veterans formed close units and fought their way toward the relative safety of the nearby hills, even they were thwarted by the arrival of the English foot soldiers, who set about them with ruthless efficiency and maximum aggression.

'Robert,' shouted Cynan, mounting his horse, 'send a signal to the cavalry we have left: they are not to engage the enemy but leave the field immediately. Tell them to rendezvous at Builth in two days' time.'

'What about you, my lord?'

'I will not treat you like a fool, Robert, this is a disastrous rout for us. De-Lacey has out-thought us this time and good men are being slaughtered without mercy. I am going back to Denbigh to gather our garrison; we need to salvage what we can if we are to have any chance of continuing the fight. Once we have mustered at Builth, we will see what paths lay before us.'

'But that means relinquishing Denbigh.'

'Denbigh is but a name on a map, Robert. We wrested it from the English grasp but always knew it couldn't be held, at least, not unless there was a complete Welsh victory. That outcome took a step backward today but all is not lost, we need to consolidate and look to our options once more.'

'So be it,' said Robert Byrd and both men rode in different directions while deep in the valley below, thousands of men lay slaughtered in the mud.

Henry de-Lacey reined in his horse and lifted his blood splattered visor. Men lay dead all around him but even though they were vastly outnumbered, many Welshmen fought on in isolated groups. The earl knew the day was won and despite his anger, even his blood lust had limits. He ordered the signal sounded to ease the attack and at last, the few hundred surviving Welshmen were given time to consider terms.

Within the hour, all fighting had stopped and any surviving rebels were marched out of the valley at spear point, prisoners of Henry de-Lacey and uncertain what fate lay before them. The battle had been a one-sided rout and the English knight knew that at last, the fight back had truly begun.

In the north the siege had been in place for three weeks and Madog knew the castle garrison must be on its last legs. Over the past few days they had witnessed several ships trying to land supplies at the castle quay but of the many sent, only one had managed to dock, the rest being blown away by the ever-present storms. One had even crashed upon the rocks and the whole of Madog's army cheered wildly as the ship broke apart sending men and supplies to the bottom of the river.

Despite this, Madog was growing impatient and had sent word to Criccieth to send the trebuchets but just as he thought the castle was about to surrender, a rider was escorted into his campaign tent with devastating news.

—

'My lord,' said the rider, 'a well-armed column of English cavalry ride hard toward us as we speak. It seems they crossed the river yesterday and have lost no time in riding north to relieve the castle.'

'What is their strength?' asked Madog.

'About a thousand or more and warriors to a man. I am told that behind them, an infantry force twice their number escorts a supply column taking the same route.'

'And you are sure about the number?'

'I am, my lord.'

Madog turned to face Meirion.

'What do you think?'

'If we stay here, we will be cornered as were the English.'

'We could defend the town walls; they are only cavalry and will have no idea about siege tactics.'

'Perhaps, but don't forget there is an infantry force a day or so behind them. On top of that we have another English army within the castle. If we were to engage those attacking the town, what's to stop Edward opening the gates and falling upon our rear? No, if this man's news is accurate, we have no other option than to abandon the siege.'

Madog stared at Meirion, knowing his friend was correct yet loathe to admit defeat. Finally he sent the messenger on his way and after strapping on his sword belt, walked out of the tent.

'Where are you going?' asked Meirion.

'To see the prize one more time, my friend,' he said. 'To get a lasting memory in my mind of how close we came to killing the King of England.'

--

Hours later a knight knocked on the door of the chapel in one of Conwy's towers and burst in on the King as he knelt in prayer alongside the castle priest.

'Who dares to interrupt the King's worship,' shouted Edward over his shoulder.

'My lord, you told me to keep you informed about any changes in the Welsh army.'

'What about them?' replied Edward.

'They've gone, my lord, the town is empty.'

--

Edward climbed to the top of the tower and gazed out over the town below him. Sure enough the streets seemed empty and, in the distance, he could see the last of the

Welsh column as it snaked over the hill. The news was true, the Welsh had called off the siege.

'Thank God,' he whispered to himself, 'thank God.'

Chapter Twenty

The Southern Road

Geraint rode his horse slowly on the southern road. Behind him, Fletcher drove a small cart in the back of which lay Garyn on a bed of hay. It had been over a month since Garyn had been injured and though the fever had broken, the wound still hadn't healed properly. Finally, due to the increased presence of the English across the north, they had taken the difficult decision to move Garyn as soon as he was strong enough, to avoid the consequences they may face once their nationality was discovered.

The news across north Wales wasn't good. Longshanks had survived a siege by Madog at Conwy and the castles at Denbigh and Criccieth re-taken from Welsh hands. Edward's armies now dominated the northern quarter of the country and the brothers had to take the lesser known paths to avoid capture. The going was slow but eventually they approached Builth and set up camp within a copse. As Fletcher set the fire, Geraint fed Garyn some soup on the back of the cart before raising a waterproof cloak above him. When his brother finally slept, he returned to Fletcher by the fire.

'He needs an apothecary,' he said quietly. 'The wound has reopened and I fear there is infection deep within.'

'It is another two days before we reach Brycheniog,' said Fletcher. 'Can he wait that long?'

'I fear not, he already burns with fever.'

'What are we going to do?'

'I am going to ride into Builth and seek aid. Hopefully it still lays in Welsh hands but if not, I am just going to have to take my chances.'

'You could be killed,' said Fletcher.

'We could be killed at any time,' said Geraint, 'such is the world in which we live, but I will not stand idle and watch my brother die when help may be just a few leagues away.'

'Do what you have to do, I will stay with your brother for as long as it takes.'

'You have my gratitude but I suspect if I'm not back by tomorrow night, it will be too late anyway.'

Geraint mounted his horse and rode out onto the road before spurring the animal and galloping toward the town of Builth.

—

Two hours later, he tied his horse to a rail and entered a tavern knowing full well that when seeking information in a strange place, the tavern was always a good place to start. The single room was full of men but fell silent within moments as Geraint approached the innkeeper standing by an open cask of ale. Before he reached him, a large man stood to block his way.

'Stop right there, stranger,' said the man. 'Your face is unknown to us, state your name and your business.'

'I am Geraint ap Thomas of Brycheniog,' came the reply, 'and I come here seeking aid.'

'Your accent is not of Brycheniog,' said the man. 'How do I know you are not an English spy?'

'I have lived these past ten years in the north but my family is Brycheniog born and my allegiance is to Madog.'

'I hail from that town,' said another man standing up, 'and know most families. Name your kin and their trade so I can vouch for your claim.'

'My father was Thomas Ruthin and he was the blacksmith in Brycheniog for many years before he was murdered at the behest of the Abbot Williams.'

The man's eyes narrowed.

'I remember there was a blacksmith's forge on the edge of town that burned down around that time. Is that the family you speak of?'

'It is. My parents and sister were murdered that night though my brother survived.'

'Yes, I remember now,' said the man. 'Both sons left soon after but were thought long dead.'

'We both still live, sir, and when I get back to Brycheniog I can provide witnesses to support my claim, but that is why I am here. My brother is wounded most grievously and needs the aid of an apothecary, lest he dies in the night. I implore you as a fellow Welshman, delay me no longer and direct me to the man I seek for every moment I waste is surely weighed against the balance of his life.'

'I believe you stranger,' said the man eventually, 'but alas I know of no such physician hereabouts. Many have died these past few months and we count the medical men amongst them. Despite your need, there is nothing we can do.'

'There must be someone,' said Geraint in desperation, 'a priest, a monk, anyone.'

'There is one,' said another man from the back of the room, 'though it is unlikely he will attend your brother.'

'Why not?' asked another.

'For he is in the close company of Cynan himself and has no time for commoners such as us.'

'Your words lack worth,' came the reply, 'for if this man speaks true then his brother fell in the service of Wales and surely by Cynan's own promises, every man of Welsh birth is equal.'

'Perhaps so, but many have fallen in service and no matter how helpful the apothecary, he cannot attend them all.' He turned to face Geraint. 'I am sorry about your brother but I feel you have had a wasted journey.'

'Wait,' said Geraint, 'where can I find him, it has to be worth a try.'

'He is at the manor in the top meadow,' said the man, 'but you will not get past Cynan's guards.'

'What if I pay?'

The man sneered.

'Cynan has accumulated and discarded more wealth in these past few months than any of us will see in a hundred lifetimes. What do you have that makes you think he will listen to you?'

'Something he has craved for a long time,' said Geraint. 'The Sword of Macsen.'

Geraint waited impatiently before being shown in through the large doors of the manor. Inside he expected to see the opulence and grandeur that such places usually contained but was shocked to find the place had been ransacked and much of the interior ravaged by fire. He was taken through the ruined hall and into an antechamber. Three men sat against the walls, sipping on flasks of ale while a pile of furniture burned in the centre, the smoke billowing out of the damaged shutters. The soldier turned and left the room, closing the door behind him.

'So, you are the man who claims to know the whereabouts of the Macsen Sword,' said a voice from the shadows.

'I am, my lord, but seek a favour in return for giving up the knowledge.'

The man stood and walked across to stand before Geraint. His face was gaunt and smeared with blood, dirty from weeks of rough campaign. His hair was tangled and fell unkempt about his face and his deep-set eyes reflected the weariness of fighting a cause long lost. He took another drink from the flask before speaking again.

'Ah yes, the attendance of my physician, is that correct?'

'It is, my lord,' said Geraint, 'but my need is dire and he has to leave with me straight away.'

'And where is this sword?'

'I have it back at our camp in the forest and will gladly hand it over to your men as soon as we arrive.'

'What makes you think I have need of it anymore? I don't know if you realise but the resistance throughout Wales crumbles around our feet and I suspect such a bauble holds little worth to those now struggling just to stay alive.'

'I realise this, my lord,' said Geraint, 'but thought that should there be a reckoning before Longshanks, then its possession may hold you in good stead.'

'What makes you think this?'

'It is well known that Longshanks enjoys the study of the mystical and especially the history of the Roman invaders many generations ago. Caernarfon itself was selected for its proximity to Segontium and the design of the fortress is taken from those in Constantinople, once the heart of the Roman Empire. To have such an artefact in his possession may just open his mind to negotiation.'

Cynan considered the argument for several moments.

'Your words have merit,' he said. 'Return to your horse and wait there. My apothecary will attend you soon. Once he has treated your brother, send him back with the sword. Be gone, Geraint of Brycheniog, for I have ale to drink and victories to recall.' He returned to the shadows and resumed his place against the base of the far wall, comforted by the dancing flames and flasks of strong ale.

—

'Who's there?' hissed Fletcher, standing up and drawing his sword.

'Ease your sword, Fletcher,' replied Geraint, 'it is me and I have brought a man of medicine.'

Fletcher lowered his knife and lost no time in leading the apothecary to the cart where Garyn slept a fitful sleep.

'Remove the bandages,' said the apothecary, 'and let me see the wound.'

They did as they were told and the physician leaned forward to smell the wound, recoiling quickly at the stench. Similarly he smelled Garyn's shallow breath before reaching for a leather wrap and retrieving a sharp blade. Carefully he scraped the pus away from the wound before gently pulling the unhealed skin apart. Seeing the black flesh beneath he glanced up at Geraint and slowly shook his head.

'I'm sorry,' he said, 'this man's wound is riddled with the demons of infection. There is nothing I can do.'

'No,' said Geraint, 'you are wrong. You are an apothecary and must have powders or potions to kill the rot.'

'It is too late,' came the reply. 'If I had seen him a few days ago perhaps he would have had a chance but he is too far gone, the poison is in his blood and he has the smell of death about him.'

'There must be something you can do,' snapped Geraint angrily, 'anything.'

'I can clean the wound and ease the pain but he is too weak to fight the fire in his veins. All I suggest you do now is make him comfortable until the time comes.'

'How long has he got?' asked Fletcher.

'If I clean him up and ease the pain, I reckon he could last a day or so, no more.'

'Can we move him?'

'No, the strain will finish him off. Set up a shelter and make him as comfortable as possible. Also, if he is a godly man, try and find him a priest.'

Geraint looked down at his brother and fell to his knees, taking Garyn's hand in his.

'Brother,' he said, 'I am so, so sorry. After everything you did for me in my life, when you needed me, I fell short. My life is cursed.'

'Geraint,' whispered Garyn, 'do not fret, this is not your doing and truth be told, I outlived my given span many years ago. Be comforted that I will die a happy man knowing that you still live.'

'Forgive me brother,' said Geraint and placed his head on Garyn's chest.

Garyn raised his hand weakly and placed it on his brother's head.

'Nothing to forgive, Geraint, nothing to forgive.'

--

Ten minutes later, Garyn had fallen into a pain-filled sleep and Geraint rose quietly, realising Fletcher was nowhere to be seen. He heard a noise in the bushes and as he walked through to find the cause he saw Fletcher astride Garyn's horse, about to ride out.

'What are you doing?' demanded Geraint. 'You can't leave now, my brother can't be moved.'

'Perhaps not,' said Fletcher, 'but there is something I can do. Keep the apothecary here, Geraint, and task him with keeping Garyn alive as long as possible. I will be back as soon as I can.'

'Why, where are you going?'

'I hesitate to tell you, my friend, in case it raises a false hope, just keep him alive as long as possible.'

'But...'

'No time to explain,' shouted Fletcher and spurred the horse to burst through the trees onto the southern road.

'Where is he going?' asked Geraint.

'I have no idea,' said the apothecary, 'but wherever it is, I fear it will be a fool's errand. Come, help me make your brother's last days more comfortable.'

Chapter Twenty-One

Montgomery

William De-Beauchamp was sitting at a table in his campaign tent when the news he had been waiting for finally arrived. For weeks, the Earl of Warwick had chased shadows through the forests of Mid Wales, sending out patrols to seek Madog's army but always the rumours had proved false and the Welsh prince stayed one step ahead. De-Beauchamp had even engaged hundreds of farmers and woodsmen to lay waste to huge swathes of forests across the region, cutting down thousands of trees to deny the enemy shelter, but despite this Madog remained at large and rumours abounded that he intended to attack English interests along the border. This was a disturbing turn of events and the earl had doubled his efforts to locate the Prince before he could do any lasting damage. Finally the news he had been waiting for had arrived and two Welsh spies were ushered into the tent.

'Welcome,' said William, standing up, 'I hear you have good news for me.'

'We do, my lord. Madog and his army lay camped in a field a few leagues hence. They head south-east and intend raiding into the Welsh Marches within days.'

'Show me on the map,' said William, walking to another table.

'My lord, he is here,' said the man indicating a spot on the chart, 'along with perhaps a thousand men.'

'How can he still keep such a big army in the field?' asked William. 'His supply lines must be yet intact.'

'His support column is indeed well stocked, my lord, for he still enjoys the allegiance of many villages. They empty their food stores to feed his cause.'

'A cause on its last legs,' spat William, 'yet one that clings to life with an unparalleled stubbornness. We will deal with these villagers' misguided loyalty soon enough but in the meantime, our concentration must focus on the Prince himself.' He looked at the map again. 'What is the name of this place?'

'It is a valley called Y Fygin,' said the man.

'Is it suitable for a cavalry attack?'

'It is.'

'And how long do you think it will take a column to reach Y Fygin?'

'If you march through the night, you can be there by dawn.'

'And you think he will still be there?'

'He has been for several days and doesn't look like moving anytime soon.'

'Then that is our plan,' said William and turned to his aid.

'Sir Henry, muster the men, marching order only. I want to be on the road within the hour with our full command.' He turned to the two men once again. 'Do you know where he hides his supply column?'

'We did not see it with our own eyes but I am reliably informed it lays in this wood, two leagues north of his camp.'

'Then we will launch a two-pronged attack,' said William, 'and deal with this man once and for all. If your information proves true, gentlemen, then I will personally make you very rich men. In the meantime I want you each to accompany a column with my officers. One will take us to Y Fygin while the other will lead us to the forest that contains the support column.'

'Aye sir,' said the men.

'One more question,' said William, pointing at a name at the centre of the valley, 'this place called Nant Moydoc, what does it mean?'

'It mean's Madoc's stream,' said the spy. 'A coincidence only for it was named after a different man many years ago.'

'How ironic,' said William, 'the place where Madog will finally meet his demise already bears his name.' He stood up and faced the men in the room. 'This is it, gentlemen, our path is clear. Tomorrow morning, Madog ap Llewellyn pays the price for his traitorous rebellion. Form up the men, Henry, take us to Nant Moydoc.'

—

The following morning was overcast and a fine drizzle of rain fell on the encamped Welsh army. The sun still lay beyond the horizon and the mist lay heavy in the valley. One of the sentries yawned and pulled his cloak tighter around him, looking forward to the end of his guard duty when he could find some warm food and grab a few hours' sleep in the back of a cart. Behind him, hundreds of worn tents were pitched haphazardly throughout the valley and he could see signs of life as yawning men started to appear from within the shelters to relieve their bladders and find what food had been brought up from the supply column in the rear.

Jon Evans looked up at the horizon, almost willing the first rays of sun to appear and signal the end of his duty. He yawned again, watching the patterns the mist made as it rose from the valley floor to disappear in the warmer air above, revealing the straight lines of small trees lining the far slopes.

He blinked hard and stood a bit straighter. Though they were yet indistinct in the remains of the mist, he was sure there were no trees on that slope yesterday, no matter how small.

As he strained his eyes, his heart beat a little faster as the swirling mist patches offered glimpses of what it concealed. Slowly, the mist lifted and he realised his worst nightmare had come true. Waiting patiently on the slopes was the biggest English army he had ever seen.

He stepped backward several paces, not believing his own eyes but within moments had turned to run as fast as he could down to the camp.

'Alarm,' he shouted, 'we are under attack, stand to your weapons.'

In an instant someone blew on a horn and the camp erupted into activity as men scrambled from their tents grabbing frantically for their weapons.

Madog's eyes sprung open as he heard the horn, his tired mind struggling at first to recognise the significance but seconds later he sprang from the cot in the back of the wagon and jumped to the floor below.

'Sergeants,' he roared, 'gather your men and someone tell me why the alarm has been sounded.'

'English on the north slope, my lord,' called a voice.

'And on the east,' answered another.

The Prince pulled a cloak over his head and grabbed a spear before running up onto a knoll at the centre of the camp. The mist had almost disappeared and he looked around in horror as he realised there was a strong enemy presence on three of the four sides.

'Where do you want the lines, my lord?' shouted Tarian.

For a few seconds Madog was at a loss, unsure from where the attack would come but he knew he had to provide an answer. Even if he was wrong, the men had to be led.

'To the west,' shouted Madog, 'three lines deep, archers to the rear. Meirion, take your detachment and set up at the far side of the camp, watch we are not flanked. Keep close together and be prepared to support any line, move.'

The English army stood in silence watching the panic ensue, knowing they had their enemy trapped and though they would have been better served attacking while the Welsh were in disarray, William De-Beauchamp knew that no matter what they did, there was no way the enemy could escape the carefully laid ambush.

'My lord, the men are ready,' said Sir Henry minutes later. 'Do you want me to give the command to advance?'

'Yes, Henry,' said William, 'let's show this upstart what a real army can do.'

The sounds of dozens of horns filled the air and the entire western slopes seemed to move as half of the Earl of Warwick's army descended to engage the Welsh.

'Here they come,' shouted Meirion, 'archers look to your bows, lancers to the fore.'

'Men to my left,' shouted Madog, 'deploy to Tarian's front, the threat is from the west.'

Soldiers ran everywhere and no sooner had the lines been strengthened than the first of the arrows rained in on the defenders.

'Archers return fire,' roared Tarian from beneath his shield. For several minutes both sides exchanged volleys of arrows and though men fell on both sides, the numbers of English archers far exceeded those of the opposition and the Welsh fell in their dozens.

'Cavalry,' shouted a man and Tarian looked up to see fifty horses galloping toward them.

'Pike men form a line,' he roared and those regular soldiers who had trained for this sort of defence, rapidly swung around to provide a wall of steel, forcing William's cavalry to swerve at the last moment rather than impale their mounts on the pikes.

At the far side of the camp, English infantry descended on Meirion's lines and both sides fought ferociously at close quarters. Blood and bone flew everywhere and the morning air echoed with screams as steel and iron hacked into living flesh.

At first, the fury of the Welsh ensured they were more than a match for the English but as each fresh attack came, the defenders tired while the soldiers of Warwick were regularly replaced with their reserves and thus were fresh for the fight. For many hours the waves of attacks came, interspersed with long periods of withdrawal but gradually the strength of the English army and constant attacks began to tell and the Welsh lines were forced backward. During a lull in the battle, Tarian took the opportunity to run over to the exhausted Madog.

'My lord,' he shouted, 'over half of the men are dead or wounded, we can't go on like this.'

'We cannot surrender, Tarian, every man would be put to death and they do not deserve that. Better to die fighting for freedom than at the end of a rope.'

'I do not advocate surrender; I suggest we break for the forest at the end of the valley.'

'Don't you think I have considered that?' asked Madog. 'If we break from here, we will be run down by their lancers. At least here we have the comfort of broken ground.'

'If we stay, we will be slaughtered, my lord, can I suggest we form a schiltron yet move whilst still in formation. If we can keep a tight wall, we will be safe from his cavalry.'

Madog stared at Tarian, considering the proposal.

'Tarian, my men are familiar with the formation whilst static but have never used it on the move. The slightest lapse in concentration will mean the ranks collapse and our whole force will be open to their cavalry.'

'I know,' said Tarian, 'but if we stay here, we die anyway. What have we got to lose?'

'So be it,' said Madog, 'task the men to gather every pike and spear they can and form the square. The English infantry could attack again at any moment.'

Soon, every man formed into a square with all the spears and pikes facing outward in an impenetrable defensive wall. Those men in the centre of the square held whatever shields available above the heads of the others, protection against the arrows that would inevitably follow.

'Listen to me,' shouted Tarian when they had formed up, 'our target is the forest at the end of this valley. Once there we will disperse and rendezvous three valleys to the west. However, if any of us are to escape, we have to remain disciplined so heed my words, or we will fall as surely as leaves in autumn.' For the next few minutes, Tarian explained the tactics while high on the hill nearby, William watched with interest.

'What are they doing?' asked William. 'Why have they formed a schiltron, surely he is not expecting relief?'

'Perhaps he knows he is beaten and makes a last stand,' said Sir Henry.

'No, this man has tenacity and he doesn't give up easily. Give the men a few more minutes' rest then signal a fresh attack. Let's see what this rebel has up his sleeve.'

'Here they come,' called a voice and Tarian looked over the front rank to see another attack racing across the ground toward them.

'Archers, use up what you have left,' he shouted, 'at least we can weaken their number.'

The last of the Welsh arrows flew through the air, most missing their targets but some hitting home and dropping a handful of the enemy.

'Present,' shouted Madog from the centre of the square and hundreds of spears appeared over the shoulders of the front rank.

'Brace,' shouted Tarian and as the enemy crashed into the Welsh formation, they found a solid wall of steel and shields waiting for them. The pressure of those behind forced the front English ranks onto the spears and dozens were impaled onto the lethal spikes.

Within minutes it was clear the wall was too strong and an English command echoed across the field.

'Withdraw a hundred paces and reform.'

The English walked slowly backward, leaving their dead and wounded behind them.

'It worked,' shouted Madog, 'catch your breath and await my command, prepare to move.'

For a minute or so the Welsh watched the English withdraw and as soon as the enemy had turned their backs, Madog gave the order the Welsh lines had been waiting for.

'Ready,' he called, 'now!'

Instantly the whole schiltron formation broke up and as a man, the Welsh army turned to run as fast as they could down the valley.

'What are they doing?' shouted William. 'The Welsh are escaping, sound the recharge.'

A horn echoed across the valley but the soldiers below looked up in confusion at the contradictory command;

their sergeants were organising a withdrawal yet the horns sounded the advance. For a few moments, confusion reigned until the realisation dawned and they turned to see the retreating Welsh.

'After them,' shouted a sergeant, 'don't let them get away.'

By now the Welsh had managed over half the distance to the trees and kept running as the English pursued. Tarian looked over his shoulder, waiting for the right moment and as the English closed in, he gave the fresh command.

'Form up,' he screamed, 'schiltron formation.'

Immediately the fleeing men stopped and reformed the square they had been in only minutes earlier. Again the English fell upon the well-formed walls and once more men fell needlessly at the impregnable defence. The attackers withdrew again, realising they were in an impossible situation.

'Ready,' shouted Madog, 'same again, break!'

The formation scattered again and fled further down the valley, making good ground as the English ran in pursuit.

'Oh he's good,' said William in admiration. 'He knows our men can't breach that wall and gains every yard he can between attacks.'

'Send the cavalry, my lord.'

'Even horses will baulk at the lances, Henry.'

'Yes, but at least it will stop them fleeing. If the Welsh break formation my lancers can run them down.'

'Agreed but send in the archers as well.'

'The archers may be found wanting, my lord, for by the time they form their ranks the Welsh will move on and if my cavalry ride amongst them, our arrows will not discern between friend or foe.'

'Tell them not to form ranks but to join the assault as individuals, mingling with our infantry.'

'My lord, is that wise? Everyone knows that arrows are more effective when fired in volleys.'

'The ground dictates the tactics, Henry, and at the moment their bows are useless to me. At least amongst the fray their weapons may add to our strike. Tell them to get as close as they can amongst our infantry and seek out individual targets at close range.'

'So be it,' said Henry and turned his horse to ride down into the valley.

–

By the time the English cavalry had reformed and raced back into the valley, Madog's men were within five hundred paces of the treeline. They were once more formed up into a schiltron though by now it was significantly smaller due to the amount of men they had lost. Tarian looked up in dismay as the riders came into sight.

'My lord, he deploys his riders once more. Once they engage, we will no longer be able to break out without being run down.'

'Agreed,' shouted Madog, 'this is as far as we can go with this tactic.' He looked around desperately, knowing that safety was so near yet too far to reach in formation. Finally he took the only option left to him if any of his command was to survive.

'Men of Wales,' he called, 'together we have thwarted the might of the English for despite their strength we are still here. Your valour does you great credit and your names will be spoken by the bards for years to come but this is where it ends. If we stay, we will die, it is as simple as that and there are many amongst us who yearn to see their families once more, so my decision is this. Upon my command, we will break for the last time and seek the sanctuary of the trees but this time there will be no call to reform. Every man is to do whatever he can to save himself for I have no doubt that the English will be amongst us as wolves amongst sheep, but do not hesitate, the dream of liberty still lives on but right here, upon this field, our day is done. Men of Wales, it has been an honour to serve you.'

As the remainder of his army cheered, Madog turned to Tarian.

'Give the order, Tarian, send them home.'

'Men of Wales,' roared Tarian for the last time, 'to the trees and may God be on our side… *Advance!*'

The ranks broke up and most of the men ran as fast as they could toward the safety of the treeline. Many discarded their heavy weapons whilst others stood their ground to face the pursuing enemy. Within moments the English infantry were amongst them, cutting down the stragglers with impunity as their fresher legs carried them amongst the exhausted Welsh.

In amongst the English, individual archers paused their advance to pick off those escaping the pikes and swords of the infantry and their arrows cut men down with lethal efficiency. Horses galloped past the foot soldiers and decimated the Welsh army but though hundreds fell, many still reached the trees to stumble gratefully through the undergrowth.

Madog crashed through a thicket and paused for breath behind the trunk of a tree, gasping for breath after the exhausting run. Some men still stood upon the battlefield, making a last stand against the enemy but within moments the last had fallen to English steel. He looked around and could hear the sound of those who had survived the run crashing through the trees and he knew that though the situation was far better than moments earlier, the day was still not over.

—

Up on the ridgeline, William De-Beauchamp looked down in satisfaction. The Welsh army had been routed and after today, would no longer be a major threat. As he watched, a rider galloped toward him before reining in and giving the earl the customary salute.

'My lord, I ride on behalf of Sir Robert Greenwood. He sends his regards and tells me to inform you that at dawn this very morning the Welsh supply column was ambushed and engaged as requested. Our casualties are minimal while the enemy was routed with extreme savagery. The column was taken, my lord, victory is ours.'

Sir William smiled and looked back down into the valley as the last of the enemy were struck down. At long last, Madog ap Llewellyn had been defeated and even though he may regroup elsewhere, it was only a matter of time before the rebellion collapsed completely.

—

Further south, Garyn ap Thomas grew weaker and Geraint sat alongside him in the cart, the two brothers alone deep in the heart of the Welsh countryside. As promised, the physician had been sent back to Cynan along with the Sword of Macsen and the remains of the emperor and though he had been gone for almost three days, Fletcher was nowhere to be seen.

Geraint talked quietly, recalling the shared memories from their childhood. He knew his brother's life could be measured in hours and he wanted it to be as gentle a passing as it could be. The potions from the apothecary numbed his brother's pain but were useless against the poisons that now flowed through Garyn's veins. Garyn's eyes closed once more and for a second Geraint thought that he had finally died but with relief he felt the slightest of breaths upon his hand. He pulled the sheepskin cover closer about his sleeping brother but looked up suddenly at the noise of someone crashing through the undergrowth.

'Geraint,' called a voice, 'it's Fletcher, tell me he still lives.'

The Fletcher appeared on his horse closely followed by two other riders.

'He does,' said Geraint, 'but his light fails as we speak, I fear he has hours only.'

Fletcher dismounted and climbed into the cart.

'Garyn,' he said quietly, 'wake up, I have someone here to see you.'

Garyn's eyes fluttered open and he looked up, his eyes glazed through pain and tiredness.

'There you are,' said Fletcher, 'look who's here.'

He moved aside and Garyn gazed into the eyes of Elspeth Fletcher, the woman he had loved all his life.

'Oh Garyn,' said Elspeth quietly, 'taking his hands in hers, what have they done to you?'

'Elspeth,' said Garyn, 'how are you here?'

'My father came for me,' she said, 'and told me of your plight. He has told me everything, Garyn. About how you left all that time ago, simply to protect me. All these years and I have thought you a rogue, yet little did I know you did it because you loved me.'

'And still do, Elspeth,' said Garyn, 'I have never stopped loving you.'

'Oh Garyn,' said Elspeth, the tears running down her face, 'I am so sorry, I should never have doubted you.'

'Don't be sorry, Elspeth, be happy for me. I am going to see my family at last and will dwell alongside them in paradise.'

'Garyn,' said Elspeth through her tears, 'listen, we have little time and there is something you should know. Do you recall the last time we spoke back in the castle a few months ago? When I told you my son was not yours, that he was sired by another?' She paused as she brushed a lock of hair from his face. 'Well I lied, Garyn, he is indeed your kin. You have a son, my love, a fine boy called Thomas and you would be very, very proud of him.'

Garyn moved his head slightly to look at Fletcher.

'It's true,' said Elspeth's father gently, 'and he is growing into a fine young man.'

'Does he know about me?' asked Garyn.

'He does, we have told him everything.'

'And has he forgiven me for leaving him?'

'There is nothing to forgive, father,' said a voice and Garyn turned his head to see a young man standing at the end of the cart.

259

Everyone fell quiet as father and son stared at each other for the first time in their lives.

'Thomas,' said Garyn quietly and held up his hands.

Thomas clambered into the cart and as Elspeth moved aside, he held his father tightly in his embrace.

'My boy,' said Garyn weakly and as the tears started to flow, Garyn ap Thomas passed away clinging tightly to the son he never knew he had.

Chapter Twenty-Two

Conwy Castle

Longshanks stood in one of the northern towers, peering at the town below. The Welsh had long gone and the residents of Conwy who had sought refuge amongst the hills during the siege, had returned to repair their homes and businesses. Out in the river, dozens of barges lay at anchor, waiting their turn to be brought into the harbour where they would be fitted out ready to carry the King's troops to Ynys Mon under the protection of a squadron of ships and a substantial land army. In addition, dozens of pontoon bridges had been constructed in Chester and were due to arrive any day in readiness to build a crossing to the island in place of the one burned months earlier. Ynys Mon was crucial in the control of the north and though Edward now held most of north Wales in his power, he knew that possession of the island was important if he was to stamp out the rebellion once and for all. He had heard of the defeat of Madog a few days earlier and though the news had caused great celebration, he knew there were still many smaller armies at large under the command of lesser warlords and the war was still not won.

A knock came on the door as he sipped his wine and he turned to see Nicholas Fermbaud enter the room.

'My lord,' said Fermbaud with a slight bow, 'a word if I may.'

'Of course,' said the King, 'come in.'

The past few months on campaign had been hard for Fermbaud yet he had risen to the task and Edward was happy with his contribution and it became known that he'd rather spend time with his men than around the heavily laden tables of the King's court. Subsequently, as he became leaner and battle hardened, his demeanour changed back to that which had gained him a knighthood many years previously.

'Any further news from the Earl of Warwick?' asked Edward, pouring the knight a goblet of wine.

'Not yet, my lord. They scour the Welsh hills as we speak but Madog has disappeared. I'm sure it is only a matter of time.'

'Perhaps,' said the King, 'but it is a concern. There are still many rabid Welshmen refusing to lie down across this cursed country and if he manages to link up with some of them, this struggle could extend into the summer and that, Fermbaud, is something I cannot contemplate.'

'I understand Gascony weighs heavy upon your mind, my lord.'

'It does but I will not sail forth until the affairs of the Welsh are well and truly settled. We may be in control along the northern coast and Mid Wales, Fermbaud, but Ynys Mon evades me as does the south.'

'Yes, well there is news regarding the south, my lord, and I fear it is not good. Morgan ap Maredudd heeded a plea for aid from the people of Brycheniog and assaulted the castle there. The castellan, a man by the name of Gerald of Essex, was absent at the time and though the garrison put up a fight, it is understood there was an uprising from the servants within, who overpowered the guards and enabled the warlord to breach the walls. As we speak, Brecon castle lies in the hands of the Welsh.'

'So where is the Earl of Gloucester?'

'He engages on seeking those responsible for sacking the castles at Ogmore and Llantrisant,' said Fermbaud, 'a secondary force of Morgan, yet one just as deadly. To be fair, it seems the uprising in the south is still as strong as ever and the earl chases shadows most days.'

The King sighed.

'Send a message to the Earl of Hereford,' he said, 'and request his engagement on my behalf. Ask him to send his forces south and deal with the situation in Brecon. I cannot spare the time at the moment for Ynys Mon lays heavy on my mind.'

'My lord, the island is the main reason I came here this evening. I understand you are assembling a fleet to invade the island yet are concerned there is still a large force encamped along the shore.'

'Indeed there is,' said the King, 'though we know not where. That is why I employ caution for if we attack and are under strength, they will repel us with ease and I cannot take that risk. In a few weeks the barges will be complete and we will smite the enemy with unmeasurable force.'

'What if I was to say there is a way to bring that day forward and, in the process, lower the chance of defeat?'

'I would welcome your views,' said the King. 'Share them with me.'

'My lord, last night while my men were patrolling the shore west of here, they came across a fishing boat hidden amongst the reeds. The fisherman was still on board and it became apparent that during the storm yesterday, he lost his sail and was cast upon the rocks. His boat was damaged and he was trying to effect repairs so he could return whence he came.'

'And where was that?'

'Ynys Mon.'

The King lowered his wine glass and looked at Fermbaud with renewed interest.

'Continue,' he said.

'Well, at first my men were just going to despatch him as a spy but he begged for his life in return for information.'

'What information?'

'He told us the location of the Welsh army on the island.'

'Where is he?' demanded the King. 'I would speak to him immediately.'

'Alas, after he told my men, they were bringing him back when he tried to escape. An arrow brought him down, but he did not survive the journey here and now lies dead.'

'Damn,' said Longshanks, 'his information could have proved crucial.'

'My lord, it still could,' said Fermbaud. 'I have a suggestion and would beg your indulgence.'

'Go on.'

'My men grow impatient at the continued inaction and ask continuously for a chance to seek out the enemy. I have explained there is a greater plan but this is an opportunity that could benefit you, them, and indeed me.'

'In what way?'

'I note that there are several barges already finished and I request permission to land my men on Ynys Mon under cover of darkness to seek out the enemy camp. If successful, we can engage them prior to the main army and inflict what casualties we can. We may not defeat the entire force but even the presence of your men on the island will strike fear into their hearts and any ensuing invasion will find the defences much thinner.'

'Fermbaud, you do realise that if they lay stronger than you think, then your entire command could be wiped out?'

'It is a possibility,' said Fermbaud, 'but the island is a big place and we should be able to evade them if we keep on the move, but I do not think it will come to that. The fisherman told of a force no more than a thousand strong. I believe we can get in, cause havoc amongst their number and get back to the barges before they can reorganise.'

'This is a big ask, Fermbaud,' said the King. 'I'm not sure I can allow it.'

'My lord, consider the benefits. The enemy will be severely weakened which means when you lead the assault, fewer of our men will die. Even if I lose some of my men, it will be significantly lower than if you face ranks of archers as you disembark the barges. The assault will take less time which will release you to campaign south and put this rebellion to bed once and for all.'

Edward stared at the knight, considering the proposal.

'My lord, there is one more thing,' said Fermbaud, 'and it is a personal one.'

'Continue.'

'Many months ago you expressed a desire to see me display the mettle expected of a knight. I will be honest and say your words cut me to the core, not because they were harsh but because they were true. When I lost my men to the blades of Cynan ap Maredudd, I was guilty of arrogance and an expectation that just because I bore a title, I was deserving of victory. It was a conceited stance to take and cost the lives of many men. Since then, I have suffered many sleepless nights and realised I had grown fat and lazy, afflictions caused by comfort and abuse of my position. However, I believe I have seen the error of my ways and have worked hard to find the knight within.'

'You have indeed become a valued asset in this campaign, Fermbaud.'

'Perhaps so but it is not enough. The war will soon be over and I worry that I will not have done enough to redeem my name, not just in your eyes or the eyes of the court but in the eyes of my men. Subsequently I believe this may be my last chance and beg permission to lead this assault in your name.'

Edward walked around the room, thinking about the implications.

'How many men would you require?'

'I will take only those under my command, about a thousand.'

'Barges?'

'Ten.'

'And you truly believe you can inflict a defeat upon the enemy?'

'If not a defeat, certainly cause them severe casualties.'

'And when do you intend this to take place?'

'If you are agreeable, tomorrow night.'

'Why so soon?'

'The weather is fair and we do not risk stormy waters. If we wait, who knows how long it may be before the circumstances are so favourable?'

'You do realise that if you find yourself outnumbered, we will not be able to come to your aid?'

'I do, my lord, and it is a risk I am willing to take.'

Edward stopped his pacing and stared at Fermbaud.

'Are you sure about this?'

'I am, my lord, more certain than I have ever been in my life.'

'So be it,' said Longshanks, 'and may God be with you.'

—

The following night, Fermbaud crouched in the bow of a barge as it bumped against the far shore of Ynys Mon. Either side of him, other vessels landed silently and the soldiers climbed out quickly to wade through the shallow water. Within minutes, over a thousand men ran to the treeline and lay down in the dark shadows, awaiting further orders.

Fermbaud and eight other men spoke quietly between themselves before they split up and four groups of two went in different directions, each seeking the encampment they knew was somewhere close by while the knight returned to his officers.

'What now, my lord?' asked one of the men.

'Now we wait,' said Fermbaud and pulled his cloak further around him.

Hours later the last of the scouts returned and to Fermbaud's great relief, reported they had found the location. Immediately the sergeants were informed and they made their way amongst the men, waking those who slept. Cloaks were discarded along with any loose equipment that may make any noise and soon the entire landing force crept through the forest and formed up in the bushes above a depression in the landscape. Fermbaud crawled forward to join the scout peering down at the camp.

'Their tents stretch up to the far campfire,' whispered the scout, pointing across the valley, 'it seems they feel very safe here for there are sentries only on either end of the valley. At the far end, there are about fifty horses but apart from that, it seems they enjoy an ale fuelled sleep.'

'Then let's see if we can interrupt their sweet dreams,' said Fermbaud and crawled back down the slope.

Fermbaud briefed his officers and the sergeants.

'The plan is simple,' he said, 'the scouts have been despatched to kill the sentries. Once done, our men will descend on the camp as quietly as they can. Tell them they are to stay silent as long as possible. Take no swords or maces, this night belongs to our knives.'

'But if there is a counterattack, we will be at their mercy,' said a sergeant.

'If we do this right there will be no counterattack. I want to be down there for as little time as possible. We will strike as quickly and silently as an adder and get out before the alarm is given. By the time they realise what has happened we will be back on the boats and they will not know if we are still a threat. Any questions?'

When none were forthcoming, the sergeants were sent to brief the men until finally one of the scouts appeared out of the darkness.

'The deed is done,' he gasped, 'all sentries are dead.'

'Then muster the men,' said Fermbaud and within minutes, a thousand men at arms crept as quietly as they could down the darkened slope toward the tented camp.

—

The following few minutes saw carnage ensue amongst the Welsh camp. Men in groups of four would pounce upon a tent, collapsing it on those sleeping inside before frantically plunging their blades as fast as they could into anything beneath. Any groans or shouts were muffled under the heavy linen and hundreds died before anyone managed to shout the alarm.

Immediately the camp seemed to come alive but to add to the confusion, the attackers threw tents on the flames of the campfires and overturned the enemy carts, spreading their contents over the floor. The sounds of battle echoed through the night but the Welsh had no idea what was happening, only that they were under attack.

The night belonged to the English and even as the screams of dying men echoed through the darkness, a flaming arrow soared into the night sky and they knew it was time to leave. Every attacker ran back to the hill, many pausing to grab what booty they could before climbing up the slope. Within minutes they were racing back toward the shore and soon the barges pulled into the estuary, their cargo of men ecstatic with the success of the mission.

As soon as they reached the mainland the celebrations began and the air filled with the sound of men congratulating each other on their success. Any items taken from the camp were placed on waiting carts and one by one, the sergeants reported their losses to Fermbaud.

'Seven dead and thirteen wounded in total, my lord,' said one of the sergeants, 'and I reckon over five hundred enemy lay slain in the enemy camp. It has been a good night.'

'A tally worthy of any man,' said Fermbaud. 'Let's get back to Conwy as quickly as possible and once there, let the men loose on the casks of ale. This night has been one of note and once the King hears of our success, I'm sure he will be the first to sing their praises.'

'So be it,' said the man and turned to arrange the march.

Fermbaud smiled to himself before drawing his blade and wiping it on the sleeve of his jacket to clear the Welsh blood.

Chapter Twenty-Three

Builth Castle – July 1295

Longshanks rode slowly through the devastated town of Builth. All around him the air stank of fire where Cynan's men had torched the buildings before fleeing into the hills.

The Earl of Warwick had done a splendid job over these past few months for not only had he defeated the Welsh prince at Nant Moydoc but also hounded the armies of Cynan throughout Mid Wales. Now neither was a major risk anymore and though some rebels fought on across the country, they were isolated and their days were numbered.

It was a good time for Longshanks. The island of Ynys Mon was completely in his control as was the whole of the north. Mid Wales would be cleansed of the rebels within days and he had received news that the Welsh leader in the west, Maelgwyn ap Rhys Fechan had fallen in battle at the hands of Henry de-Lacey.

That just left the south and though Brecon castle still lay in the hands of Morgan ap Maredudd, it seemed that he posed little threat to local English interests and could be dealt with in due course.

Longshanks continued to the castle and dismounted before being led into the great hall.

'My lord,' said the Castellan bowing deeply, 'welcome to Builth. I am sorry it is not in better circumstances but we have done all we can to make your stay comfortable.'

'It will suffice,' said Longshanks. He paused before getting straight to the reason he had travelled so far. 'Take me to him.'

'Of course,' said the Castellan and he led the King out of the hall and across the courtyard toward a corner tower. Longshanks followed, eager to see the man whose capture had brought him here. The two men descended the staircase and stopped before a cell guarded by two armed soldiers.

'Open the door,' said the Castellan, 'and make way for the King.'

One of the guards turned a key and taking a candle from a holder on the wall, walked inside the room, closely followed by Longshanks.

Against the wall a naked man laid on a pile of stinking straw, matted with faeces. Around his neck was a heavy metal shackle secured by a chain fixed to a loop in the dungeon wall.

'Is this him?' asked Longshanks.

'It is,' said the Castellan.

'Are you sure?'

'He freely admits his identity.'

'It could be an imposter willing to die in his cause. Stranger things have happened.'

'I don't think so, my lord, he has been identified by several independent sources.'

Longshanks stepped forward and kicked the prisoner.

The man lifted his head wearily and stared at the King.

'So,' said Edward, 'you are the great and feared Cynan ap Maredudd.'

'And you are the tyrant Longshanks,' replied Cynan, 'defiler of women and murderer of children.'

Edward stifled a laugh.

'The man still has spirit,' he said with amusement.

'The spirit of Wales will always remain even though you slaughter our brethren.'

'I don't think so,' said Edward, 'for this time I will not repeat the mistakes of old. You are indeed honoured, Cynan, for I have travelled many leagues to meet you face to face. To see the man responsible for so much death and suffering.'

'The blood is on your hands, Englishman, not mine.'

'I think not,' said the King, 'but it amuses me that you think so. Still, you have been a distraction for me these past few months, but isn't it interesting how the natural order of things always returns and men such as you are placed back down amongst the filth?'

'Go to hell,' whispered Cynan and spat on the King's boots.

The Castellan drew his knife but Edward reached out to restrain him.

'No,' he said, 'stay your arm. Let him have his last moment of glory for I have something special lined up for him.' He turned back to Cynan. 'Enjoy the rest of your life, Welshman, though I suspect it will be a very short one.'

He turned and left the dungeon, glad to be out in the fresh air but as he crossed the courtyard, a horse came galloping through the gate.

'Fermbaud,' said Longshanks, 'I hope your urgency is merited for you almost knocked me off my feet.'

'My lord, forgive me,' gasped Fermbaud, 'but I have momentous news. Our forces cornered Madog in the Welsh Marches. He and his men put up a fight but he was outnumbered and soon surrendered to John De-Havering. We have him, my lord. Madog ap Llewellyn is in custody.'

Further south, the Earl of Hereford sat at a trestle table before the gates of Brecon castle. Inside the fortress hundreds of armed men peered down from the castellations, waiting for the attack they hoped would never come. Down in the courtyard hundreds more stood behind barricades of piled furniture, each bearing whatever weapons they could muster from pikes to pitchforks. These were the citizens of Brycheniog, the men and women who had finally had enough of the English tyranny and had risen up against the cruelty of the local lords. Together with the forces of Morgan they had conspired to seize the castle from the English and had done so with remarkable ease. Since then they had waited until the inevitable arrival of Edward's forces.

Eventually that day had come in the form of the Earl of Hereford and his army. At first, the earl had considered besieging the castle but knowing the uprising was coming to an end, offered the rebels terms for surrender. Morgan ap Maredudd himself was in the castle and upon receiving the communication had agreed to talk.

Slowly one of the gates opened and four men walked across to stand before the table.

'Are you the warlord known as Morgan ap Maredudd?' asked the earl.

'I am.'

'Then please be seated for there is business to discuss.'

Two weeks later, Brecon castle was back in the hands of the English. Morgan ap Maredudd had agreed terms and all those occupying the fortress were granted amnesty. Farmers and labourers returned to their fields, while any trained soldiers were enlisted into Edward's army, destined for the battlefields of Gascony. Morgan himself submitted to the custody of the Earl of Hereford though he enjoyed far greater comfort than Cynan, still languishing in a filthy dungeon in Builth. Subsequently an uneasy truce had descended over Brycheniog and life in the town gradually returned to normal.

Eventually the uprising was all but over and by September, the English could once more ride the ways and tracks of Wales with impunity.

Longshanks rode the length of the country, visiting every castle to convey favours and rewards to those who had remained loyal while dispensing brutal justice on those guilty of supporting the rebels. Eventually he headed toward Brecon knowing full well that the final act in the war was about to play out.

Elspeth and her family had returned to their home, fully aware that Gerald of Essex was dead. Geraint had joined them and though there was still an air of nervousness in the town, they set to repairing the damage to their former home caused by the fire. At first, they slept in the church and Geraint spent many hours telling Thomas about his father. The boy listened carefully, drinking in the tales of adventure from the Holy Land but in particular, questioned Geraint about the manner of the family's downfall. At first Geraint was forbidden by Elspeth to share the tale of Garyn's feud with Father Williams but finally she agreed that it was important he knew everything about his father, including those things that still hurt.

'So what happened to the abbot?' asked Thomas one evening.

'We are not sure,' said Geraint. 'We know that when the people of Brycheniog first entered the castle, they found him hiding in a secret room and though he was a hated man, nobody had the nerve to kill a man of God so he was sent back to the abbey.'

'Is he there now?'

'We don't know. He was a very ill man and I suspect he died many weeks ago but that is no longer our concern. The war is over, Thomas, and we have to focus on rebuilding our lives. I suspect there will be reprisals from the English but if we can rebuild the business your father once ran so successfully, I suspect we may just get through this alive.'

Chapter Twenty-Four

Brecon Castle

'My lords,' announced Fermbaud in the great hall, 'be upstanding for our monarch, King Edward.'

The many knights in the hall rose as Edward entered to stand before the top table. He was adorned in the finery of the court and wore a gleaming tabard over his ceremonial armour. Every knight, lord or constable who had played a major part in putting down the rebellion, was there for one thing, the trial of the rebel leaders.

Longshanks sat as did the rest of the gathering. When the noise died down, Fermbaud stood and turned to the captain of the guard.

'Bring them in.'

Minutes later, three men were brought in in chains and led to the centre of the floor before being forced to their knees. Two were bedraggled and wore the ragged clothes of the most destitute of peasants while the third was clean and in relatively good health. All around them the court jeered and mocked them but all three just stared at the King in defiance.

Fermbaud stood again and unfurled a scroll.

'Knights of England,' he announced, 'Lords of the Marches and Wales. Hear the account of the rebellion led by these men before you, known as Madog ap Llewellyn, Cynan ap Maredudd and Morgan ap Maredudd. The fourth man, Maelgwyn ap Rhys, fell at Kidwelly at the hands of Henry de-Lacey.'

A cheer went around the room and all eyes turned to see the smiling Earl of Lincoln sat near the King. Fermbaud continued.

'These past few months these men waged war and rebellion against the King. During this time they slaughtered many loyal servants including the Sheriff of Caernarfon, hanged before the walls of his own castle. Uncountable numbers of citizens were slaughtered in their cause, mainly of English descent. Many castles fell at their hands including Caernarfon, Denbigh, De-Bere, Howarden and Criccieth. In the south, Llantrisant, Ogmore, Morlais and Brecon were amongst dozens taken and ransacked whilst across the country, many more were besieged and damaged to a great extent, including Harlech, Caerphilly and Pembroke. The men before you are stained with the blood of thousands, both English and Welsh, and stand here today charged with treason and murder most foul. What say you to their fate?'

The room broke into uproar as the knights and others roared their hate toward the three men in the centre and though the reaction was one unbefitting the court of a king, Longshanks allowed them to vent their anger, after all, it had been a long and hard campaign. Finally he stood and held up his hand. Slowly the noise died down and the knights regained their seats as the King walked toward the prisoners.

'Which of you is Madog?' he asked quietly.

'I am,' said one of the bedraggled men.

'Stand up.'

Madog staggered to his feet and stared into the King's eyes.

'So you are the one who covets my crown.'

'I desired no crown of yours,' said Madog, 'my aim was always the freedom of the Welsh people.'

'Ah, freedom, that oft misunderstood word.'

'There is no misunderstanding,' said Madog, 'people are free or they are not. Under your rule, that privilege was denied them.'

'But surely freedom is relative to the times,' said Longshanks. 'Since William landed on these shores over a hundred years ago, the concept of freedom has changed, such is the way of the world. To the victor falls the definition of freedom. The Welsh are allowed to farm, marry, drink, live and die in the place of their choosing as long as they pay the tithe. Why is that thought so abhorrent to you?'

'Because our people once lived across the whole of Britannia. We are the true rulers of this country and as far back as we can remember, our language was the one spoken by any man of these isles. However, over the generations those with covetous eyes came to our lands and forced us back into these mountains and valleys but even that was not enough, and people like you always wanted more. You pushed and squeezed until there was no room to breathe. You took our farms, forced us into the hills, and took our young men to fight in wars not of their making, yet those who came back were taxed unto starvation. That is why we fight, Longshanks, and that is why you will never truly control this country.'

'A pretty speech, Madog, but one of empty words. These lands are mine. They were my father's before me and will belong to my son when I am gone. That is the way it is, Madog, and that is the way it will always be.'

'If that is the case,' said Madog, 'then prepare your sons and their sons for a struggle unending for never will we lay down our birth right.'

'So be it,' said Longshanks and turned away as Madog was forced back to his knees.

'Enough discourse,' announced Edward as he walked back to take his place behind the table. 'The charge is treason and murder, how find the nobles?'

'Guilty,' roared the men in the hall and again Edward had to raise his hand to still the noise.

'Despite your crimes you have been granted trial by fellow man and they have passed judgement. Each of you will now have the chance to plead leniency. Morgan ap Maredudd, state your case.'

Morgan got to his feet.

'My lord, my case is simple. Yes I took the sword against the English but not against your rule.'

'Explain,' said Edward.

'Years ago Gilbert De-Claire was given lands by your father in return for gallant service. Many of these lands belonged to my family but we accepted the decision. Since then, the earl has pushed the borders of his lands further into ours, forcing our hand against him. Hands that have always been loyal to the crown and are willing to be so again.'

'But you wreaked havoc amongst our southern allies,' said Edward.

'Indeed we did, and I stand proud of my record but have your staff check the records, for the only properties that drew our attention are those who fell under the control of Gilbert De-Claire.'

The King looked around and saw Fermbaud frantically checking the list of properties destroyed or attacked by Morgan. Eventually he looked up.

'It is true, my lord,' said Fermbaud with surprise, 'everything he attacked is run by the De-Claire estate.'

'This is appalling,' said a man standing up, 'and all the more reason to hang him. It is certainly no defence for he has cost me a fortune in coin and the lives of many good men.'

'Sit down, De-Claire,' said Edward. 'The point is made but there have been many others who have suffered just as much, if not more than you. I will hear this man out.' He turned back to Morgan. 'Continue.'

'My lord, my case is done except to say that now this war is over, allow me the chance and I will once more prove to you my allegiance.'

Cynan looked over to Morgan with anger on his face.

'You speak cowardly words, Morgan, and I am shamed to witness them.'

'I am no rebel, Cynan, I am a wronged man who sought justice in the only way left open to me.'

'As did we,' growled Cynan, 'for we are a wronged nation and also sought justice in the only way open to us. What is the difference?'

A soldier kicked Cynan across the face and sent him sprawling to the floor.

'Enough,' shouted Edward and turned to Morgan.

'I have heard your plea,' he said, 'but will hear from all before making judgement. Madog ap Llewellyn, state your case.'

'My case is clear,' said Madog. 'I am a direct descendant of Llewellyn ap Iorwerth and as such am a true heir to his dynasty. I answered a call and led my fellow countrymen in a struggle for freedom. If that is a crime then I am guilty as charged.'

'Is that it?' asked Edward.

'There is nothing more to say,' said Madog and allowed himself to be forced back down to his knees.

'And finally,' said Edward, 'Cynan ap Maredudd, what say you?'

'I say this,' said Cynan glowering up from the floor. 'I curse the day your whore of a mother spawned you and hope she rots in hell for the damage she has caused.'

The room erupted in anger and two men ran forward to attack the Welshman but were pulled back by the guards at the behest of the King.

'You disappoint me, Cynan,' sighed Edward, 'for one whose military genius caused me the most harm, you do yourself no justice in resorting to insults. However, the opportunity has gone and it falls on me to pass sentence.

'With regards to Maelgwyn ap Rhys, his grave is to be dug up and the corpse dismembered before the people of his own town. The head will be paraded around Wales before being placed upon a spike on the walls of Worcester.'

The room fell quiet as he turned his attention to Morgan.

'Morgan ap Maredudd, you were eloquent in your defence and there was sense in your argument. Your crimes were costly yet I see merit in your justification. Your punishment is this. All those lands contested between you and the Earl of Gloucester will be formally ceded to the crown to be disposed of as I see fit, never to be contested again. These same lands I subsequently hand over to Gilbert De-Claire to manage on my behalf in compensation for the damage done and costs incurred in resisting your aggression. In addition, you will attend me in London at my convenience and there you will vow allegiance before my full court and serve me on the battlefields of France.'

The men in the room murmured amongst themselves at the unexpected leniency.

'Cynan ap Maredudd, your crimes were heinous and deserve the maximum sentence. You will be taken from this place and hanged by the neck. Before you die you will be cut down and your belly opened before your eyes, and your innards burned before you upon a hot plate. Finally you will be torn apart by four strong horses with each quarter being dragged to the corners of the realm, so all will know the fate of men such as you.'

The room gasped at the sentence for nobody had been hung, drawn and quartered for many years.

'Finally,' said Edward, turning to Madog, 'you were the figurehead that sparked the fire and as such deserve the same fate. You too will...' but before he could continue, Cynan let out a shout.

'Wait!'

All heads turned to see the man struggling to his feet.

'Before you pass sentence there is something you should know. I have something of great value in my possession that may temper your mood.'

'What could you possibly have that interests me?' asked the King.

'The bones of Macsen ap Wledig, as well as his sword. These are the symbols of freedom throughout these lands and if they were in your possession, many men would think twice before raising arms against you.'

Edward stared in silence. He knew about the Sword of Macsen and had long desired it in his possession but now he had passed sentence, he couldn't go back on his decision.

'And you actually think that such a bauble would make me spare your life?'

'No,' said Cynan, 'not mine for I would gladly die before serving under you but the man alongside me did nothing wrong except become a champion for his people.'

Madog spun his head to face Cynan.

'No, my friend,' he said, 'don't do this. The Macsen Sword is worth more than the life of one man. Leave it buried for someone to find it and one day, when the time is right, it can be held aloft as our people take the field again.'

'No,' said Cynan, 'I will not see you killed, Madog. All this time I challenged your right to be called prince but now I see your claim was honourable and I bow to your lineage. Accept the gift of life as my final homage.'

'No,' said Madog, 'I cannot.'

'Enough,' shouted Edward and the room fell silent again. He turned to face Cynan.

'Your proposal interests me,' he said, 'and is acceptable. When today is done you will tell my officers where lies this sword and if it is placed in my hands before nightfall then you have the word of a king that Madog will be allowed to live. Should your words be false then he will join you on the gallows to suffer the same fate. Thus is my judgement.'

'So be it,' said Cynan and as the room erupted into raucous jeering, the two men were dragged away while Morgan ap Maredudd was released from his chains.

'So it ends,' said Edward and stood up to leave.

'My lord,' said Fermbaud, 'can I ask one question?'

'You may.'

'Even if this sword is delivered, surely you don't mean to release Madog? He could become a threat again within weeks given his freedom.'

'Freedom?' said Edward. 'Who said anything about freedom? My promise was for life only, and if that is within the deepest dungeon in the Tower of London, then my word will be kept. This day is done, Fermbaud, this war is over.'

Chapter Twenty-Five

Caernarfon Castle

Longshanks stood in a room at the bottom of a tower in Caernarfon castle. Before him was an open casket containing the remains of Macsen Wledig, now draped with a flag embroidered with the image of an eagle. Alongside Longshanks stood Fermbaud and Orland.

'Are you sure about this, my lord?' asked Fermbaud.

'I am,' said Longshanks. 'This man ruled these lands long before we even arrived here and it is only fitting that he lays in peace.' He turned and received a bejewelled sword from Orland. 'It seems Gerald of Essex employed the best craftsmen in repairing the sword but the value lays in its history not the gold.'

He laid the weapon on the emperor's chest and for a few moments all three men stood in silence as they stared down at the coffin. Finally Edward took a deep breath and turned to Orland.

'The deed is done,' he said. 'Have the casket closed and buried beneath the floor. When done, I want to see no sign it was ever disturbed and every man is to swear on pain of death never to repeat what they saw this day.'

'Is that it, then, my lord? Is there no memorial to be made to the memory of Macsen?'

The King paused for a moment and looked upward. 'What is this tower named?'

'It has no name,' said Fermbaud.

'Then let it be called after the Emblem of Macsen. His people created an empire that ruled the known world and we only follow meekly in their footsteps so in memory of Macsen ap Wledig, this tower will be named after the bird that adorned their banners.' He turned to face Fermbaud. 'Agreed?'

'It is a fitting legacy,' said Fermbaud. 'Henceforth it will be called the Eagle Tower.'

Epilogue

Brycheniog – November 1295

Geraint and Fletcher stood in the cemetery. Each held a shovel and looked down upon the grave at their feet.

'Are you sure about this?' asked Fletcher.

'No,' said Geraint, 'but it makes sense. Garyn told me that the abbot dug up the bodies of our family many years ago and had them fed to the dogs but while we were in the castle, a serving girl told me she overheard Father Williams telling Gerald of Essex that his treasures lay in the graves of common men. Knowing the way he thinks, I fully believe he would have buried some here and laughed at the thought of us praying before his wealth. If I am right, there could be enough in here for us to rebuild the forge and your house.'

'And if you are wrong?'

'Then nothing changes,' said Geraint, 'but unless we try, we will never know.'

'So be it,' said Fletcher and without further ado, pushed the spade into the topsoil of the grave of Thomas Ruthin.

–

A few leagues away, Father Williams lay in his bed within the abbey. He had suffered another bout of sickness but again seemed to be pulling through. A knock came upon the door and a monk entered.

'Father,' said the monk, 'there is someone from the village who has been sent to pay their respects. He says he has a gift for you.'

'Send him in,' said Father Williams and a few moments later, a young boy entered, closing the door behind him.

'Welcome,' said the abbot weakly, 'what is your name, boy?'

'My name is unimportant,' came the reply, 'for I am here on behalf of another.'

'And who may that be?'

'My father,' said the boy and removed his hood.

Father Williams stared at the boy's features, struggling to recall where he had seen them before.

'And who was your father?'

'You knew him as Garyn ap Thomas,' said the boy, walking toward the bed, 'and he has unfinished business.'

Realisation dawned on the abbot but as he drew a breath to call for help, Thomas leaped forward and clamped his hand over his mouth.

'If it wasn't for you, old man,' he hissed, 'I would now be working the forge surrounded by a loving family. Instead, we live from hand to mouth and the only thing I have is a fleeting memory and my father's blade. The memory will be mine for evermore but his blade I share with joy in my heart.' As he spoke, he pushed a knife deep into the abbot's stomach, watching his victim's face screw up in agony.

'You did not win, old man,' said Thomas backing away, 'for even from the grave it is my father's blade which ends your life. Make that your final thought, priest, and take it to hell where you truly belong.'

As the abbot choked on his own blood, Thomas turned and walked away without remorse, back to his family and the uncertain future that lay before them all.

Author's Note

Obviously, the story of Garyn and his comrades is a tale of fiction but many of the background events throughout the book, and indeed the three previous books, are based on real occurrences. There was a real uprising in 1294 and the rebel leader was called Madog, but though our story paints him as a young man, the real Madog was considerably older. The other rebel leaders are also based on the stories of real people at the time though embellished with artistic license to make the book work. Where castles are named as being taken by certain rebel leaders then this is based on real events. Actual facts are readily available all over the internet and for those who would like to learn more about the revolt of Madog, there is plenty of information available.

Suffice to say, Madog and his comrades rampaged through Wales in a very short space of time and many castles fell before them. Edward had to postpone his war in Gascony to put the rebellion down and at one point had an army approximately thirty-five thousand strong.

The Siege of Denbigh

Denbigh castle was held by the Earl of Lincoln and had been for over ten years. When Cynan laid siege to the castle within its walls, it is thought that he first captured the external well, denying the defenders a source of fresh water. In such circumstances, a castle would soon fall to a determined besieging force. Excavations indicate that in the years after the Madog uprising, the castles walls were extended to encompass the well.

Somewhere on the outskirts of Denbigh, history tells us of a great battle between Madog's forces and those of the Earl of Lincoln. Madog was the victor on the day but de-Lacey escaped with much of his army intact and tried to retake the town and the castle. He was unsuccessful and seemed to join forces with Longshanks at a later date.

Edward's advance into Wales

In December 1294 Edward marched into Wales, leaving a huge army at Rhuddlan while he campaigned toward Denbigh and along the north coast. A fleet of twelve boats and a galley of five hundred men set sail from Chester to try to establish a bridgehead at Ynys Mon, known today as Anglesey, but the mission was unsuccessful and as he ventured further west. Madog's forces cut off and attacked his supply column, forcing Edward to return to Conwy with all speed.

Once there, he took refuge in the castle as the main force of his army was on the other side of the river and unable to come to his rescue. For a while, Madog actually had the King of England at his mercy, albeit encamped in one of the most formidable castles in the ring of steel. How long the siege lasted is unclear but apparently the conditions were very poor and they had to ration the supplies until a ship managed to brave the storms and resupply the fortress. Records are unclear whether the siege was lifted by the Earl of Warwick or simply a break in the weather allowing Edward's own forces to come to his rescue, but eventually Madog was forced to withdraw.

The Battle of Maes Moydoc

On 5th March 1295, the Earl of Warwick marched his army through the night and surrounded Madog's forces in a valley called Y Fygin near Welshpool in Wales. The Welsh army are reported to have fought ferociously and made extensive use of the schiltron formation to repel the attacks. Though many were slaughtered, some escaped into the forests including Madog himself. The attack of the English is particularly noted due to their unusual use of individual archers amongst the infantry, a tactic unheard of at the time.

Madog went on to continue the struggle until about July of that year when he was either captured by the English or gave himself up, sources differ on the outcome.

The fate of the rebel leaders

Morgan ap Maredudd was pardoned by the King and went on to serve him faithfully for the rest of his life. Madog was incarcerated in the Tower of London and Cynan was indeed hung, drawn and quartered.

The Sword of Macsen

Though the focus on the Sword of Macsen is just part of the story, the tale of Macsen Wledig is indeed a well-known one in Wales. According to the story he was a Roman emperor and came to Wales to marry the woman of his dreams.

A mile or so from Caernarfon castle are the ruins of the Roman fort of Segontium and it can be assumed that Macsen would have at least lived there for a while as Caernarfon was Helen's hometown.

Edward the First was fascinated by anything historical and had a great respect for the Romans in particular. Caernarfon castle was built in the manner of the fortresses he had seen while on crusade in the east, and there are accounts that when the bones of a Roman emperor were discovered in Caernarfon, he had them laid to rest some-where in the castle. Interestingly enough, there is indeed a tower in Caernarfon castle called the Eagle Tower.